A Nice Little Business

by Eileen Dewhurst

A Nice Little Business

EILEEN DEWHURST

PUBLISHED FOR THE CRIME CLUB BY

Doubleday

NEW YORK

1987

RAP *194 6054*

Library of Congress Cataloging-in-Publication Data
Dewhurst, Eileen.
A nice little business.
I. Title.
PR6054.E95N5   1987   823'914   87-9129
ISBN 0-385-24313-8

A Nice Little Business

CHAPTER ONE

Cathy could see the bus through the trees which filled the curve in the road, a shiny slab of bright unnatural green moving downhill behind the winter skeletons and the dark foliage of conifers at a speed which started her running towards the point round the bend where she could request it to stop. As she ran she renewed her annoyance with her car for letting her down, and then as she grew short of breath she was unfamiliarly afraid and stopped dead, for the first time relating the momentous thing she had just found out to her everyday life. Wasn't it rather foolish to be flinging herself along in this breakneck fashion?

Less precipitately she set off again, and was still in time to catch the coach to London, if only because it had stopped anyway to let off two elderly people who were negotiating the long steps with care.

"Thanks." Gratefully she hauled herself aboard. "O-o-h, sorry!"

An insensitive start had thrown her into a seat with less than half its width unoccupied, but she decided to spare herself another violent jerk and stay put.

"A few deep breaths," suggested the small stout woman by the window. "Have you run all the way across Kent, dearie?"

"I've hardly run at all," gasped Cathy.

"*I* see." Although Cathy's glance was straight ahead as she tried to settle into the narrow space, she knew she was being looked up and down. "Have an apple."

"I don't really think . . . ." Cathy turned to face her neighbour.

"It's all right, I washed 'em."

"Goodness, I didn't mean that." The woman could be amused by her embarrassment. "I didn't like to take your apple, that's all. Thank you."

The apple was of the same cheery red as the woman's cheeks, and no disappointment as Cathy bit into firm juicy flesh. "It's as good as a drink of water."

"That's nice." She was still being studied. "You calming down now?"

"Yes, of course. It's stupid, isn't it, you almost burst a blood vessel catching a train or a bus or whatever, and by the next day it doesn't matter a bit."

"That's how it has to be, though." The woman smoothed her hands down the curved front of her coat. "We've got to believe a thing's important at the time of it, or nothing would be. I reckon that's how we keep our interest up in being alive."

"Ye-e-s." The idea was novel, and somehow surprising from the conventionally comfortable-looking woman beside her, surrounded and partially obscured by a welter of bulging plastic bags. "I've never looked at it in that sort of a way before."

"Haven't you, dearie? Well, it's just a little thought of mine." She was being examined yet again. "You've got over your rush now, but you're still het up, aren't you?"

"Het up? Why d'you say that?" It wasn't difficult, though, to believe that what she was feeling inside had leaked out into her face. Not that this woman had ever seen her as she had been before hearing the news.

"Just something in the look of you." This time Cathy watched the bright dark eyes travel from her head to her feet.

"Well . . . Oh, I'll tell you, I can't keep it to myself, anyway. And sometimes it's easiest to talk to someone you don't know."

"People find that, dearie. What are you going to tell me?"

"I'm—oh, it seems absurd, as if I was the only woman in the world . . . I've just learned I'm going to have a baby."

"I thought as much."

"You—what?" She was staring now into the knowing face, in disbelief.

"I thought that was what it was."

"But I've only just—"

"Oh, it's not from seeing. Well, not from seeing what everyone will see later on. It's just—something about you. Some people have the gift of it. Of seeing when a woman's in that way, however quiet she keeps. Like the gift of knowing death's on the way. I've got that, too."

The shiver had passed over Cathy before she knew it was coming, and the woman patted her arm with a small white hand of noticeably different texture from the rosy face. In a shaft of sunlight Cathy saw that the colour in the full cheeks was made up of a close texture of tiny veins, and as the face turned away from her, perhaps for the first time since she had fallen into her seat, the small nose was revealed to be tiptilted, probably the feature, allied to the assumption of intuitive knowledge, which was making Cathy think of an elderly elf. Certainly it was a face she would like to paint.

"Death seems—sort of unimaginable, just now," said Cathy.

"Of course it does, dearie." The woman had turned to her again, and to her artist's memory store Cathy added the short fair-white hair and the slightly lopsided smile which showed small uneven teeth. "So you've just found out, have you?" The seat rose and fell as the woman shifted her weight, and the packages on and around her stirred and subsided into different shapes, emitting as they did so a waft of disinfectant not quite masking another, mercifully weakened, smell.

"Yes. Just. Of course it was naughty of me to deceive Neil, but I just couldn't wait to be sure and I did so want it to be old Dr. Kelly. He's the doctor who's looked after my family all my life," added Cathy, forcing herself to realize she wasn't talking to herself. "I didn't even tell Mummy and Daddy I was going to see him, that I was so near home, I wanted Neil to be the first person to know. Oh!" She caught her neighbour's attentive eye above the hand she had clamped to her mouth. "Now I've made you the first person, haven't I? How horribly unfair of me. But somehow you made me . . ."

"People do confide in me, dearie. It's another little gift, I reckon. Don't you worry, though, it'll be our secret. And as you said, it doesn't count, telling a stranger . . . Neil? Your husband?"

"Yes."

"And your first baby?"

"Yes."

"You been married long, dearie?"

"Almost a year." Cathy gestured through the window. "I remember being engaged against a background of that very fine pink blossom. Almond, isn't it? We said we wouldn't have a baby for at least three years but I'm terribly glad. I know Neil will be, too." But suddenly her happiness was breached. Would Neil be glad?

"You not quite sure of that, dearie?"

"Of course I'm sure! And I don't know why I'm going on like this. Please forgive me. It's very boring as well as being bad manners."

"Bad manners! *You* forgive *me*, dearie, but I can't decide whether you're a little girl or a little old lady."

"Settle for a haywire young woman." Her neighbour was too obviously a law to herself for Cathy to take offence—which anyway wasn't a tendency with her, and her excitement was back in place.

"I'll do that." The woman smiled at her in a friendly way. "Live in London, dearie?"

"Yes. St. John's Wood." She really must remember that she wasn't the only woman in the world. "Do you live in London, too?"

"North London, I live in North London, too. There's a coincidence."

"Yes . . . I'd like to paint you."

"Paint me!" Surprise made the face alert, almost suspicious, but the look was so quickly gone, Cathy thought she must have imagined it.

"Yes. It's my living. Well, if I'm honest the living is from teaching art at school, but I do portraits if I can get the commissions. And of course if I especially like a face I ask if I may paint it and then I do it for my own pleasure."

"Well, now . . . We might be able to do one another a favour. I'm Mrs. Willoughby, by the way."

"I'm Cathy Carter."

"Well, Mrs. Carter"—Mrs. Willoughby's whole body had turned slightly towards her, dislodging itself from the back of the seat so that there was suddenly enough room for Cathy to stay on without bracing her legs—"I'm a dressmaker. And I alter clothes whether I've made 'em or not. Taking in, letting out, hems, remodelling. Not so easy these days, dearie, finding folk to do that."

"I can alter, but I'd much rather not. And especially now . . . I'd certainly like to come—"

"And paint me, eh? Well, you paint me, I'll make you a wardrobe for the next few months."

"It's a deal. And we've just broken up, I've got free days for a whole month. Are you all right?" Her neighbour was suddenly as breathless as if she had run all the way across Kent herself.

"Bless you, dearie," said Mrs. Willoughby when she could. "It's just my irregular heart. Sounds like a popular song, doesn't it? Which it isn't, it's a condition I have to live with these days, and that's a thing I'll never be used to . . . I'm all right now. What were we saying?"

"We've made a deal."

"Ah yes. And I was going to say that there's another thing, although you'll maybe not be as interested in that."

"What is it, Mrs. Willoughby?"

"That's nice, you remembered my name. It's the hands. I read the hands. There's the crystal, too, if anyone fancies that. As I said, it may not be your cup of tea—I don't do tea-leaves, by the way—but I just thought I'd mention it. You can be thinking whether you'd be interested."

"I probably would, normally," said Cathy slowly, examining her reaction. "Just now, I don't know. I mean, if you told me things weren't going to be so good for a while it would worry me, it would be bound to. You'll understand—"

"Bless you, of course I do." Mrs. Willoughby's breathing was still alarming. "Anyway, you come along with any bits and pieces of frocks and things, and any ideas for some new ones, and your paintbox if you want to, I shan't be bothered."

"I will, I'll give you a ring. Can you let me have your number?"

"I can give you my card."

Mrs. Willoughby withdrew an arm from the handles of half her carrier bags and rummaged in the one non-plastic item she had about her—a large dilapidated leather handbag. "Here we are."

The card bore the name Mrs. Charles Willoughby in its centre, with an address and a telephone number to right and left above, and in the two lower corners the words "Dressmaker and Clairvoyant." A deepening of the white to cream at the edges made Cathy wonder if it had been some time awaiting bestowal.

"It shouldn't be Mrs. Charles, it should be Mrs. Mabel." A mournful note was affecting Mrs. Willoughby's cheerful voice. "I lost my husband a few years back, but I'd had the cards done and I always feel it's a bit heartless, like, to drop your husband's name overnight just because he's been taken off of you and didn't even choose to go."

"The Americans don't do it," supplied Cathy.

"There you are! And it doesn't do any harm to let people think you still have a husband. I don't usually say anything, but with you . . . Calling myself Mrs. Charles is a bit like hanging a man's hat up in the hall, I always think."

"Yes, I can see—"

"He suffered a lot at the end," continued Mrs. Willoughby, reminiscently gloomy. "And before that he was an invalid." Her movement on the seat, this time, was sharper, and her breathing suddenly loud again. "But we managed. Still do. Your husband a teacher too, dearie?"

"Oh, no. My husband's a policeman. At Scotland Yard," added Cathy casually, wondering if a day would ever come when she would pinpoint Neil's office without a sense of pride.

"Really, dearie?" Again there was enough room for Cathy to relax her legs. "That's very interesting. Constable, is he? You hardly looking old enough to be married at all, I can't think—"

"An inspector. CID."

"Well now, fancy that! Make you uncomfortable sometimes, does it, dearie?"

"No," said Cathy in surprise. "Why should it?"

For the first time her neighbour laughed, a small sharp sound. "Just my little joke, dearie. I was only thinking . . . No cutting any little corners with a policeman for a husband."

"My husband's not a puritan, he doesn't make me feel I've got to be superhumanly good. He makes me feel rather safe, actually."

"Of course he does, dearie . . . Well, that is interesting."

"You've been doing an awful lot of shopping," said Cathy, feeling she had played enough of the defensive role in which, she didn't know why, she had cast herself.

"Shopping? These?" Mrs. Willoughby glanced round at her carrier bags, laughing more expansively. "Bless you, dearie, this ain't shopping. I've been visiting some friends and got given some sewing to do for 'em. Can't be bad, can it?" Mrs. Willoughby laughed again, making a token gesture of gathering her unwieldy hoard closer about her.

"You're going to be busy," said Cathy. "And how will you manage at Victoria? And with your heart . . . I'm sorry Neil's not coming to pick me up so we could give you a lift, but as I said he doesn't know where I've been. I can help you with the bags on the tube, at any rate, if you're going by Bakerloo."

"Bless you, dearie, none of these bags is heavy. Only awkward. All the same I'll get a taxi, it's my extravagance with not having a car. Thanks, though, for the thought. You don't have a car, either? I'd have thought—"

"I do, Mrs. Willoughby, I do. It let me down a couple of days ago as inconveniently as it could, and I'm going to collect it from the garage on the way home, I'm pleased to say."

"If you'd had it this afternoon, dearie, we wouldn't have met, would we?" Mrs. Willoughby gave her lopsided smile.

"No," amended Cathy quickly, "and that would have been a pity. I don't feel half as bad-tempered about the car as I did."

Nor did she feel, though, that she wanted less than half a seat beside Mrs. Willoughby between Victoria and the garage, to say nothing of a better opportunity of analyzing the emanations from her carrier bags. Nevertheless she took most of them into her grasp before walking Mrs. Willoughby carefully to a taxi, and strewed them over the unoccupied space as she declined the offer of a lift home.

"Thanks so much, but I've one or two things to do on the way, apart from collecting the car. I'll ring you very soon and look forward to seeing you again."

"Any time, dearie, any time. Thanks for the company, it passed the journey a treat. Now you go and tell your husband the good news."

"Yes. Of course." If Mrs. Willoughby had looked in her crystal then and there, and disliked what she saw, Cathy would have put it down to Neil about to be less than delighted with what she had to tell him. Her joy was breached a second time by a shaft of anxiety, and when she got home she had to force herself to concentrate on preparing the meal as she listened for the lift gates and Neil's key in the door. Even when he told her he didn't expect to be late he often was, and she made no comment. But tonight when she heard him, half an hour from the time she had begun to expect him, she also heard her voice ring out accusingly.

"You're late!"

"I'm sorry, darling."

At least he was surprised, and as she ran out to the hall she offered a brief prayer that he would never get used to being told off the minute he came through the door.

"I'm sorry." She was beside him, putting her arms round him, then drawing him into the sitting-room. "It was just that I want so much to tell you something and it seemed a long wait. I've been out."

"I know, you told me. Celebrating the end of term. Anne's for tea."

"No, actually . . . Sit down and I'll get you a drink, then you can listen to me."

He obeyed her in silence and she knew he was watching her as she moved about the room, trying to assess the importance of what was to come. He didn't speak until she put his drink into his hand.

"Aren't you having one?"

"No. That's what I want to tell you about, in a way. Neil . . ."

"For heaven's sake, Cathy, you scarcely touch the stuff. You may have begun to have a bit more since we got married, but you can't be imagining—"

"Of course not. Oh, it's my own fault for being all muddly as usual. I only meant . . ." Cathy cast herself down on the wide arm of the sofa, straddling it with her denim legs and trying and failing to imagine how such an instinctive action was going to become difficult, or impossible. "Darling, I didn't go to tea with Anne today, I went home."

"You went—"

"Well, not home, I didn't go and see Mummy, she didn't know I was so near, I went to see Dr. Kelly, because of having an idea . . . Neil, I'm going to have a baby, oh, darling, I do hope you're glad about it, I am if you are. I know we said . . . But we'd have been much stricter, wouldn't we, if we'd really—"

"Come here."

"Oh yes, please, and please tell me—"

"I'm a bit shaken, child, but I'm as glad as you are. Oh, Cathy . . ." She was on his lap and he was rocking her as if she were the baby. "Poor little thing, what have I done to you?"

"I'd be a poor little thing if you hadn't. I'm twenty-five, Neil, not fifteen, and you're thirty-three. Just the right time to start a family. You really are pleased?"

"I'm over the moon. It's just that I can't help always feeling that you're very, very young. If you're really happy, I am."

"Oh, I'm really happy. Absolutely, now that I know you are too. The only trouble is, I feel far too small to contain it all—the happiness, I mean, not the baby, Dr. Kelly said I ought to be fine. I specially didn't go home and see Mummy because I knew I wouldn't be able to resist telling her, and I wanted to tell you first. And then on the bus coming home—I had to go by bus, the car wasn't ready till this evening—I got chatting to an odd little woman with some smelly bags in the seat next to me—taking up most of the seat, actually, she was rather wide—and I told her. Oh, darling, I'm sorry. We both agreed that it didn't really count, but I wish I hadn't."

"I'll forgive you. When's it to be? Are you sure you're all right?"

"I'm sure I'm all right, and it's to be the end of September, beginning of October. I keep remembering when we got home after that New Year party, I'd like to think . . . It fits in beautifully, doesn't it, I can work till the end of the school year."

"And you're going to cut out even your single pre-supper sherry until after the baby's born."

"Well, yes, I thought so. All the things you read nowadays. If anything went wrong—it won't, Neil—I'd always feel it might have been that."

"You're probably right. So far as I'm concerned you've already been transformed into a piece of porcelain." Almost tentatively his hands tightened on her shoulders, making her smile. "Too attractive a piece, though. At this moment . . ."

"Oh, that's all right for ages yet. Alcohol and tearing about are the only things I'm intending to give up . . . This woman I met on the bus, she has a strange sort of a marvellous face, I'm going to paint it. Also she makes and alters clothes and doesn't live too far away, so we can organize something to suit us both. The smell didn't come from her, it came from the bags she was carrying . . . Neil . . . Well, it *is* a casserole, it can't spoil, and anyway it's got a long way to go yet . . . I've already been tempted once today, this woman gave me an apple . . ."

CHAPTER TWO

"Push the door now, dearie!"

Mrs. Willoughby's voice, sepulchral behind the buzzing of the opening mechanism, was unrecognizable. Cathy pressed the heavy, dilapidated door, once white, and it reluctantly gave, on to a small dark lobby containing, she could just make out, panelled doors to right and left and, immediately in front of her, a tall narrow staircase.

"That's right. Come on up, dearie." Mrs. Willoughby's squat shape appeared at the head of the stairs, beckoning encouragingly, and Cathy began to climb, hearing the door latch behind her, seeing as her eyes grew accustomed to the dim light the worn and dusty pattern in red, blue and green of a carpet familiar from the lesser corridors of old hotels.

"There you are! Forgive me not coming down for you, dearie, but my heart . . ." Mrs. Willoughby, appearing as breathless as if she had in fact climbed the steep stairs several times, patted the deep curve of her front. The light, Cathy now saw, came from a weak landing bulb and a grimy skylight which seemed a long way away but which she knew, from her examination of the Victorian building before pressing the buzzer marked WILLOUGHBY, could be only one further floor above. "You see your way all right? The landlord's a bit neglectful," conceded Mrs. Willoughby, "but you can't always have things just as you'd like them at your workplace. Now, you come in here, you can see what's what, at least."

Mrs. Willoughby pushed an open door to the left of the stairhead, urging Cathy to precede her into a large, bright, untidy room with two sash windows on to the street. Against the far wall a bed dressed impressionistically as a couch was covered with the unsewn portions of a dress and jacket. In the other window corner a rudimentary kitchen had a short wooden draining-board sodden dark from generations of dishes left to dry. The wall on to which the door gave was taken up almost entirely by an enormous mahogany wardrobe, the outer two of its three doors ajar and the long drawer under the central mirror open to reveal one of Mrs. Willoughby's bulging carrier bags and a bolt of bright blue cloth protruding beyond its edge. The familiar stair carpet, less worn, extended in all directions to treacle-brown floorboards, and in the centre of the room was a large round table on a scuffed Regency leg, its surface covered by a dark green cloth in crushed velvet, sporting an intermittent fringe. Despite the disorder Cathy could see that the room was clean, and there was no smell. Her instinct had been right.

"I sleep here when I'm too tired or it's too late to go home," offered Mrs. Willoughby, tweaking then smoothing the table-cloth. "It's all right, it does me. I could use my other room, but I like to keep something decent, even at my place of work. You can put your coat nicely, at any rate. Leave your paints and your frocks here and come and see."

Pulling the door to behind them so that its Yale latch caught, Mrs. Willoughby led the way across a landing devoid of feature and only a little larger than the lobby below, from which another narrow stair continued upwards, linoleum-covered.

"If you want the bathroom . . ." Mrs. Willoughby gestured vaguely towards the door next to the one from which they had just emerged. "Exclusive use of toilet and bathroom, it says in the lease, so I keep it locked. Not being self-contained, you see, if I didn't every Tom, Dick and Harry would help themselves. The people up top for a start—*very* common"—Mrs. Willoughby's voice sank to a token diminuendo— "you couldn't call what *they've* got much more than a privy. Mr. Grayson downstairs, Jim"—by the light to which she was growing accustomed Cathy saw the keen face soften and thought she heard warmth in the voice—"he's got his own proper place so *he* wouldn't be up—not that Jim's the sort to help himself to other people's toilet facilities without a by your leave whether he had his own or not . . . Mr. Bolshaw—he's the other gentleman downstairs—he's got his own facilities, I suppose. Not that anyone could know for sure, he never opens his door more than a crack and he never lets anyone in. So polite, though, Mr. Bolshaw, such nice manners, I can't think he'd ever . . . Here we are, dearie."

Mrs. Willoughby unlocked the door opposite and pushed it open, feeling for and snapping on a light switch.

"Oh!" exclaimed Cathy, not entirely out of politeness, as Mrs. Willoughby stood aside. Staring, she moved forward in response to the hand on her shoulder as the door clicked shut.

"It *is* nice, isn't it?" responded Mrs. Willoughby complacently, crossing to a deep bay window to open orange silk curtains and dissipate Cathy's disorientating reaction of having been transported back into a best bedroom of the 1930s.

Mrs. Willoughby's back room was a time capsule. A bedspread in orange satin matched the curtains, an embroidered spray of marigolds scattered asymmetrically across its shiny surface, and there was a sharp-angled matching suite in some dark, unnaturally grained wood with a long unframed mirror plunging down between the wings of the dressing-table and obtrusive barred handles to the drawers and those of the wardrobe and tallboy. The bare cream walls had a narrow frieze in green and orange, and on the carpet, geometrically patterned in orange and brown, there stood two small gilded wickerwork armchairs. On the dressing-table was an Art Deco toilet set in heavy green glass.

"Most of the things in here were wedding presents." Mrs. Willoughby lifted the net curtain and peered out. "I've got rid of a few things over the years, but never anything from my front bedroom. I still call it that, dearie, even though the other's the front room nowadays, it being the one I have to use, with having the light and a bit of life in the street. This gives on to the back, nothing to see, and I'd get the willies except it's nice in the spring when it's all white with pear blossom. At least someone put in a bay window, you don't ever get a bay window at the back with this sort of house. You can have a look out if you want to."

Mrs. Willoughby vacated the narrow gap beside the dressing-table, keeping hold of the net curtain so that Cathy could see the series of long narrow gardens separated by old walls and meeting other gardens stretching towards them from the variegated backs—some flush, some warted with small extensions—of an Edwardian beige brick terrace. Cathy liked the effect of so much mature growth and the mellow walls giving the impression of ornamental interruptions rather than boundary lines. But it was easy to understand Mrs. Willoughby preferring the bustle outside the other windows on the front of the house.

"Yes, I still think of it as my front room," repeated Mrs. Willoughby, letting the curtain fall as Cathy, murmuring a compliment, stepped back from the window. Mrs. Willoughby immediately closed the orange silk curtains, restoring the weak but harsh light from the one overhead fitting, and Cathy's unnerving sense of time travel. "Do put your coat on the bed, dearie."

"It's very nice," Cathy managed. "Beautifully kept, too." She was about to add that it was a pity it wasn't used, but it occurred to her in time that, occupied by a modern tenant, it would cease to be itself. This could be something Mrs. Willoughby knew by instinct, and was prompted by her knowledge to maintain it as a museum piece.

It was a relief to be back in the bright lived-in untidiness across the landing.

"So what have you got for me?" asked Mrs. Willoughby, as Cathy bent towards her bags.

"Two dresses and a pair of trousers as a start." She took them out. "I was going to bring a skirt that needs taking in, but then I thought I'd leave it as it is because of—of getting bigger soon." She had never felt thinner, it seemed absurd.

"That's sensible," said Mrs. Willoughby, spreading the things on the table. "Your husband pleased to hear your news?"

"Of course, I told you he would be."

"That's nice, then, dearie . . . You want these hems let down?"

"Please. I think one of them will need a false hem—"

"That's all right, no problem. And the trousers?"

"They're new and they're a bit long."

"Good. Off we go, then!"

There was no central heating, but a large gas fire was making the room suffocatingly hot. A buzzer sounded while Cathy was fastening the first of the dresses, and Mrs. Willoughby, whose back had been obtrusively turned since the undressing began, went over to a telephone on the wall by the door.

"Yes, who is it?"

There was a faint squawk.

"Hold on a minute, dearie." Mrs. Willoughby put her hand over the mouthpiece and turned tentatively towards Cathy. "One of my other lady clients, come to settle a bill. You mind if she comes up?"

"Goodness, no." She was dressed, but she wouldn't have minded, either, if she'd been in her slip. Would she mind in a few months' time, when her body had changed?

"Come up, Miss Littlewood, dearie," said Mrs. Willoughby into the telephone, pressing a button whose effect was inaudible, but almost at once Cathy heard feet ploddingly on the stairs, and then a loud rap at the door.

"Come in, come in!" called Mrs. Willoughby cheerily, opening the door and then the central mirrored panel of her wardrobe, to reveal a warren of miniature mahogany drawers, doors and spaces. When she closed it she was holding a small black book.

The woman who entered the room was so like a man, she had Cathy crossing her arms over her body in reflex modesty before she noticed the curve of bosom and width of thigh.

"You should have said you had company, Mrs. Willoughby." The voice was deep for a woman, brusque and possibly ironic.

"Bless you, dearie, Mrs. Carter doesn't mind." Mrs. Willoughby looked up from her black book. "This is Mrs. Carter. Mrs. Carter, Miss Littlewood."

"Hello," said Cathy, smiling and trying not to feel uncomfortable in the bright light of Miss Littlewood's ungracious glare.

"Mrs. Carter's a new client—"

"My coat's ready, I suppose?"

Miss Littlewood had compounded nature's work on her by a short bristly haircut, no make-up, and baggy trouser legs resting on flat heavy-duty shoes.

"Oh, yes, dearie, I was expecting you in your lunch hour." Mrs. Willoughby picked up the large carrier bag leaning against the side of the wardrobe.

"I'm taking it late today."

Mrs. Willoughby passed over the carrier bag, and received an envelope from Miss Littlewood's large red hand which she slipped between the pages of her book before making a note and returning the book to the recesses of the wardrobe. "There we are!" She closed and locked the mirrored door. "Thank you very much, dearie. My ladies are always so prompt," she said to Cathy. "They use their imagination, bless them, and understand it isn't always easy for a person in my position . . . Whole businesses can fail, you know, just because of people not paying, dormant money, they call it . . . Now, Miss Littlewood, I'm just going to put the kettle on for Mrs. Carter and myself. You'll stay for a cuppa?"

"No, thank you," snapped Miss Littlewood. This time her glance at Cathy seemed to contain speculation as well as hostility.

"Goodbye, then, dearie, for now," beamed Mrs. Willoughby, un-snubbed. Miss Littlewood jerked the door open and shut, and could be heard plunging heavily down the stairs.

"A woman at odds with herself, wouldn't you say?" Mrs. Willoughby spoke through a mouthful of pins, a feat which Cathy found alarming, particularly in view of the ever present possibility of breathlessness.

"Well—she did seem to have got out of bed the wrong side today," she responded carefully.

"She's always like that. My own view is that she was born wrong. If you follow mc, dcarie. Very sad. Well, you can see, can't you? I don't like to think about such things, let alone talk about them, but with Miss Littlewood . . ."

"I suppose it could be . . . What does she do?"

"That's fine!" Mrs. Willoughby stepped back to examine the dropped hemline. "Into the next frock now!" She crossed the room and turned on a tap, which wheezed and spluttered preparatory to emitting a thin flow of water. "Do? She's supervisor of a typing pool with some big firm up west. Most unsuitable, I always think." The gas let out a loud pop as Mrs. Willoughby turned round. "Oh, that's *very* nice, dearie, very nice indeed. But you're quite right, it could do with a couple more inches."

Mrs. Willoughby's mouth was soon full of pins again, and Cathy forbore to initiate conversation until the tin kettle began to whistle from the dark maze of obsolete gas pipes on top of Mrs. Willoughby's old stove.

"Shall I make the tea?"

"Bless you, dearie, that's all right. But it was a sweet thought." Mrs. Willoughby removed the remaining pins and crossed the room. "I don't suppose you need sugar," she said, smiling.

"No, actually. Just a dash of milk." She had been hoping Mrs. Willoughby did not intend to broach the intact packet of substantial-looking buns lying on the draining-board, and was relieved to see her remain by the table when she had deposited the two steaming mugs.

"Nothing like a cuppa, is there? I had an aunt, once, got addicted to it. *Yes.* Half-drunk cups of dark brown tea all over the house, not to mention the turn of the stairs and her husband breaking his leg over it." Mrs. Willoughby ripped expertly at the hem stitching round Cathy's skirt. "There, dearie, how's that?"

Cathy took her second twirl in front of the speckled cheval glass. "That's exactly it, thanks."

"I thought so. You were quite right, dearie, a false hem. Into the trousers now, and then—"

"And then I'll make a sketch if you've got time, Mrs. Willoughby."

"Bless you, you still want to paint me, do you, dearie?" Cathy thought she could detect surprise as well as satisfaction. Intending that first afternoon to do no more than draw, she had come without any artist's paraphernalia.

"Yes, please . . . Look, Mrs. Willoughby"—her chest reacted unfavourably to the mouthful of piercingly strong tea—"if it goes as I hope it will, I'd rather like to include you—your head and shoulders, at least—in a mural I'm doing with my pupils on a long wall at school. There's a crowd watching a procession—well, you just see the front faces in the crowd properly, and I'd like you to be one of them—a sort of look of eager interest, if you can imagine . . ." It occurred to Cathy that this was the sort of look she had been receiving from Mrs. Willoughby ever since she had sat down beside her on the coach to London.

"Eager interest, dearie?" Mrs. Willoughby's face seemed momentarily to close.

"Well—yes. I'm asking other people too, of course. About ten or a dozen recognizable faces at the front of the crowd. Three of them will be children—I've already lined up my young brother although he won't be easy . . . Then there's—"

"Bless you, dearie, that's all right!" Mrs. Willoughby beamed at Cathy. "In fact I'm quite flattered."

"Oh, don't be flattered, but I'm glad you don't mind. I want to paint a portrait of you first and foremost, but the mural face can be done from that. And I want to begin with a pencil study—"

"You just begin any way you like, dearie. More tea?"

"No, thank you." Mrs. Willoughby stood back and Cathy turned slowly in front of the mirror. "That's absolutely right."

"They suit you, but you were right, they need that bit off. That's all the work you've got for me today, then, dearie?"

"For today, yes, thanks. I'll get dressed and perhaps we can take one of those nice balloon-back chairs over to the window and then I'll arrange you."

"Anything to oblige. And I'll admit I'm ready to get off my legs. No, it's all right"—as Cathy ran over to prevent Mrs. Willoughby picking up a chair—"I can manage that much."

Mrs. Willoughby set the chair by one of the windows and sat heavily down while Cathy got back into her shirt and jeans.

"Y-e-e-s. I'll just angle you a bit . . . It's a good light."

"Wouldn't you like me to go and comb my hair, put a bit of powder on?"

"*No.* Your hair's nice and natural and the bit of shine on your cheeks shows me the bones. Just relax. Talk if you like; later on I'll be asking you to keep your mouth still."

But the situation seemed to inhibit Mrs. Willoughby's ready powers of speech and she sat silent as Cathy worked, speaking only the few times Cathy saw that her eyes were glazing and asked her a question to reanimate her face.

"Have you any children, Mrs. Willoughby?"

She had gone almost as far as she wanted to go that day, and this was the last question she would need to ask.

"I've a son." If Cathy hadn't been concentrating so exclusively on Mrs. Willoughby's face she might not have noticed the tightening of the mouth and its minute repercussions in forehead and jawline.

"Ah. D'you see him much?"

"I don't. He's abroad."

"That's a pity." Cathy left it there, both because the voice, she thought, was suggesting it would be best if she did, and because the subject of conversation was not enlivening her sitter's face as her earlier questions had done . . . If she had a son and one day he went to live abroad, would she resent it, feel badly done by? She hoped not, but there might be more to Mrs. Willoughby's resentment than mere distance.

"There, that's it for today."

"Have a look, can I?"

"It would be too mean of me to say no. But please remember it's not much more at the moment than something for me to work on."

Mrs. Willoughby heaved herself out of her chair and came to stand beside Cathy.

"Looks clever," she said after a moment.

"That's diplomatic of you." Cathy closed her sketch pad and got up smiling from the other balloon-back chair. "I'd like to bring paints and a canvas next time, if that's all right."

"That's fine, dearie . . . I'm so glad your husband's pleased about the baby." Mrs. Willoughby was looking through the window on to the busy street. "Did he ever find out that you'd deceived him?"

"Deceived him? Neil? Goodness, I'd never—"

"You said on the bus that it was naughty of you to have deceived your husband."

"Oh, yes." Cathy burst out laughing. "Whatever have you been thinking of me? It was just my silly way of talking; I pretended to him that I was going out to tea because I didn't want him to know I was going to see my old family doctor until I knew what the doctor would tell me. About the baby, or not. Of course as soon as I got home I told Neil where I'd really been and what I'd done, so it wasn't much of a deception."

"Of course not, dearie, it was just my joke. You and your husband don't have any secrets from each other, I'm sure."

"None that count . . ." Suddenly, even as she deplored it, Cathy decided to give in to the impulse she'd wrestled with beside a sleeping Neil in the early hours of the morning. "There's maybe going to be another small one . . . Mrs. Willoughby, I know I said I didn't think, just at the moment, that I'd want to ask you—"

"To look in the crystal, dearie? You did say it, and I could understand why, but if you've thought after all that you'd like me to have a peep, there's no harm in that. It's not as if we're making something happen that wouldn't happen naturally, is it, we're only looking to see what's there."

"I suppose so." Cathy wished Mrs. Willoughby's face had been as bright and animated while she was sketching it. "Well, then, if you've got time . . ."

"Bless you, dearie, of course I have. I've another lady popping in at any moment—her jacket's ready—but my time's my own. It is the crystal, is it, rather than the hands?"

"Well, I've never encountered a crystal."

"Haven't you, dearie? Nothing to worry about. See . . ."

Mrs. Willoughby was back at the heart of her wardrobe, bringing out a plain glass orb on a black base, which she set respectfully in the centre of the table. "Take the other chair again, dearie . . . That's right. Now, we'll just relax, shall we, make our minds blank. You can close your eyes if you'd rather, but there's no need . . ."

Cathy closed her eyes in an attempt to clear her mind, but the immediate inrush of vivid and irrelevant images made her open them again and focus on Mrs. Willoughby's intense face and small hovering hands. The contrast between the rosy face and the smooth white hands struck her even more strongly than on the bus from Kent. Mrs. Willoughby clearly cosseted her hands for her activity as clairvoyant, smooth hands would be especially desirable when reading palms . . .

"Gently does it . . ." Mrs. Willoughby's voice had softened to a croon. "Oh, yes, dear, a very good atmosphere, very good indeed. Right away your husband's there with you, you're sitting together, talking, laughing . . . Wait a moment, though, dearie . . . There's something . . . Something troubling you, something you want to say to him but can't quite manage . . . can't quite decide . . ." Mrs. Willoughby looked up, and keenly across at Cathy. "Is there something that's worrying you, dearie, something you want to tell your husband but feel you can't quite . . ."

"Goodness, no, nothing like that."

"All right, dearie," said Mrs. Willoughby soothingly. "Perhaps it's something I'm picking up from nearby, from someone else. That sometimes happens, if there's something very strong . . . It's all right, you're smiling together again, you're—God in heaven!" Mrs. Willoughby struggled to her feet, rocking her chair back behind her and raising her arm in front of her face as if to ward off a blow. Up till then she had been talking easily and fluently, the word "patter" had crossed Cathy's mind, but all at once, unless the clairvoyant was a consummate actress, there was no mistaking her shock and unpreparedness for what she had apparently seen. Or her struggle for breath.

Cathy too was on her feet, frightened and remorseful. "What is it, Mrs. Willoughby? Are you all right? Oh, I wish we hadn't . . ."

"It's all right, dearie." Mrs. Willoughby was obviously working as hard to reimpose her self-control as to regain her breath. Slowly she sat down again, and to Cathy's relief the working of her chest subsided. As if reluctantly, she bent her head once more over what looked to Cathy like the unchanging dull globe, and her eyes showed no reaction to what they now saw. "It's gone," said Mrs. Willoughby after a long moment, raising her head to stare unseeingly at Cathy. "It's all gone." Her eyes refocused, and Cathy saw the flash of concern. "I'm sorry, dearie, I didn't mean to frighten you. What the crystal showed . . . It wasn't to do with you. Really, dearie. I think, though, we'll leave it there for today."

"I think I'd rather we did." Cathy had no impulse to confess her absurd instinct that punishment could be hovering for those who tried to see what was meant to be hidden. And perhaps if there was a further revelation Mrs. Willoughby's breathing wouldn't recover . . .

This time the telephone buzzer shocked her into a little moan.

"I'm so sorry, dearie. It's only the front door again, probably the lady I told you was coming."

Mrs. Willoughby appeared to have recovered, but there was less contrast than usual between her face and her hands and it seemed an effort for her to walk to the telephone. "Come up, dearie," she said into the receiver.

The feet this time were slower and softer, the knock on the door faint.

"Come in, Mrs. Lawrence, dearie." Mrs. Willoughby, the black book again in her hand, crossed to the door and pulled it wide.

On the threshold was a dark attractive woman just out of first youth, notable for large blue eyes which failed to respond to either of the faces in the room. It was as if Mrs. Lawrence was blind, but she knew where Mrs. Willoughby's hand was waiting to receive an envelope.

"Thank you very much, dearie. Another conscientious customer!" said Mrs. Willoughby, then made a note and placed book and envelope carefully back in the wardrobe. "Your jacket's all ready." She crossed to the bed and picked up a carrier bag, taking it over to the door where her latest visitor still stood. "Here you are, dearie. No need to try it on. The skirt'll be ready next week. All right?"

Mrs. Lawrence took the plastic handle from Mrs. Willoughby, letting her hand fall to her side without glancing at the bag. Cathy thought she slightly inclined her head, and then she had slipped out of the room and her feet were just audible on the stairs—hesitant, irregular.

"Well!" said Mrs. Willoughby, when there was no more sound. "You *will* be thinking I've some funny customers, Mrs. Carter. Mrs. Lawrence is all right, really, just a bit of a melancholy disposition."

"She *can* speak? And see?"

"Bless you, yes! But I'll grant you she's a woman of few words. Only speaks where she really feels it's necessary. I reckon there's some of us could take a leaf out of her book, and I'm not saying I'm not one of them."

Mrs. Willoughby smiled at Cathy, as rosy and jolly as she had ever been. It seemed a good moment in which to leave, and Cathy collected her scattered belongings, somehow glad that Mrs. Willoughby crossed the landing alone to bring her her jacket from the gold satin bed.

"Same time next week?" asked Mrs. Willoughby, perhaps anxiously.

"Of course!" Cathy heard the heartiness of her voice, trying to make up for her realization that she would really rather not come again, and regretted the instinct which would deprive an old lady of some company and interest. And she still wanted to paint the portrait and include Mrs. Willoughby in the mural.

"Thank you, dearie, that'll be nice, I'll look forward to that. You see your way, now?"

"Fine," said Cathy untruthfully, gripping the banister rail. She was at the foot of the stairs before her eyes were accustomed to the poor light.

"Au revower!" called Mrs. Willoughby, and Cathy heard the click of the Yale lock upstairs as she went through the heavy street door.

On to a *tableau vivant* of shouting, screaming people bunched in one spot against the bright red background of a stationary bus.

A man in London Transport uniform stood slightly apart from the cluster, raising his arms and calling out, tears glinting on his cheeks. Cathy tried to think "street theatre," but she knew the man wasn't acting, and when the group of people broke up to let two other people in, she saw there was someone on the ground. A woman on her side, her legs at an angle no legs would naturally go, one hand as if groping in a spill of blood, a white face staring up at the sky, large blue eyes . . .

"Mrs. Lawrence! It's Mrs. Lawrence!"

"There's nothing we can do. Come in here."

A man had appeared beside her in the doorway. As his arms took her weight the bus driver shouted, "She didn't give me a chance!" and sank to his knees. Then mercifully the curtain came down, the heavy door closed with her and the man who was supporting her on the inside, and she was letting herself be helped the short way into a downstairs room.

"Mrs. Lawrence! It's Mrs. Lawrence!"

She had heard the words several times, like the refrain of a song, and as she sank on to a sofa she realized it was she who was saying them.

"Mrs. Lawrence?" asked the man's voice. "Ma has a client called Mrs. Lawrence."

"Yes! She just left, she went down the stairs just before I did. Mrs. Willoughby said she wasn't blind but she looked to me—"

"She wasn't blind, I'm sure. Here. Drink this." It was a small tot of brandy, on which she choked. "I hope Ma didn't see . . ."

"What? See what? Is she . . ."

"She was dead, I think," said the voice softly, and Cathy at last raised her head to look at the man who was speaking.

He was sitting forward in a chair quite close to her, his hands dangling between his knees and an expression of gentle concern on his thin pale face. He had thin pale hair, untidy, and was about the same age as Neil, with a comparable intelligence in his worried eyes. She was disposed to like him without reference to his having probably saved her from passing out on the pavement.

"The baby!"

"I'm sorry?"

"*I'm* sorry, I'm still saying things I don't know I'm going to say. I haven't been pregnant very long and I just remembered . . ."

The skin round the man's eyes crinkled more deeply. "Do please go on sitting there as long as you want. Are you comfortable?"

"Yes, of course." She was able to smile at him. "I'm Cathy Carter, I've just been with Mrs. Willoughby."

"I'm Jim Grayson. I'm glad I was at home, I'm not usually at this time of day. Please don't look round too much, this is an awful dump, but I came here when I was young and poor and just got used to it."

The large room was sparsely furnished but what was there pleased Cathy—two jewelled Persian rugs on a plain pale carpet, a long white structure full of books facing the windows, comfortable-looking chairs and on a side wall a pattern of topographical prints. The two windows looked out on to the garden.

"And now you're rich, if not old?"

"As a private eye? Hardly, although at least I've got a salubrious business address these days . . . Ah, you have a reaction."

"My husband's a public eye. In the Met." She stood up, testing herself. "I'm all right now, really I am. Thank you for being so kind and quick."

"There was nothing to it." Jim Grayson was on his feet too, preceding her to the door. "I don't suppose I'll be in the next time you come to see Ma, but in case I am, do please knock to tell me you're all right."

"Thank you, I will." She felt fine again, with no legacy from the shock. "Is Mrs. Willoughby a relation?"

"No." His face softened, as Mrs. Willoughby's face had softened when she spoke of him. "I just keep an eye on her. She's a nice old thing."

"I hope she's got someone like you to look after her at home as well."

"Oh, no!"

"What is it?" She had obviously said more than the words she'd used: Jim Grayson was looking a mixture of exasperation and regret.

"It's only—Ma hasn't anywhere else to go. This is her home as well as where she works."

"But she told me—"

"I know. She told—another of her clients, who told me, so I suggested to her, as gently as I could, that she shouldn't do it, that she didn't have to be ashamed of where she lived. I told her I wasn't ashamed—white lie—and she promised me she wouldn't do it again."

"I suppose it was a reflex action, don't be cross with her."

"Oh, I won't. I won't even tell her you and I've mentioned her. She was more put out to find she'd been the subject of discussion between me and one of her clients than that I'd learned about her fantasy. And she prefers to keep her clients to herself. Well, I don't suppose she's got much else, these days."

"She's got a son." Cathy tried not to look hopeful of learning something. Mrs. Willoughby intrigued her.

"Who seems to bring more pain then pleasure, so far as I can tell. Which isn't far, as she won't talk about him."

"My experience, already. I'm painting her portrait, by the way. But she'll tell you."

"A Yard man's wife and an artist, all in one day! And all in one person!"

Jim Grayson smiled as he pulled back the heavy front door for her, his face transformed. The bus had gone but there was a screen round the place in the road where Mrs. Lawrence had lain, two policemen standing beside it and looking sternly at the persistent small crowd.

"You're sure you're all right?"

"Certain. I don't usually over-react like that. But somehow . . ."

"It was a shock, you'd just seen her. And your condition, no doubt." This time his smile was a grin. "Au revoir."

"Goodbye and thanks again."

Cathy crossed the road beyond the grim obstruction, looking straight ahead. When she reached the far pavement she glanced back at the house. A man with a lot of grey hair dodged away from one of the ground-floor windows. The mysterious Mr. Bolshaw? Behind the net curtain at a window above she thought she saw someone standing motionless.

CHAPTER THREE

Each time Cathy came back to the flat where she had lived before her marriage she gave herself the pleasure, as she turned the key in the door, of contrasting her home-comings then with her home-comings now. Then, her entry had been invariably preceded by a roll of the eye and a lurch of the heart towards the identical door opposite behind which Neil was living as a sociable bachelor. Now she went eagerly inside without a glance around her, and although she still usually returned, at the end of afternoon school, to an empty place, it held the promise of Neil's presence and the proof of it in his belongings mingling with her own.

"So much the same," said Cathy aloud, letting everything she was carrying fall to the floor as she raised her arms in thanksgiving and, this particular afternoon, an unfamiliar sense of relief. "And so different."

The hat trick of shocks was Neil lounging in the sitting-room doorway, looking wary and defensive until he saw that she was alone.

"Talking to yourself *again?*"

"Was I? If I was, it was because I didn't think there was anyone else to talk to. What are you doing here?"

"I was on a job which ended up round the corner. There was a lot of paper work and nothing else particular to be out and about. And I'd forgotten you wouldn't be here."

"If there was a lot of paper work, it's just as well that I wasn't." She was in the air, at the end of his arms. "You won't be able to do that in a few months' time."

"I'll be much too scared to." He was searching her face with that new look of anxiety which had her wanting to laugh at him. "Cathy, I'm really not imagining it, you don't look very well."

"I've had—a shock." She had been going to say a couple of shocks, then remembered she had decided not to tell him about the crystal. "It's all right," she went on quickly, as the anxiety in his eyes approached panic, "nothing to do with me. I went to see that woman I met on the bus the day I saw Dr. Kelly—you remember, Mrs. Willoughby—to have a few things altered and start painting her. She lives in two rooms on the first floor of a dingy old house quite near Archie's junk-shop." She peeled off her coat and dropped it too before taking his hand and leading him to the sitting-room sofa. "A couple of other clients came up while I was there. They both came and went rather quickly, and I went myself just after the second one and when I opened the front door . . . Neil, she'd just been run over by a bus."

"Oh, darling." He put his arms round her and she felt her concern for Mrs. Lawrence ebbing away.

"It was awful," she said, conscience-stricken. "She was quite young and pretty, and then she was dead."

"Did you find out what had happened?"

"Not really. I started to go all silly and fainty when I saw her—I saw her in the road, Neil, in an impossible sort of position, and there was blood and the poor bus driver . . . Then there was suddenly a man there who pulled me back into the house and into a downstairs room which turned out to be his flat. Oh, darling, don't look so miserable, I suppose he *could* have been a white slaver and in the shape I was in I couldn't have put up much resistance, but he was just one of the two men who live downstairs and he was kind and considerate, gave me a brandy and told me to take my time. He's fond of Mrs. Willoughby and keeps an eye on her, she's a widow with delusions of—well, not grandeur exactly, but of living on a bigger scale than she actually does. She kept talking about her rooms in that house as her work-place and about going home, but this man—Jim somebody, he told me his other name but I've forgotten it—Jim said she hasn't got anywhere else and it's just a pretence. A bit sad, I thought. Especially as one of her rooms is a thirties best bedroom and quite enough for her to show off with, she obviously thinks it's the last word in elegance. It gave me the creeps, somehow. Perhaps because it reminded me of that guest-room of Grandma's where I used to be sent to calm down when we went for Sunday lunch and I got too excited . . . Neil . . ."

"What is it, darling? You look awful."

"I'm all right. Could you just get me a glass of water?"

While he was out of the room she tried to subdue the impact of her fourth shock. Was it Mrs. Lawrence's violent death that Mrs. Willoughby had seen in her crystal? *The gift of knowing death's on the way. I've got that . . .*

"You're all shivery."

"The proverbial goose, that's all. See." Forcing herself to smile, Cathy set the empty glass down and held her hands out in front of her, overcoming all but the tiniest tremor. "I'm fine now, Neil, honestly."

"It was a nasty shock, though. Will you go and see Dr. Kelly?"

"No. It hasn't affected the baby, I know it hasn't. Neil . . . The woman who was run over, Mrs. Lawrence, she was rather strange."

"Strange?"

"Well, she didn't say a word while she and Mrs. Willoughby did their transaction, and she didn't seem to see either of us. I'd have thought she was blind and maybe deaf as well, only Mrs. Willoughby told me she wasn't. Mrs. W talked for the two of them, and Mrs. Lawrence just put whatever she owed Mrs. W into her hand, and Mrs. W put a plastic bag into *her* hand and she turned and went out and down the stairs. Almost as if she was sleepwalking."

"Which could argue both for and against it having been an accident," said Neil eagerly. Cathy saw that he was all at once professionally alert, and that the hand on hers could as well have been resting on the arm of the sofa. "I mean, if she was ill or upset she could have walked under the bus without seeing it, and being ill or upset could have made her *decide* to walk under it. It'll be interesting to see the verdict on the death." His eyes saw her again, his hand lifted hers against his face. "I'm sorry, Cathy, I'm reverting to type. But don't think I'm not aware it was a horrible thing."

"And interesting too. I agree with you. Perhaps Mrs. Willoughby'll be able to tell me something when I go next week. I can still see it, though . . . Have you been here with your paper work all afternoon?"

"Since about four o'clock. The first half-hour was wasted at crosspurposes with some fellow wanting to deliver a parcel at 36 Westcote Road and trying to persuade me 36 Westcote Gardens, Westcote Road, was the same thing."

"At least it makes a change from not having things delivered because they've gone to 36 Westcote Road. But I thought the GPO had got us sorted out at last."

"This wasn't a GPO delivery, it was one of those ultra-speedy expensive private enterprise jobs. A dark grey uniform and probably a dark grey van to match. You see them more in the City, plying between prosperous firms. But I suppose there's still plenty of money about in St. John's Wood, even though we don't see much of it."

"And those old houses the other end of Westcote Road, they're pretty palatial. Any other interruptions?"

"Only this last one."

"Which isn't going to go on any longer. I'm trying something new for supper and I'm going to start now."

It was a spur-of-the-moment decision, born of her need to take the goose-flesh out of Mrs. Willoughby's horror at the crystal being followed by Mrs. Lawrence's death. She had to talk herself into believing it had been a coincidence, and she was more likely to manage it on her own. Reading and obeying her recipe on a series of reflexes, Cathy tried hard to convince herself, but kept coming back to her conviction that Mrs. Willoughby, in the midst of her smooth talk and her routine comments, had suddenly seen something which had terrified her.

Mrs. Lawrence, lying dead in the road?

The gift of knowing death's on the way. I've got that . . .

And if it *had* been a coincidence . . . Something terrible to do with her client? Mrs. Willoughby had reassured her, but how much had that been a true reflection of what she had seen, and how much simply an attempt to correct the impression made on Cathy by her terror?

She was making herself feel worse rather than better. The only thing was to force her menu to the forefront of her mind so that she could reaccommodate her usual happy background preoccupation when she was alone in the kitchen: the wonderful contrast between the old days when Neil had dropped in for coffee and sympathy on what might as well have been the boy as the girl next door for all his awareness of her, and stood around the kitchen talking out as many of his day's trials as he could while she tried to persuade him to stay for a Welsh rarebit or at least some homemade biscuits; and her knowledge, now, that he was in the sitting-room awaiting his supper and she was not going to suffer in an hour or so's time the dreadful bereavement of standing in the hall alone after closing her front door on him . . .

She was at last feeling better, and the new dish was successful enough for Neil to suggest it go into the repertoire. When they had cleared away and washed up and he was back with his paper work, Cathy, on an unfamiliar mingling of urgency and reluctance, brought out her sketch of Mrs. Willoughby, making herself look at it as if for the first time and discovering she had already captured the essence she had sought.

"May I interrupt for just a minute?"

"A downy old bird," said Neil, after a long look. "Do you feel you've caught her?"

"As well as I've ever caught anyone. I could really manage everything from this—the portrait and the mural."

"But you want to find out about the mysterious victim of the bus."

"*You* want me to. Oh, anyway, Neil, of course I'll do a much better portrait, at least, if I have the living person under my eye as I start to paint."

"The face is very typical of a certain sort of bright, instinctive person," said Neil, picking up the sketch pad again. "Yet at the same time it's got some sort of extra thing—I mean, although it's a type, I feel I'd always remember this particular example of it."

"That's what I felt, although I hadn't put it into words. She's got heart trouble, by the way, although she makes light of it. There's something almost gallant about her, the way she seems to make the best of things. Although I don't really know why I'm saying that."

She knew, though, even while she disapproved, why she wasn't saying that she had patronized Mrs. Willoughby as clairvoyant as well as dressmaker—because to match Neil's inevitably amused reaction she could only tell him on a laugh, and she could not make herself find Mrs. Willoughby's crystal funny. And she was even less prepared to make that further confession, not so much because Neil might then find her funny as well, as because it would be to admit that she was taking Mrs. Willoughby's self-proclaimed powers seriously.

As Cathy hugged her husband in a contrition she was happy for him to misinterpret, she determined not to call on Mrs. Willoughby as clairvoyant again.

Even so she climbed the steep stairs the second time with a sense of apprehension, and found herself relieved to discover that her dressmaker was not alone: behind her as she stood smiling in her doorway was a girl in a tacked-up dress who seemed to be so obviously alive, she was an extra light in the sunny room.

"Hello," the girl said, rippling with movement although she was standing carefully still. "You must be Mrs. Carter."

"I'm Cathy Carter, yes." Cathy smiled and nodded to Mrs. Willoughby and walked up to the centre table, close enough to the source of the brightness to be able to penetrate its dazzle. There she discovered Mrs. Willoughby's current client to have unremarkable features in a pale face under a precarious pile-up of lank brown hair and a tall body which was just too thin. Yet the impact persisted. *Life*, thought Cathy again, *warmth*. Then, to her surprise, *courage*.

"Cathy," said the girl, her voice lingering on the word. "I'm Sandra Fane."

"Sandra Fane, actress," said Mrs. Willoughby, through the pins. "She's got herself a nice little part in the West End, haven't you, dearie?"

"After ten years of rep," said Sandra Fane, radiating from Cathy to Mrs. Willoughby and back. It was, of course, the larger-than-life effect so often generated by the acting profession, but it was an abundance of goodwill as well. And the voice was beautiful, the sort of voice which would never appear to be uttering a banality. "Not that I'm complaining about that, I loved it. You're juggling several productions at once, and you and your audience get to know one another."

"Exciting, though," said Cathy, beginning to wrestle as discreetly as possible with her collapsible easel, "getting to the West End. Where and in what?"

"It's a rather good new play by Gerald Lovatt, *The Magic Horseshoe*. At the Touchstone. I don't suppose you've heard—"

"I read about it. That must be why your name sounded familiar. It certainly hasn't opened unnoticed."

"Thank you! Mrs. Willoughby's been telling me about your painting."

Proud of her young women, thought Cathy, realizing she had shaken off the sense of dread engendered by her return to the scene of Mrs. Willoughby's reaction to the crystal. "It's nothing much yet," she responded, "just a sketch. I was hoping to start painting today if Mrs. Willoughby has time."

"Bless you, dearie, I always have time for my young ladies." Mrs. Willoughby completed the setting in of a sleeve and stood back to inspect the effect. "That's all right. I'll put the kettle on now and it'll be boiling by the time I've finished this frock, we'll have tea before Miss Fane goes off to the theatre. No, you'd better leave it to me, Mrs. Carter dearie, it's a bit temperamental."

Sticking pins back into the pincushion she wore as a bracelet, Mrs. Willoughby bustled across to her kitchen corner, and Cathy saw that Sandra Fane had turned to watch her as she bolted the easel into place.

"You teach art, I believe?" Cathy was aware of being under a close but restrained scrutiny, and that it contained an element she could only define as compassion. Neil sometimes said she looked like a waif, but it could hardly be that. And if Mrs. Willoughby had told Sandra Fane she was pregnant that, too, was scarcely a reason for pity. The only other explanation she could think of for the look on Sandra Fane's face was that Mrs. Willoughby had mentioned the crystal episode without adding the assurance that it had had nothing to do with her client.

"Yes, at school." Vigorously she shook her fair cap of hair, to rid her head of its absurd suspicions. "But I like doing portraits when I can get the opportunity."

"And Mrs. Willoughby has an interesting face," said Sandra Fane, softly.

Mrs. Willoughby looked over at them as the gas popped. "Miss Fane's a very good little actress. You'd be surprised."

Cathy was sure she had no intention of being either rude or patronizing and Sandra Fane showed no reaction, unless the sudden astonishing assumption of Vivien Leigh's Scarlett O'Hara, as Mrs. Willoughby tightened the waist of her dress, was a form of restoration for hurt pride. For a moment the colourless young woman was the brilliant Southern belle, fighting the tight laces in Mammy's hands.

"There now!" said Mrs. Willoughby with a proprietorial smile, as if she had just been manipulating the strings of a puppet. "The waist comfortable now, dearie, in spite of all that acting?"

"It's fine, Mrs. Willoughby, thank you." The performance was over as abruptly as it had begun.

"I'd like to see your new play," said Cathy.

"Would you? I'd love it if you would. I think Mrs. Willoughby enjoyed it."

"It was a very nice evening," said Mrs. Willoughby. The kettle began to complain and she went back to the stove. "Very nice indeed."

"There you are!" said Sandra Fane, turning to Cathy and opening her eyes wide. She could not have looked less like the unfeminine Miss Littlewood, but Cathy was reminded of the woman she had seen the week before in the possibility of irony.

Sandra Fane was dressed in a skirt and jumper, and Mrs. Willoughby was bringing the first two mugs to the table, when there was a rap on the door. Cathy saw Sandra Fane jerk and bring her hand up to her face.

"Who's this, then?" queried Mrs. Willoughby as she crossed the room.

"I expect it's Jim," said Miss Fane casually.

"Jim, is it?" asked Mrs. Willoughby, a fraction before opening the door. Cathy decided there was something in the atmosphere of the room she didn't understand. "Jim!"

"Hello, Ma." The man in the doorway kissed Mrs. Willoughby on the cheek as she stood aside to let him in, and Cathy thought she drew away. "Sandra. And the artist!"

"Oh, yes," said Mrs. Willoughby, returning to the stove. "You two met, didn't you?"

Now the moment had come, Cathy found it difficult to speak. "Jim —I'm afraid I can't remember your other name"—she cleared her throat—"was very kind to me last week when I—when I saw what had happened in the street. He let me rest until I'd got over the shock. But I expect he told you, Mrs. Willoughby. I was so very sorry . . ."

"He's Jim Grayson. He did say something about what happened. Yes."

"Have you got a cup of tea for me, Ma?"

"If you don't mind all the women and women's things," said Mrs. Willoughby mysteriously.

"Of course not." He spoke perfunctorily. All his energies, Cathy thought, were expended on trying not to look continuously at Sandra Fane. "I just popped in really to see if Sandra was ready for a lift to the theatre, but I'd love to stay to tea." He paused, and Cathy saw him turn his attention successfully to Mrs. Willoughby to the extent of walking over to her and putting his arm across her shoulders. Sandra Fane followed his progress with her eyes, and a smile which Cathy was about to call anguished when she saw it was serene. "And," continued Jim cajolingly, "I also wanted to make sure you were coming down to have supper with me tonight."

"Bless you, Jim, of course I am! I've been looking forward to it." Mrs. Willoughby's breathing was noticeable again, but Cathy thought she relaxed for an instant against Jim Grayson's arm. "That's why I decided I'd stay here tonight rather than go home, because of you always keeping me so late and all . . ." She had turned away to pour another mug of tea, her voice uncharacteristically slurred and low. Jim Grayson made no response, merely looking with the ghost of a sad smile from one young woman to the other. Cathy decided Mrs. Willoughby was probably on the way to being cured of her pretension and that she had just witnessed its dying reflex kick.

"Cathy's going to paint Mrs. Willoughby," said Sandra Fane. She too sounded short of breath.

"So I hear." Cathy was able to read the predominant emotion of the room since Jim Grayson's arrival. It was of two people having to discipline themselves to remain physically apart. But there was still something else beyond her interpretation. She was glad when the lovers or incipient lovers prepared to depart, although she knew she liked them both.

"Be good!" said Mrs. Willoughby, her eyes on Sandra Fane.

"What else, Ma?"

"Of course," said Sandra Fane, returning the level gaze. "Goodbye, Cathy."

"May I fix you by the window again?" asked Cathy, when a few minutes had gone by in which Mrs. Willoughby reflectively drank tea.

"Of course, dearie!" Mrs. Willoughby bustled noticeably to attention as Cathy picked up a balloon-back chair and followed her across the room.

"It's paint today, but again it's general rather than particular and I'm not asking you yet to keep your mouth still."

Mention of last week's tragedy in the street might inhibit Mrs. Willoughby's expression, but she was merely blocking in the scope and shape of the portrait to be. Cathy suspected, though, that even if she had reached the stage of detailed work on the features she would have been unable to hold back on the subject dominating her thoughts.

"Jim really was kind to me last week, Mrs. Willoughby. I opened the door right on to—what had just happened, and when I saw—when I saw it was Mrs. Lawrence I think I was going to faint but he had hold of me and took me into his flat. I hope you weren't watching—"

"I saw what happened." Yes, the face had tightened almost into a different face. But Cathy had to go on.

"I'm sorry, I'd hoped you hadn't. Have you heard anything about it? What *did* happen? I must say when I saw Mrs. Lawrence here just before . . . I thought she looked odd, as if she couldn't see or hear us. Perhaps she was ill—"

"What happened, happened, Mrs. Carter. All the wondering in the world won't bring Mrs. Lawrence back." Mrs. Willoughby paused, and for the first time Cathy saw a tiny muscle in movement under her eye. "More's the pity," she brought out on a whisper, as if against her will. "I think we're better not to speak of it."

"Of course. Forgive me. Tell me about Miss Fane's play."

The reversion was instantaneous, and the beginnings of the portrait went so well, she was able to rough in the features. As she was finishing Cathy risked one more question altering her sitter's face again.

"Miss Fane and Jim Grayson are old friends?"

"I let Mr. Grayson take me to Miss Fane's play on the second ticket she gave me." The change this time was more subtle, and Cathy thought she heard regret in Mrs. Willoughby's voice. *She really prefers to keep her clients to herself.* Well, that at least was understandable. "Miss Fane had insisted I go round backstage at the end." Mrs. Willoughby shrugged. "So that meant Jim too, of course . . ."

"Of course, yes." If she had made Mrs. Willoughby suffer, she had no wish to prolong the ordeal. "Mr. Grayson's a private detective, he told me."

"Yes. He's got a lovely office off High Holborn, he took me once to show me."

"That was nice of him. But he's obviously very fond of you. Well, he told me so." Too late Cathy realized that what she had offered as a compliment was also an example of the discussion of Mrs. Willoughby by Jim and a client which he had told her Mrs. Willoughby disliked. But there was no adverse reaction. "I think that'll do for today."

"You're sure, dearie?"

"Yes. I've made a very good start."

Cathy and Mrs. Willoughby looked at one another, the possibility of Mrs. Willoughby's other skill trembling between them. Cathy experienced another moment of temptation—to ask Mrs. Willoughby to read her hands—but it passed.

"You sure there's nothing worrying you, dearie?" asked Mrs. Willoughby, before Cathy could break the mutual gaze.

"Only when you ask me a question like that." She tried unsuccessfully to laugh. "You make me feel that perhaps there is, but truly there isn't." There was, though, an opening for her to seek another reassurance. "I *was* a bit upset of course last week when you saw—what you saw—in the crystal, and then Mrs. Lawrence . . . You'd told me on the bus that first time that you had the gift of foreseeing—death—and it made me think . . . And then of course I worried that perhaps what you'd seen *had* been to do with me after all and you hadn't wanted to say . . ." Oh yes, there was something worrying her.

"Bless you, dearie!" Cathy couldn't read Mrs. Willoughby's exaggeratedly amused reaction. "No, that was nothing to do with you. I'm not going to say straight out, like, that it was Mrs. Lawrence I saw, because although I know I've got the power, it isn't always comfortable to face it . . . No, before—before you and your husband disappeared from the crystal, dearie, I thought I saw that there was something worrying you, I think I said—"

"You did, Mrs. Willoughby, but really there isn't. Nothing I know of at the moment, anyway . . ." Oh, she must refuse this line of country, it could do harm. It could make her remember how Neil had been before he had loved her.

"That's all right, dearie, there are so many influences coming in, maybe we got our lines crossed." Mrs. Willoughby beamed at her. "I'm very glad, very glad indeed, that there aren't any clouds on your horizon. Just you remember, though, that if anything ever bothers you there's an old woman here you can always talk to."

With a son who had gone abroad. "Of course I'll remember, Mrs. Willoughby." Cathy forgot herself on a surge of compassion, and felt immediately better. "And I'll be back the same time next week, if that suits you."

"Bless you, dearie." Mrs. Willoughby carried the mugs to the draining-board as Cathy dismantled her easel. "I'll look forward to it."

Which Cathy thought she might do, too, now she had overcome temptation.

CHAPTER FOUR

There was nothing in Cathy's second visit to Mrs. Willoughby which she preferred Neil not to know, but somehow, when she had told him of her failure to learn any more about Mrs. Lawrence, it was difficult to find words for anything else, even while she wanted to share the impact of Sandra Fane and her awareness of the feeling between her and the man downstairs.

"I thought Mrs. Willoughby must have acquired her through meeting her with Jim Grayson, but it turned out it's the other way round. Something I think Mrs. W hopes everyone will remember. No, I don't quite mean that . . ." Cathy leaned forward to help herself to her third apple, pausing as she was about to sink her teeth into it. "Neil, I think I've got a thing about apples, I could go on eating and eating them. Well, I've always liked them, but not to this extent. I suppose it's one of those pregnant fancies, lucky it's not cream buns. Which reminds me to tell you that I wasn't sick this morning, I didn't even feel sick. But I did have a bit of trouble fastening my waistband."

"Are you scared?"

She was back in the curve of his arm and he leaned away from her to look at her curiously.

"N-o-o. Well, only the way one's scared on a plane once it's airborne, because of there being no turning back. More scary than scared, it's a sort of excitement, really, knowing I've burned my boats and have got to go through with it. Oh, I know one doesn't have to these days, but you and I do, as we feel, so here I am, landed . . ." Rapidly demolishing the apple in her hand, Cathy eyed the last on the dish. "I'm extra aware of myself all the time, even my hands and parts of me which aren't going to change. I know it sounds silly, but I am." She took a scrunching bite, then paused again to consider. "In a way I feel separated from my body, as if it's struck out on its own and I'm watching it. What's reassuring about the process is that I still feel completely myself—the me that's always the same, that's doing the watching, it still feels the whole me, not as if it had lost anything because of the body having gone independent. An argument for the existence of the soul, would you say?"

"It's a good thought. A mild version of the inspiration which sustains martyrs?"

"Yes! How marvellous of you to have seen that, you've given me a whole new way of looking at it. Only just now I'm suddenly too tired . . ." She took the last apple. "Neil, this Sandra Fane, when I first went into Mrs. Willoughby's room she had quite an impact, some-one you had to be aware of. I thought she must be beautiful but when I went up to her I saw she wasn't, not at all, a poor complexion and a big mouth and the sort of hair which shows when it wants washing, which it did. But all adding up. There was something else, too. I got the feeling she was disciplining herself all the time in some way—I don't know how to describe it, but I felt that if she'd let herself go she'd have started shouting or weeping, or—or showing that she was terribly sad. She smiled once in a painful sort of way, and then I realized it wasn't that at all, it was calm, a really calm smile . . . Oh, this sounds ridicu-lous. The only thing I was sure of was that she and Jim Grayson were aware of one another. Well, more than that, they could hardly manage to keep apart. I'd rather like to go to her play."

"We will. How's the portrait?"

"I think I've made a good start. No attempt to get a likeness yet, of course, but I'm sure I've chosen the right angle, not quite full face. Like the sketch."

"How long will it take?"

"Beyond the beginning of term. So I shan't be able to go on Tues-days then, you'll have to do without me for a few Saturday afternoons."

But meanwhile it was Tuesdays and she was becoming the absorbed artist, relieved that there were no more distractions from other clients, anxious each time to get finished with the fitting of the maternity clothes Mrs. Willoughby had begun to make for her, so that she could settle down to the portrait. Jim Grayson didn't appear again, and Mrs. Willoughby, standing at the top of the stairs, waiting to greet her or say a final farewell in the shaft of daylight which Cathy let in when she opened the street door, was hardly conducive to her calling on him as he had suggested—and anyway, she had already seen him a second time to acknowledge his kindness the day Mrs. Lawrence had died.

It was on the last Tuesday of the Easter holidays that Cathy saw him again, and that was only because a man strolling from the other direction stopped at the door of the house almost at the moment she did, pressing the buzzer marked GRAYSON as she drew back from summoning Mrs. Willoughby.

"We could hardly have coincided more exactly," said the man, who was about Neil's age and extremely good-looking, "if we'd arranged it."

"Probably not," agreed Cathy as easily, basking despite herself in the type of smile which appears to proclaim an exclusive interest in the person at whom it is directed, but which her experience had taught her is more likely to be at the instant and indiscriminate command of its owner.

"Is that you, Mrs. Carter, dearie?"

"Who is it?"

The robotic voices twanged together. The man smiled his instruction to Cathy to answer first.

"Yes, Mrs. Willoughby."

"Who is it?" repeated the metallic echo of Jim Grayson, faint behind the noise of Mrs. Willoughby's activated buzzer.

"It's Dave. Okay, I'm in."

The man pushed the heavy door for Cathy and followed her into the lobby. Mrs. Willoughby appeared at the head of the stairs as Jim Grayson opened his door.

"Dave . . . And Cathy Carter." A grave, concerned look, making her think of Sandra Fane.

"Hello, Jim," said the man.

"Is there anybody else down there?" called Mrs. Willoughby.

"Only Dave Earnshaw, Mrs. Willoughby. Your visitor and I arrived together."

"*I* see. Good afternoon, Mr. Earnshaw. Come on up, dearie."

"Cathy," said Jim Grayson, "this is my partner, Dave Earnshaw. Not often to be seen"—he lowered his voice—"in these unsalubrious surrounds."

"I've been on the Abbey Road job." The voice was as intimately attractive as the smile, and playfully reproachful. "And as I was so near I thought I'd look in on the off chance you might be here. I want to talk out one or two aspects before they get mixed up with other things."

"Of course, Dave, come in."

"You coming up, dearie?"

"Right away, Mrs. Willoughby."

"How's the portrait going?" asked Jim Grayson abruptly, as if making an effort. Perhaps it was just the contrast with his sleek colleague, but Cathy decided he was too pale and thin.

"Quite well, I think." Dave Earnshaw, with his well-groomed hair and immaculate suit, made her think of private eyes in pre-war films. Mrs. Willoughby could let him sleep in her best bedroom without disturbing its atmosphere. "I'm enjoying it enormously, at any rate, and Mrs. Willoughby's very patient. I'd better go up . . ."

"See you, Mrs. Carter." Cathy blinked in the radiance of Dave Earnshaw's valedictory smile.

"I'll help you with your easel," said Jim Grayson. "Go on in, Dave."

"It's all right, really . . ."

But Jim Grayson was taking her easel from her and preceding her up the stairs. Cathy, without turning round, was aware of Dave Earnshaw watching her climb.

"All right, dearie? I thought you were never—Oh, it's Jim. That's nice of you, Jim."

"Where d'you want it, Ma?"

"Just lean it up against the couch, will you? That's right. You coming up for a cup of tea with us later?" Again Mrs. Willoughby was breathing as if the exertion had been hers.

"If you'll excuse me. I only came home to catch up on some paper work." Cathy bit her lip to keep from smiling to hear one of Neil's favourite phrases used in his favourite context. "Things have slid a bit these last few days." She noticed effort, again, in the way Jim Grayson raised his head to look at Mrs. Willoughby. There was a tension in his face she hadn't seen before.

"Of course, Jim, I understand. Just let me know when you have time and feel like a bit of company again."

"Will do, Ma." Jim Grayson didn't turn round as he slipped out of the room.

Mrs. Willoughby crossed to the door to make sure it was clicked shut.

"Poor Jim, he's just buried his grandpa, hasn't he? I'm sure he's had a perfectly good set of parents, but his grandpa was something special."

"I could tell there was something . . . When was it, Mrs. Willoughby?" Cathy was so anxious to start painting, she was already out

of her shirt and jeans and waiting for Mrs. Willoughby to slip her new
flowing party dress over her head.

"Middle of last week or thereabouts; it's really cut him up, he hasn't
wanted to talk about it. Unwise that, I always think, but there you are."

"I'm so sorry." *But he has Sandra.* "Have he and Dave Earnshaw
been partners long?"

"A good few years." Mrs. Willoughby advanced with a billow of
emerald green across her extended arms. "As long as I've been here,
anyway. I don't really know Mr. Earnshaw, I only see him by chance or
if Jim gives a party. Always asks me to his parties, Jim does, he's ever so
kind. I hope he'll feel better soon, he's been quite changed these last
few days . . . There you are, dearie . . . Jim's not often at home
during the afternoon, Mr. Earnshaw was lucky."

As she had been the day Mrs. Lawrence died.

"Goodness, it's really quite glamorous, Mrs. Willoughby." Cathy
turned slowly round in front of the glass. There was as yet no visible
change in her to make a pirouette inappropriate, but with the maternity dress, pretty as it was, she felt she had assumed a different persona,
as if she was also trying on the clumsier body of the coming months. "I
still can't imagine it fitting me, though."

"Just take each day, dearie . . . Everything all right with you?"

"Oh, yes, thanks, fine. Term starts next Tuesday, I'm even looking
forward to it. And it'll mean starting work on the mural. But I shan't
be able to come to you on any more Tuesdays. Would you be able to
have me on Saturday afternoons? Starting this week, perhaps? We need
a few more sittings and I'd like to keep it going."

"Bless you, dearie, I'd miss you if you didn't come." Mrs. Willoughby draped Cathy in a more serviceable flow. "I don't usually have
clients on Saturdays, but you're a special one and it'll suit me, really,
just as well as Tuesdays. And of course come this next Saturday."

"That's marvellous. I'm going to try and capture you this afternoon,
turn the picture if I can from a portrait of a lady to a portrait of Mrs.
Charles Willoughby. And if I don't manage it I'll only have to last out
five days before getting another chance."

She thought she did manage, and Mrs. Willoughby seemed disposed
to agree with her—"Although goodness knows, we never see ourselves
as others see us, do we, dearie?"—but Cathy had no sooner left than
she was longing for her next sight of Mrs. Willoughby, which she knew

would tell her truthfully, fresh to her subject from the few days' break, whether or not she had caught her.

Saturday was cold and grey, a vicious wind whipping away the heavy prunus blossom which had replaced the tiny almond flowers blooming when she had first met Mrs. Willoughby, making her feel sorry for the bowed heads of the tulips the gardening committee had planted against the north wall of Westcote Gardens. Mrs. Willoughby's front door was in a wind funnel, and Cathy had never been more aware of it than she was this Saturday afternoon after leaving Neil sprawled on the sofa in their warm sitting-room, particularly as her finger on the button failed to elicit the now familiar "Is that you, Mrs. Carter, dearie?"

A second attempt proved as fruitless. Cathy rang Jim Grayson's bell and there was no response. Nor from the bell marked BOLSHAW. After propping her easel against the doorpost and flexing her cold hands she pressed the top, unidentified, button.

"Yes? Who is it?"

It was a woman's voice, tired and irritable.

"It's a client of Mrs. Willoughby's, she's expecting me but she isn't answering. Perhaps her bell isn't working. I know you can't just let me in, but if you could be kind enough to go down to her flat and—"

The buzzer snarled. Cathy was leaning against the door in an attempt to get out of the wind, and felt it move inwards. "Thanks so much," she said into the top grid, making sure the door stayed open. "I really wasn't expecting you actually to . . ." She sensed there was no longer anyone there.

If Mrs. Willoughby had forgotten about their new arrangement and gone out she wasn't much farther on, but at least she could escape the wind for a few moments while she made sure it wasn't just the bell out of order. Cathy parked her easel under the row of hooks round the back of the stairs opposite Jim Grayson's front door, where a battered trilby —Mrs. Willoughby's perhaps?—hung alone. Then, feeling her ears and nose tingle in the comparative warmth of the unheated lobby, climbed the stairs, imagining the small squat figure emerging to stand at the top.

But of course there was no one there, and no one on the second flight up to the mysterious multi-peopled abode above—she had thought the woman who had let her in might at least have taken the few steps necessary to have a look at her.

Cathy stood a moment in the silence, postponing the disappointment of knocking at Mrs. Willoughby's door and finally being forced to realize she wasn't in. Without her lively presence the dinginess of the little landing was more depressingly apparent: the peeling dark green walls, the threadbare drugget, the absence of furniture, picture or ornament to show that someone, sometime, had considered the place and its impact.

Shivering as her spirits plummeted, Cathy stepped up to the front-room door and knocked.

There was no response, but she wasn't listening for one in her surprise at finding the door opening inwards under the pressure of her hand. Mrs. Willoughby had gone out without locking up. Unless her heart . . .

Cathy pushed the door wide and ran into the room, feeling her own heartbeat subside as she realized there was no one there. Mrs. Willoughby had had to pop out for something and had been in such a hurry she'd pushed her door to without latching it. She'd probably be back in a moment, the best thing was simply to stay in the warm bright room and wait.

After having gone to knock on the bathroom door.

"Mrs. Willoughby! Are you there, Mrs. Willoughby?"

There was no sound from inside and the door was locked, but when she got down on her knees on the drugget Cathy found she could see through the worn keyhole across to the minute bright window, the view unimpeded above what looked like several clothes-horses loaded with washing. She couldn't think Mrs. Willoughby was in there, unconscious . . .

She would wait a quarter of an hour or so. Try on her dresses if she found them waiting for her. Which would indicate that Mrs. Willoughby was expecting her.

She hadn't noticed from her first anxious entry, but the day dress and the emerald party dress were on top of the pile of work in progress on the couch. Perking up, listening now in a hopeful way for sounds from the lobby, Cathy latched the door and tried on the dresses, pleased and surprised to find them both apparently ready for her. Mrs. Willoughby was fulfilling her side of the bargain and more, she hadn't indicated that a point had arrived where Cathy should start paying her for making up her materials, but enough was enough—this time she would offer something more than a stint at her easel . . .

Back in the clothes she had arrived in, Cathy wandered to the window and lifted the curtain, looking for the dumpy figure making its way through the Saturday afternoon throng of shoppers towards the house. People looked cold, heads were lowered against the wind, hands clasped throats. Bad weather for Mrs. Willoughby to battle against . . .

She'd been there almost half an hour and there was still no sound in the house beyond an occasional thump overhead punctuating the faint steady beat of pop. Cathy wondered whether to go downstairs and try Jim Grayson again, and then thought of Mrs. Willoughby's best bedroom.

She was a fool, how did she know Mrs. Willoughby didn't use that room herself for an afternoon nap? Nothing, now she thought of it, was more likely, particularly as Mrs. Willoughby had told her she wasn't used to having clients on a Saturday. And once in there, with the door to and dozing off, she would hardly hear the bell.

Being careful to leave the front-room door on the latch, Cathy ran across the landing and knocked firmly on the door opposite.

"Mrs. Willoughby! Are you there, Mrs. Willoughby? It's Cathy Carter."

This door was partly engaged and didn't yield immediately to her hand on it. But when in response to the continuing silence she pressed it harder the catch released and it swung inwards.

It was the wall by the bed she saw first, and her first sensation was surprise that Mrs. Willoughby should have breached the integrity of that plain cream decor with a spray of red petals to form a triangular burst across its centre. Then she saw, once and forever, that Mrs. Willoughby was on the bed by that wall, on her back with something glimmering against her cheek and her fingers spread on her breast and patterned like the wall and the front of her grey dress with more of those bright red bits of flowers.

Cathy's brain clung stubbornly to the image, it didn't want to let it go, move on as it then must to the realization that the red spray was Mrs. Willoughby's blood, forced out of her throat by the pointed thrust of her long slender cutting-out scissors, driven home with such force they seemed to have skewered her to the bed beneath her . . .

She was on her knees moaning and retching, her head bowed to the ground, hugging herself and praying that a nightmare so terrible must wake her up, that she wouldn't have to go on dreaming when she lifted her head . . .

Mrs. Willoughby's stockinged feet were neatly together and her eyes were closed. That was merciful, thank God for that. Her mouth was closed too, she hadn't shouted for help, screamed out her terror, but the division of the lips was marked in red, some of which had trickled down from the corner of her mouth, and her nostrils were blocked with it . . .

She was telling herself, aloud, that she must get away, but she was standing by the bed, in her hand the black book she had scarcely noticed and only dimly remembered, as she realized she was holding it, had been lying beside Mrs. Willoughby.

She thought of the black book Mrs. Willoughby used to take out of her wardrobe in the innocent world which had now closed against them both, but this wasn't it, this was smaller and more square. She found herself turning the pages, thinking she saw her name and going back to discover that she did. *Mrs. Cathy Carter*, with her address and a line of letters which didn't make sense . . .

Her bag was on the carpet beside the bed, there were no red petals on the carpet, and she was down on her knees again, opening the disguised compartment underneath and stuffing the book in. Not thinking what she was doing, just doing it, managing to do it in time before the sounds behind her turned into a bellow of outrage and disbelief.

"Oh, no!" shouted Jim Grayson, knocking her aside as he ran up to the bed. "Not this! Oh, no! Oh, Ma, no!"

"I just found her," said Cathy. Her voice sounded strange to her, strangled in her throat. Her throat . . .

Cathy darted out of the room and across the landing and over to the sink, just in time. When she turned round, gasping, Jim Grayson was in the doorway, staring at her in horror.

And hostility?

"I found her," she said again. She knew, as she spoke, that she was explaining herself for the first of several times. "She was expecting me at three, there was no reply—none from you, either—the people on the top let me in, this door was open and I waited. Then I thought she might be having a nap. It can't be true, I've got to wake up."

She was reaching out to the tea-stained mug on the draining-board, as heedlessly as she must have reached out to the notebook, and Jim Grayson had crossed the room and was taking her by the shoulders and telling her it was all right, it had been a terrible shock for them both, and they had better not touch anything, in that room either.

Then he helped her to the easy chair and dialled the three nines.
"Police, please."

No need, of course, for an ambulance.

Jim Grayson had difficulty with his voice, too, as he reported the
details of Mrs. Willoughby, deceased, and the outline of what had
happened to her. "We'll latch the doors," he said then, "and wait for
you downstairs in my flat on the ground floor. Press the button marked
GRAYSON. Come on," he said to Cathy, and when he had picked the set
of keys off the centre table in his handkerchief, and used it to close
both doors, she followed him dazedly downstairs and into his flat.

"Lie down on the sofa," he ordered at once, and the alarm in his
eyes made her remember the baby. The lurch of her own alarm, she
told herself, was no more than a response to his, but obediently she lay
back.

"If I could just stop seeing her." At least her voice was normal again.
"I'll have water, please," she said as he went to the cupboard from
which he had already given her brandy.

When he had brought her water Jim Grayson poured brandy for
himself and walked about the room with it.

"It wasn't me," she said eventually. "For a moment you thought it
was."

"I don't know what I thought. She always kept her doors locked
. . . I can't understand it."

"The people upstairs. They let me in without coming down to look
at me. Perhaps they let someone else in as well."

He whirled round, to stare at her. "Perhaps they did."

"But she could have let anyone in herself, couldn't she?"

"What?" He was prowling again. "Yes, of course. Yes."

"She loved you," said Cathy, starting to cry, realizing Jim Grayson
was crying already.

"Such a waste," he said. "Such a waste." He blew his nose and at last
sat down, leaning forward to look at her as he had done that first time.
"You say—you waited."

"Yes. In the other room."

"How long?"

"About half an hour, I suppose. It's hard to say exactly, I didn't look
at my watch."

"Of course. You didn't—hear or see anyone?"

"No. Except for vague sounds from upstairs."

He was on his feet again, pacing. "Perhaps I should have rung your husband."

"It was more important to ring emergency. I think I'd better ask him to come for me, though, when we've seen the police."

His face tightened. "You realize—there'll be questions?"

"Of course." She couldn't make herself worry about that, even though she could see, with as much clarity as she could see Mrs. Willoughby, that she would have to be suspected of killing her. The thought of anyone so much as imagining her capable of that terrible movement made her need to be sick again, and she was in Jim Grayson's bathroom when the police arrived. They were an inspector and a sergeant and when they came downstairs from Mrs. Willoughby's the sergeant had to go into the bathroom, too. While he was there the inspector explained that, although he would welcome statements from them, they were not obliged to give them.

"Oh, but we will, of course," said Cathy, and Jim Grayson nodded.

"Perhaps you'll also agree to answering a few questions first." The inspector was still asking a favour. But by British justice, innocent until proved guilty.

"Yes, of course." It was Jim this time.

The sergeant came into the room, murmuring apologies, his fleshy face still greenish white.

"Who discovered her?" asked the inspector, after a wry glance at his subordinate.

Cathy said, "I did," and Jim Grayson, "We both did," on an instant.

"I did," repeated Cathy, hoping Jim's gallant gesture wouldn't make the inspector start imagining there was something which needed covering up. "I'd been in the room for a minute or two, I suppose—it was such a shock, I'm not sure—when Mr. Grayson came in." She told them why she had been there, and how she had got into the house, and the inspector sent the sergeant to the top floor to bring down whoever was up there. Jim explained that he had come back to the house ten minutes or so before going upstairs to say hello to Mrs. Willoughby and maybe join her for a pot of tea. He did that most days, at some point.

The inspector turned to Cathy. "You heard him come in?"

"I didn't, actually." She was going to say it was perhaps surprising that she hadn't, as she had been listening for Mrs. Willoughby, but she stopped herself. She had closed Mrs. Willoughby's door while she tried the dresses on, and the comment might make the inspector wonder if Jim Grayson had been in his flat the whole time.

Had he?

"I'd closed the front-room door . . . Forgive me, Inspector, I'm feeling a bit faint."

"Mrs. Carter is pregnant," said Jim severely.

"If my husband could be asked to come for me . . ."

"Of course, Mrs. Carter . . . We can take your statements here, but it would be helpful if you would be prepared to come to the station so that we can take your fingerprints as well for purposes of elimination. I must tell you that there is no obligation on you to do this, but you will appreciate—"

"Of course," said Cathy. "Perhaps I should mention that my husband's in the Met. Detective Inspector Neil Carter. I'm quite well enough to go to the station if someone—"

"We'll take you, Mrs. Carter, of course." The inspector hadn't reacted as if he knew Neil, but she was aware from some indefinable change in his manner that her observation had lifted her out of the ruck of the general public. "If you're certain you wouldn't prefer to wait until you feel better?"

"Goodness, no."

The sergeant came back into the room behind a youngish woman and a girl about seven years old. The woman was what Cathy would have expected from the voice on the intercom and the things Mrs. Willoughby had said—boldly attractive, not very well groomed. The child was wearing a short-sleeved pink cotton dress, and shivering.

"Mrs. Monkton," announced the sergeant. "And daughter Daphne. Mrs. Monkton confirms she let a woman into the house about an hour ago."

"I don't have to look, do I?" was Mrs. Monkton's anxious reaction when the inspector had explained matters. "I don't want to see the old lady—like what you say." She pulled the child against her, as if for her own protection. "I haven't got nothing to tell you. And my brother always says not to sign your name to anything, you don't know where it'll end up."

"There's no need for you to see Mrs. Willoughby," said the inspector reassuringly. "Nor for a statement at this juncture if you don't want to give one. Perhaps you'll just answer a couple of questions, and we'll leave it at that for the time being."

The last four words brought a look of hostility to the woman's face, but the inspector was smiling so pleasantly, she sniffed and relaxed.

"I don't know what I can tell you, I'm sure."

"You and your little girl have been alone in the flat all day?"

"Except for going out this morning to do some shopping."

"What time did you get back?"

"Twelve, quarter past, I don't know."

"Did you see Mrs. Willoughby?"

"Haven't seen the old dame for a couple of days, now."

The inspector turned to Jim Grayson. "How long since you saw her, Mr. Grayson?"

"When I was leaving this morning, at about half past eight. She was on the landing and I called up to say I'd see her if I came home for lunch."

"You didn't, though?"

"No, I got caught up. But I was here about half past three or so and went upstairs as I told you to see if she was all right . . ." Jim Grayson passed his hand over his mouth.

"Do you see much of Mrs. Willoughby in the normal way?" the inspector asked Mrs. Monkton.

"Might pass her twice in a day, mightn't see her for a week. We didn't go out of our way to meet. I wasn't good enough for *her*, and *she* didn't interest *me*."

"What about your little girl?" The child, sucking her thumb, seemed oblivious of the proceedings.

"Oh, the old lady never took any notice of *her*, 'cept to shoo her off like she was a cat."

"Did you let anyone else into the building today?" asked Jim Grayson, then mumbled an apology as the inspector coughed.

"Did you?" repeated the inspector.

"I didn't let no one in, 'cept the one woman, and I didn't hear no one, neither," retorted Mrs. Monkton on a barrage of negatives. "And that's the truth."

"Very well. Thank you. That will be all for now."

The sergeant walked to the door and held it open, and with a suspicious glance at the inspector Mrs. Monkton swayed out of the room, pushing the child in front of her.

"Mrs. Carter and Mr. Grayson have agreed to come to the station," the inspector told the sergeant when he came back from seeing Mrs.

Monkton out of Jim Grayson's front door. "To give their statements and be fingerprinted for elimination purposes. Are you sure you're all right, Mrs. Carter?"

"I'm fine now, thanks." And she didn't feel so bad as she sat up and slid her feet to the floor. But she was floating along beside events rather than taking part in them, in some strange grey inversion of the world of light and colour.

Someone had helped her into her coat and the flat door was open. Jim said, "Your easel and your canvas, Cathy, I'll take them inside for the time being."

She wasn't going to have another chance to study Mrs. Willoughby's bright keen face. All at once she was a step nearer taking in that Mrs. Willoughby was dead. She herself felt reanimated for a moment, but only in order to relive her time in the best bedroom . . . Jim grabbed her arm.

The forensic team was forming up on the doorstep as the sergeant opened the front door. "It's pretty wacky," he said, as he led the way upstairs.

"Now that they're here," the inspector called after him, "you might as well come back with us, Jenkins."

They waited for him in the lobby. Cathy noticed that this time he went no further than the top of the stairs.

She asked if she could ring Neil herself and they took her to a telephone as soon as they reached the local station. She told him merely that she had been a witness to an incident. The statement was easy, she just said everything she remembered having seen and heard and done, and she had signed it before she also remembered she had picked up the black notebook and put it in her bag. If she hadn't imagined it. And if she hadn't, there was nothing she could do about it now, she had to go on perverting the course of justice. She had to sit with her head between her knees before going to be fingerprinted, and she was escorted back to the station lobby by a large pleasant man who told her he was Detective Chief Inspector Farley and that Mr. Grayson, knowing her husband was coming for her, had left.

Neil was at the counter with his back to them, her warmest coat over his arm. Also at the counter, his back to Neil, was the sergeant who had come to Mrs. Willoughby's, in excited conversational flow to a uniformed constable.

" . . . turn up for the book, Derek, eh?" Cathy heard. "Copper's pregnant wife prime suspect in sadistic murder case, can't you just see those headlines?"

The constable's warning look had him swinging round, into the ideal position to take Neil's swift uppercut to the jaw. There was a cracking sound as the sergeant's face changed shape, then a thud as he fell against the counter, striking his head. When he had slid to a sitting position he stayed still.

Neil, with no particular expression on his face, caressed his knuckles and looked round as Cathy cried out. She had run up to him and taken his arm before Chief Inspector Farley moved forward.

"A pity about that, Inspector Carter."

"He's breathing," said the constable, on his knees. The duty sergeant, behind the counter, was summoning medical assistance.

"He was way out of line, Governor," said Neil to the chief inspector.

"So were you." The chief inspector looked at Cathy. "You'd better take your wife home. She didn't need another shock."

"I'm all right," said Cathy, leaning against Neil's noisy heart.

"And you'd better stay at home on Monday," continued Chief Inspector Farley to Neil. It was hard to believe he had recently looked kind. "I'll be in touch with your superior officers and they'll let you know the course of events."

"Yes, Governor." Neil hesitated. "Whatever is to happen, may I ask for press silence?" He glanced at the man on the floor, who was groaning and coming round, one side of his jaw swelling and darkening as Cathy looked at it. "We're neither of us important, and from what the duty sergeant has just told me there's going to be enough publicity already as a result of today."

The chief inspector's hesitation was brief. "I think we can agree to that, Inspector. Unless"—the malevolent eyes had just opened—"there is an unauthorized leak."

"Thank you, Governor," said Neil. He ushered her firmly and steadily out of the station and along the road, but when they were in the car he dropped his head on to the steering wheel as she dropped hers on to her breast, and they sat a long silent moment, hand in hand.

CHAPTER FIVE

"Suspension pending a disciplinary hearing," said Neil. "There just isn't any way round it."

"And the sergeant?"

"A dressing down."

"It isn't fair!" said Cathy, and his heart leapt in relief at the flare of indignation lighting her uncharacteristic languor. "It's like the house-holder being prosecuted for attacking the man who's broken into his home."

"Not quite, love." But he appreciated the comparison. And the fact that she had recovered enough to think it up.

"Oh, darling, what else could you have done? Well, I suppose you could have grabbed him by the tie or the jacket, and shaken him or something. But I was proud of you, you didn't stop to think."

"That tends to be my trouble. And Chief Inspector Farley knows it, we've met before. Even so, he only did what he had to."

"If only I hadn't pressed that top button. I just couldn't accept the idea of not being able to get on with the portrait." He felt her shiver. "Oh, Neil. The world's changed in a day."

"Not if you're all right." He moved his hands gently over the body hunched on the sofa beside him, stopping at the still sharp pelvic bones and looking his sudden anxiety. To his relief again, she smiled at him.

"The baby's all right, I'm sure of that, although I suppose it's been lucky. The shock—"

"I know. Dear Lord, I know. But try not to think about it. You've talked it out to the police, try now to push it away."

"I can manage to for bits of the time. The worst will be when we're in bed and have said good night . . . But I'm not taking tranquil-lizers!"

"Don't you think you should see the doctor, though, be on the safe side . . ."

"*No.* I know I'm all right, I only begin to think perhaps I'm not when anyone suggests it. I felt quite normal driving home."

Cathy had insisted, when eventually they felt ready to drive away, that they go there and then to collect her car from the car-park near Mrs. Willoughby's where she always left it. She had also wanted to collect her things from Jim Grayson's flat, but Neil had drawn the line at that, trying not to acknowledge that mingled with his concern for his wife was the realization that to leave her belongings where they were was to leave the pretext for calling on Grayson on his own . . .

If he had been working, his oblique personal connection with the murdered woman would have precluded any possibility of his being assigned to the search for her killer, the killer who had threatened the life of his unborn child. There would have been no way he could have done anything to help reveal the calumny in what the big-mouthed sergeant had implied. Suspended, he would be unable to pursue any of his own current investigations (for none of which, mercifully, he had any proprietorial feelings), he would be left severely alone with time on his hands . . .

At the back of his mind an idea stirred. He might just be glad to find himself officially idle at this particular moment, and he wasn't afraid of having time in which to think. Although the disciplinary process would have to take its course and be forever a mark against him, he wasn't ashamed of what he had done (nor, he thought, would his colleagues be ashamed when they discovered why he hadn't come to work), he knew he would do the same thing again. He wouldn't, of course, feel so equable about it on Monday when awaiting the reaction of his Chief, but the idea of enforced leisure was presenting itself as an opportunity rather than a condition to dread . . . And anyway, at the moment he wasn't much more than a living, breathing thanksgiving that Cathy seemed to be unharmed.

"I'm afraid I'll want to tell it all to you, Neil," she was saying, and he was registering another dual reaction: the hope that he would be able to help her to come to terms with it, and a sense of satisfaction that he would begin his period of idleness with as much information on the Willoughby murder as was in the possession of his colleagues on the job. If not more.

"Neil!" She jerked against him. "Something I forgot, I honestly forgot, to put in my statement. Not that I could have done, even if I'd remembered in time . . ." Here it was, already. But all other reactions were swallowed up in his concern at her sudden intense distress.

"What is it, darling?"

Her face, a moment ago so white, had flooded crimson.

"Neil, I can't—yet, anyway—I can't remember it all exactly as it happened. There seem to be—gaps. I mean, I found I'd knelt down when I first saw . . . And then I found I was standing by the bed. I don't remember getting up and I don't remember picking up the book. I didn't know I'd even noticed a book on the bed. Near her hands. She had such white hands . . . Neil . . ."

"Don't say any more now," he urged, feeling unselfish as professional considerations began to seep back. "Wait until you feel stronger."

"No, I've done something dreadful, really dreadful, and I've got to tell you, even though you're bound to be angry." Ice touched his spine; had she compromised her innocence? "When I found I was standing by the bed and holding a black notebook I started to turn the pages, I don't know why, it seems crazy in the midst of . . . Anyway, I thought I saw my name, and I went back and I *had* seen it, with my address. And—and—Neil, forgive me, please, a policeman's wife . . . I got down on the floor again and I—I stuffed the notebook into my bag. The hidden compartment at the bottom, so I was being dreadfully devious even while I wasn't even thinking what I was doing. It's still there, if I haven't imagined it."

Excitement mingled with his relief. "You didn't mention it to anyone?"

"No! Even if I'd remembered while I was writing my statement I'd have realized I couldn't do anything about it by then, that I'd just have to keep it hidden and feel awful."

"Grayson didn't see you?"

"I'm sure he didn't. I suppose I might just still have been fastening the bag when he came tearing in, but the notebook was out of sight and anyway he only had eyes for . . . for . . ."

Cathy just made the bathroom, and Neil, disrespecting one of the few taboos they had put on their intimacy, followed her in and held her shoulders.

"It may have been—seeing it again in my head," she said as they came out, "or it may have been the baby. I'm all right now, I'm even hungry."

He wasn't, he was too eager to get at the black notebook, but he managed not to remind her about it while, under what he knew was his fussy supervision, she made omelettes and they ate them. She accepted his offer of removing the trays and making the coffee, and when he brought it in with some biscuits he saw she had the book in her hands.

"I didn't imagine it."

She put it into his outstretched hand and he received it with hyper-sensitive awareness of its shape and texture. Forbidden fruit. It was open near the centre, and in capital letters he read her name and address, alone on a page save for a line of letters in uneven groups.

"That's the only page with me on it. So far I've glazed on what else is there."

"I suppose this is the book you saw her take out of the wardrobe when a client called."

She looked startled. "No, it isn't. I'd forgotten that. While I was standing there looking at . . . I still realized it wasn't that other book, the other one was bigger and longer, quite a different shape, although it was black, too. It was the shape of a diary which has a couple of weeks to a page, while this one is more like one which has just a couple of days. Only it isn't a diary, is it?"

"No. It's just a blank notebook."

"The other one may not have been, either, of course. It just looked like it. But there's no doubt at all that they're two separate books. May I have it again? I'm in a state to read it, now, and I may recognize names."

Cathy advanced her hand, then pulled it back as if the small black square Neil was holding out to her had darted a forked tongue.

"Fingerprints! We're going to have to get it back some way, aren't we?"

"Yes. And before we do, we'll have to put gloves on and clean every inch of it. Which won't be all that easy, your hands will have been clammy . . . No point in worrying until then, though."

"Neil, what a dreadful thing for me to have done."

"You wouldn't have done it if you hadn't been in shock. Here, have a look."

Gingerly she took it, opened it at the beginning.

"Nothing to connect it with Mrs. Willoughby, but perhaps we could hardly expect a 'This Book Belongs To.' Here's a name and an address and some letters. The same format as me, but the name's crossed out." She moved on a few pages. "The same thing again, crossed out as well.

Women. Perhaps they moved. Amanda Littlewood . . . That's the Lesbian-looking lady I saw the first time I went. Lots of letters by *her* name. *Amanda.* Neil!"

"What is it?"

"Here's Sandra Fane. Even more letters. Then—there's me and another name crossed out. Nothing else. Wait a minute, I missed one. Stella Lawrence. Crossed out."

Cathy shuddered and threw herself into his arms, where she clung like an animal and shed copious tears.

"If I can just forget it some day, what she looked like . . . Poor Mrs. Willoughby, why should something so absolutely obscene have happened to *her?* To anyone? The vicar said once in church, when people ask 'Why me?' they might as well ask 'Why not me?'—that one has to be thankful awful things *don't* happen. I suppose that's the right way to look at—well, ordinary things that go wrong—but *this* . . . Everyone in the world should be able to be certain something like this won't happen to them. And the person who actually did it, that's worst of all. Like with the baby seals and the badgers. It's dreadful for the creatures, but they can only die once, it's over for them. The people who do it, they go on being able to live with themselves . . . I'll be all right, darling, but just for this minute I can't bear it . . ."

He was glad to see her weep, she had been too normal. He realized as he rocked her in his arms, increasingly reassured as she was increasingly comforted, that it had been worrying him. "There, darling," he murmured, seeing himself, in one of those rare moments of long sight, murmuring to an unhappy son or daughter. "It's all right, it's all right . . ."

"Neil!" Mercurial as ever, she had leaned away from him and was wiping her eyes with her hand. "Miss Littlewood could have done it. Or the woman on the top floor, perhaps wanting someone to find her . . . Or the mysterious Mr. Bolshaw. Or Jim. Or Sandra Fane, although I can hardly—"

"Or any friend or acquaintance of Mrs. Willoughby's, ringing her doorbell and being invited upstairs."

"Mrs. Lawrence must have been crossed out because she was dead. Perhaps the other three people crossed out are dead, too. And now Mrs. Willoughby . . ."

"Mrs. Willoughby's name isn't in the book," Neil reminded her. "If only we could compare the writing with the writing in that other book you saw. Well, that's what they'll do, of course, when they get this one back. And compare them both with things known to have been written by Mrs. Willoughby."

"How will they get it back?" Cathy stood up and stretched, then settled back on the sofa beside him.

"Posting is the only safe way. GPO Head Office. And, as Mrs. Willoughby's name doesn't appear in the book, addressed to the officers in charge of the Willoughby case. If the book had been found where it had been placed"—he squeezed her hand—"the connection would have been obvious, so we have to make it for them."

"I'm sorry, Neil."

"Don't be. I've always wanted to cut out letters from a newspaper and paste them into an address. We'll copy out everything from the book before we send it off."

He knew she had darted a look at him. "There's something here I missed—all on its own on a centre page." Cathy held out the book and they looked at it together. Written sideways down the inside of a page, close to its junction with the page opposite, was the sequence 1C13AV. "What could it possibly mean?"

"It could be the key to the text used to make a code. Those uneven groups of letters, they look to me like a code. See . . . The letter *E* occurs on its own a few times. And the letter *T*. One of them could be *I*. The other could be *A*. But not knowing what the text is, we won't get very far. When they have the book they'll put it all into the computer." He tried to feel pleased that the mystery might then be solved, rather than depressed that he would not be involved in its solution.

"It's a challenge, Neil."

"What a girl you are. Right, here's for a start. RPG occurs a few times. So does TFU. 'And'? 'The'? I said the letter *T* could be *A*. So TFU could be 'and.' But heaven knows what it could be linking. That's the way those simple codes are made up, though. Find a text and set it against the alphabet. The computer will break it down according to the comparative recurrence of letters in the English language—and it will be all the easier because whoever wrote in the book has obligingly retained the gaps between the words—unless of course he or she has made arbitrary gaps in the middle of them. Which will make it harder for the computer, as well. The one real chance for you and me is to read the message of those numbers and letters on their own and find the text."

"I think I'd feel happier if we copied it all out before we did anything else, and got the book ready for posting in the morning."

"You're right, of course. We'll do it now."

He wrote and Cathy checked, and they went through the book again, reversing their roles to make sure they hadn't missed anything.

"One thing does surprise me a bit," he said diffidently, when they were sure they had finished. "You say it was on the bed near her hand and that there was blood about . . . On her hands?"

"Yes."

"But not on the book."

"Isn't there?" She looked at it with the horror back in her eyes, and he was glad he had managed to suppress his comment until she had held it for the last time.

"I'm pretty sure not. Forensics will go over it, of course, but I can't see any sign at all. It could mean that the book was put on the bed after she was dead."

"I don't think there was blood on the bed, actually, just on her dress and hands . . . Neil, I think I'd like to tell you about it now. Then perhaps we can play Scrabble—or something—before we go to bed."

"Of course, darling." He tried to moderate his eagerness.

"I'll just—go through it—and you can say whatever you want to when I've finished."

He thought she squared up to every least thing, in an attempt to accept and absorb it, so that he was surprised she hadn't said anything about the anguish of the face.

"What about her face?" he asked gently, when she seemed to have finished.

"I was glad her eyes were closed." Cathy's voice was muffled, her head now was buried in his side. "And her mouth. She almost looked peaceful, except for the blood between her lips and in her nose. I remember now, I thought at the time, thank God she hadn't seen it coming, had time to know . . . Perhaps she was asleep."

"Perhaps . . . It's rather strange, actually, I would have thought her eyes and her mouth would have been wide open . . . As you say, darling, perhaps she was asleep," he added quickly in response to her shudder. He tried to counter the sting of frustration by reminding himself that even if he hadn't been suspended he wouldn't have been in any sort of position to seek answers to the mystery of Mrs. Willoughby's violent death. That, in fact, left to his own devices . . .

The idea stirred again, more vigorously.

Cathy lifted her head to look at him, and he smoothed her rumpled hair. "Neil, I've got another confession to make."

"Oh, darling."

"No, nothing like the other one. It's just . . . I didn't tell you before only because I felt sure you'd laugh and I couldn't have laughed with you because I couldn't find it funny . . . The day Mrs. Lawrence was run over I asked Mrs. Willoughby to look in the crystal for me—it was a silly thing to do because if she'd said anything worrying I'd have thought of the baby. She was going on about seeing you and me sitting happily together and so on—I wasn't impressed—and then she suddenly leaped up and put her hand in front of her face as if she'd seen something too terrible to look at and shouted, 'My God.' She tried to pass it off, but I'm convinced she *had* seen something. Her eyes weren't focused normally for a moment or two, but then she started saying it wasn't anything to do with me, and then Mrs. Lawrence came in, and five minutes later she was dead. Neil . . ."

"No, I don't feel like laughing."

"Mrs. Willoughby didn't actually say she'd seen Mrs. Lawrence, but she told me she had her powers . . . It frightens me to think what that might mean."

"It means nothing," he said. Not because he was certain of that but because he was sure Cathy had been frightened enough. "It's just the jargon of her trade. A bus is a lethal object if you wander into a road when it's coming along . . . Get the Scrabble out, darling. I'm sorry you felt you couldn't tell me about the crystal at the time." He was, he hated the thought of her holding back from him something important to her. Especially if it was down to his own insensitivity. Would he have laughed, at something which had shaken and upset her? "I don't think I would have laughed, knowing the whole story." But if there hadn't been a story, if Mrs. Willoughby hadn't seen her ghost and Mrs. Lawrence hadn't died, perhaps Cathy, afraid of his scorn, still wouldn't have told him . . . For the moment he was glad of the distraction of other unwelcome thoughts.

By the morning the thought of the Chief was the most unwelcome, run a close second by the nearer prospect of the Sunday papers. He had already padded barefoot to the front door three times before he heard the plop of his paper on to the mat.

"What is it?" Cathy hadn't heard him those earlier times, but as he came back with the paper she was sitting up.

"The paper," he said as casually as he could, wrenching back a curtain. "I just wondered how it had been reported."

"Oh, Neil, I hadn't thought of that!"

"I'm glad you hadn't, at least you've had a couple of hours' sleep." He spread the paper, seeing at once he had no need to open it. "Front page, I'm afraid. Well, it might actually be something new under the sun in the way of murder."

The headline was WIDOW'S BIZARRE MURDER and underneath, scarcely smaller, THE WORST CASE I'VE SEEN, SAYS FORENSIC EXPERT. Neil read quickly down, pausing at the place he had been afraid of. *Mrs. Willoughby, a dressmaker and clairvoyant, was discovered by a client yesterday afternoon.* It was the worst his paper had to offer, and probably indicated the worst to be expected from the other qualities. The tabloids, though . . .

Neil pulled trousers on over his pyjama legs, shrugged into a sweater, and ran down to the news-stand in the road outside the flats. Cathy had used his two or three minutes' absence to make coffee, and carried it into the bedroom as he stripped off his top layers. Back in bed they drank coffee and went through the stack. As he had hoped, the other qualities scarcely differed from the first report he'd read—the police spokesmen had been wisely prolific where they could be, and reporters hadn't been frustrated into probing further. Even the tabloids had forborne, but they had, of course, as he had known they would, pointed up Mrs. Willoughby's profession of the occult at the expense of her dressmaking, two of them not even mentioning that she made and altered clothes. One tabloid headline, to his grudging admiration, ran ART DECO DEATH, another spoke of the client who had discovered the body *cringing from a revelation far more terrible than she had ever trembled to receive from the dead woman's crystal.*

So the worst was that Mrs. Willoughby had been found by a female client, the client's gender, he suspected, being a reporter's deduction from the nature of Mrs. Willoughby's talents rather than a part of the official handout. It was all as it should be, of course, but sometimes things went wrong . . .

Neil's relief was already giving way to a sense of the day ahead as a lifetime to be lived through before he could discover what the Chief thought of him. He hadn't even got the job of preparing the black book for posting, he'd done it the night before, going to bed confident that his long slow work on it had expunged all evidence of his and Cathy's illicit connection.

At eleven o'clock he was mooching about the flat, getting in Cathy's way, when the telephone rang.

He fell on it.

"DI Carter?"

"Sergeant Currie?"

The tone of the sergeant's brief question had already reassured him.

"Yes, governor. Chief Inspector Larkin's been in this morning, and I'm to tell you he's on his way to see you."

"Here, Bill? Now?" But he had for some time suspected that his Chief's frequent forays into the quiet, sparsely staffed Sunday morning office had something to do with escaping his wife's alternative plans for him. And to move on to St. John's Wood at eleven or so would be to gain himself a whole free morning.

It didn't tell Neil anything, though. It could as well mean an impatience to bawl him out as to reassure him.

Cathy came into the sitting-room, dressed for going out on a cold morning, a plastic bag dangling from her gloved hand. "I'm off now, Neil. Who was that?"

"The Chief. He's on his way here."

"Oh, darling. But it works out rather well, doesn't it? He won't want to be asking me how I am and so on, which he'd feel he had to if he knew I was in the flat."

"Where have you gone, so far as the Chief's concerned?"

"Church. I'll slip into post-matins Communion at St. Barnabus. Not just to save you a lie."

"All right, love. You should be able to park quite near St. Martin Le Grand with it being Sunday. Leave the book in the bag until you're ready to get out of the car, and make sure you've got your gloves on."

"I won't take them off until the package is in the box. I expect you'll be glad the book isn't in the flat when the Chief's here."

"I expect I will." He kissed her nose. "Thanks for doing this." She had insisted on it; she had taken it and she would put it back.

He had only about ten uneasy moments before the doorbell rang. He would have liked to linger over the caricature of the Chief presented through the spyhole in the front door, but delayed only long enough to ascertain that the ears were the dominant feature and that the Chief was alone.

A good sign, he thought desperately, losing his cool in the moment of opening the door.

"Good morning, Governor. Please come in. I'm sorry I've put you to this inconvenience."

"Inconvenience, Carter?" repeated the Chief questioningly as he followed Neil into the sitting-room, making the word sound uniquely ill chosen.

"I very much appreciate your coming here. Please sit down."

Tactfully he indicated the highest and firmest chair, and grudgingly the Chief lowered his bulk into it. "Sergeant Jenkins is an unmitigated sod, Neil," he said, after what seemed to Neil a very long pause. "But you should never, never have laid a hand on him."

"I know, Governor." And he knew the Chief was with him. Strongly so, it must be, or he would have surely been played with for some time before being reassured. It would, as he had hoped, be a matter of sitting it out *(of working it out?),* and eventually going back to something of a hero's welcome. Provided, of course, he didn't let the Chief see the resurging of his confidence. "I know Chief Inspector Farley had no choice but to suspend me. You know why I did it?"

"We have a roughly verbatim report," grudged the Chief. "But Sergeant Jenkins has a broken jaw and concussion."

"He fell against the counter," said Neil gently.

"I know what he did, Neil. He was hit with force, and he fell with force. A disciplinary hearing, you understand?"

"Yes, Governor. I know what I did, whatever mitigates it in my own mind."

"Mitigating circumstances will be in most minds, or you'd be in deep trouble. As it is . . . You realize how difficult you've made life for us all? I can ill afford to lose you at the moment, and Inspector Ryan's already up to his neck. There are certain things you may not get back, Neil."

And certain things I may get. "I realize that, Governor. Perhaps I ought to mention it now, by the way. I shan't be apologizing."

"If Sergeant Jenkins apologizes first?"

"I suspect that's a rather large if. But in no other circumstances."

The Chief shifted in Cathy's elegant chair, making it groan. "I understand that, Neil. If others appear not to, I'll see it's explained to them."

"Thank you, Governor."

"Because of those mitigating circumstances I won't go on," said the Chief, after a further ten minutes or so of oblique chastisement. "I hope it won't be long, Neil, but I can't tell you the timetable as yet. Meanwhile full pay, of course. But you realize you'll have to keep away from the office."

"Of course, Governor. I take it I'm not under house arrest?"

He regretted the silly joke the second he had made it, not only because it might indicate too jaunty a mood. But the Chief responded mildly enough. "That's up to your wife. How is she?"

"All right, I think. I was worried about the baby, of course, with the shock, but that seems to be all right, too."

"I'm glad to hear it. What was she doing there, Neil? In that house in Pleasant Street?"

"Like the papers said, Governor, she was a client." The Chief's question had obliterated his regained assurance at a stroke. It had the edge to it he had learned to interpret as professional. "A client of Mrs. Willoughby dressmaker, not clairvoyant, but the papers didn't make that distinction. She met the lady on a bus when she was coming back from her mother's a month or so ago. They talked, and she learned she could have clothes made and altered. Mrs. Willoughby was making her some maternity gear." He was going to mention the portrait, then realized that if the Chief asked to see it he would have to say it wasn't there, and where it was. It could then be that the Chief would tell him arrangements would be made by the police to get Cathy's things home from Grayson's flat, depriving him of the excuse to collect them himself.

"I see. I'm glad to know the shock hasn't affected her too severely. Out, is she?"

"Gone to church."

"Ah," said the Chief respectfully. Neil judged the moment appropriate for the offering of sherry. The Chief accepted it, and one to follow. Neil's restored relief at this symbolic ratification of support was flawed by thoughts of Cathy trying to keep warm in the car, but she came in just as the Chief broached his refilled glass, flooding the room with warmth and light. The Chief appeared to bask in it, and left on an almost violent acceleration of pace when he saw the time. Neil would have liked to be a fly on the wall during the confrontation with Amelia Larkin and the Sunday lunch past its prime.

CHAPTER SIX

"What are your plans for today, love?" asked Neil casually, as they concluded an andante breakfast. Despite the circumstances he had to acknowledge an awareness of pleasure in being able to eat slowly enough on a Monday morning to savour his toast and linger over the paper and a second cup of coffee. But it wasn't as though he had the prospect of an aimless day.

"Well, with term starting tomorrow, I thought I'd do the flat a bit specially this morning—would you feel like cleaning the windows?— and this afternoon—I'm sorry, darling, of course I didn't know you'd be here—I've got a portrait in Highgate. Two little girls, and a puppy which grows by the week. Will you go out?"

"Not very far, if I do." Forty-eight hours earlier it would have been impossible to imagine the sense of relief he now felt at the prospect of a little time without his wife, but forty-eight hours earlier it would have been impossible to imagine his new situation. "Don't worry about me, I've been promising myself I'd get a few things out of the way, and this afternoon will be an opportunity. And yes, I'll clean the windows."

He also washed the kitchen floor and climbed a step-ladder to brush ceilings and light fittings. Cathy told him over a cheese and biscuit lunch that between them they'd managed a mini-spring-clean. "It didn't hurt, did it?"

"Not a bit. But then it had novelty value."

"Not all that much. It wasn't the first time you've washed the floor."

"No . . . You've never quite got used to discovering I'm not the complete male chauvinist, have you?"

"I didn't expect you'd be so ready to share the so-called woman's role. It means more to me that you *are* prepared than to have you actually do it—which isn't to say you haven't been a godsend this morning. I suppose I should have realized from the way you kept your own flat, but I rather thought that might only be because there wasn't a woman—a regular woman"—she half smiled at him—"to do it for you." Her eye caught the clock above his head. "Goodness, is that the time?"

"I'll wash up the two plates and the cups and saucers," he said. "You scoot. Anything to prepare for dinner?"

"If you're absolutely dying to scrape potatoes and carrots. Otherwise there's really no need, I'll have plenty of time when I get back. Thanks, though."

"When will you get back?"

She hesitated, and he felt himself tensing as he waited to be told how much time he had. "The sitting always takes ages, what with the dog moving all the time and the children getting bored so quickly. Then I'm invited to tea afterwards, it's quite a ritual, although I'll have to break it next week when I'm back at school, and just go straight there for the actual sitting."

"So you mustn't break it today. As I said, I've several things I want to do. I won't expect you a minute before five."

"You're thoughtful, Neil, thank you."

In one whirl she had kissed him and left the flat. Hearing the lift, he had a sudden sharp moment of empathy with her as Cathy McVeigh, sitting alone in the kitchen where he was sitting now, listening for his feet crossing the public landing and the sound of the lift, her heart sinking. When they got engaged she had told him, laughing, of her involuntary vigil, but just before he became aware of her he had begun to suspect it . . .

His battered old case with the odds and ends in it was somewhere in the deep cupboard at the top of the built-in wardrobe in the spare bedroom. The step-ladder was still in the hall and he took it close to the wardrobe to climb up and investigate, so eager to get at the case he slipped as he grasped its intrinsic weight of old-fashioned leather and heavy fittings. He had to sit on the bed a few seconds to nurse his ankle before snapping the case open and tumbling its contents on to the crisp white cover. Yes, there was everything he had hoped to see: the wig, dress and shoes he had worn as the high-class tart in last year's office revue, the stuffed bra and the theatrical make-up. The wig would do for the experiment, although if it worked he would find himself a short dark one, as well probably as a less showy dress or a jumper and skirt. And except as a base the theatrical make-up would be too heavy, he'd have to raid Cathy's dressing-table drawer.

He did a pirouette in front of the cheval-glass when he'd pulled on the tights, then when he was doubled up with laughter suddenly remembered the two plates and the cups and saucers in the kitchen and went through in his stockinged feet to get them out of the way. He'd take Cathy at face value on the potatoes and carrots.

When he got back into the spare room he put on the bra, then the slip and the dress. The dress was really too elaborate for his purpose that afternoon, but he could lessen the effect with one of his cardigans and Miss Prince would be unlikely to notice that it buttoned from the left . . . He hoped Miss Prince would be at home. If she wasn't he would knock on another door, but Miss Prince knew him and was interested in him and would offer the most stringent test.

The dress fitted really well. He went back into their bedroom to do his detailed make-up after he had covered his face and neck with the theatrical foundation—that morning he'd had an extra-careful shave. He used Cathy's paints sparingly, as she used them herself. When he had finished he looked like Neil Carter with make-up, but in the moment of crowning himself with the long corn-coloured wig he became an attractive woman smiling a mysterious smile at herself in the glass, appearing to be thinking far deeper thoughts than merely what marvellous women men made, while women attempting men always remained women in drag . . . His voice would be the one doubtful element, but he had been complimented on that, too, following his showing in the office revue. Although unambiguously masculine when he was dressed as a man, it had a light timbre which a female outfit could apparently delude people into accepting as a sort of Dietrich contralto.

"Oh, excuse me," he said to the mirror in an outrageous falsetto, and had to laugh again. "Oh, excuse me," he said in his own voice, but breathily and with a sort of lingering emphasis, and thought it didn't negate his appearance. "I was looking for Cathy Carter, actually." Yes, it was all right.

After putting on Cathy's showiest bracelet and dabbing a generous amount of her heaviest perfume on his wrists and behind his ears Neil went to rummage for a cardigan, reminding himself that it hardly mattered what Miss Prince's detailed reaction was to a friend of Cathy's she would not see a second time . . . Every cardigan he dug out was impossible with the flamboyant dress, and he was just deciding to put on an anorak and be done with it when he remembered the fluffy jumper an old aunt of Cathy's had knitted her and which was so enormous they had wondered, before putting it away in a bottom drawer to await a jumble sale, if it was perhaps an indication that the aunt was failing. If only Cathy hadn't done anything with it in the meantime.

No, it was still there, where they had stowed it together helpless with laughter, and it fitted him to perfection, allowing a demure awareness of the padded bra and turning the vamp's dress into a blue flared skirt. All he had to do now was to find a handbag and transfer to it a few of the things in his trouser pockets and one of Cathy's handkerchiefs, then pick up her loose mac and a pair of warm gloves in acknowledgement of the weather in the streets.

He hadn't seen or heard Miss Prince going out, so there was a good chance she would be at home. There was no need to wait for conventional tea-time, he knew from his own reluctant experience that she was ready at any time of the day with tea or coffee to prolong the possibility of company, and it was barely three o'clock when, having made certain through his spyhole that the landing was deserted, he came out of his front door and shut it quickly behind him—immediately to realize that he had condemned himself to a choice between a couple of hours in Miss Prince's company or a shorter period followed by a descent to the outside world to fill in somehow or other the rest of the time until Cathy's return. Miss Prince might well be already regarding him through her spyhole, and he could no more change his mind and go back indoors to wait awhile than he could let himself back into his flat at the end of the afternoon.

It was part of his role to be unsure, so when he had unavailingly rung his own doorbell a couple of times he practised his female walk by wandering about the landing, peering uncertainly at the other three front doors. When he eventually rang Miss Prince's bell her door was opened at once.

"Please forgive me," said Neil hesitantly, smiling and then wondering if she would recognize his teeth. "I was hoping to see Mrs. Carter —opposite—but she doesn't seem to be in . . ."

"Oh dear," fluttered Miss Prince, no trace of suspicion diluting her concern. "You're quite right, yes, Mrs. Carter went out an hour or so ago, she goes out on a Monday afternoon during the school holidays and doesn't usually get back until about five o'clock. I'm so sorry . . . She must have forgotten . . ."

"She wasn't expecting me, actually, I just found myself in this part of the world and thought I'd call on the off chance. Never mind, it was a gamble, I could hardly expect—"

"Oh, but you must come in and wait for her!" Miss Prince was almost indignant, thought Neil, at the idea of this course of action not being taken for granted. "And you'll have some tea, I was just putting the kettle on."

"How very kind of you." For the first time on Miss Prince's doorstep it had seemed a long wait for an invitation. "But I really don't like to—"

"Of course! Come in, come in!" Miss Prince stood aside from her doorway, putting a limp and merely symbolically persuasive hand on his arm. "I should welcome a little company, and it seems such a pity to miss Mrs. Carter just by an hour or so . . ."

"Well, then. Thank you."

"Oh dear, forgive me, I think I'm a little bit untidy in here. I'm going away tomorrow and everything is rather . . ." Miss Prince was murmuring non-stop as she led the way into her sitting-room—so different, with its pale north light, from their own bright place, and so much stuffier.

"No, no, please . . ." murmured Neil in his turn, suddenly realizing he had no idea what his name was.

"There!" said Miss Prince, patting the seat of the chair from which she had just removed a piece of knitting. Fussily she altered the angles of two of the small tables dotted about the centre of the carpet. "Please sit down, Miss . . ." She had darted a glance at his left hand, which had shed its glove, and he found himself glad that it wasn't particularly hairy.

"Bartlett," he heard himself saying. "Rosemary Bartlett." Had he dredged it up from some past encounter, or invented it?

"Do sit down, then, Miss Bartlett"—she had looked at his hand again, perhaps her faded eyes hadn't been quite certain the first time that the gold ring was on his little finger (heavens, it was as unchangeable as his teeth)—"and I'll just go and make us a pot of tea. I shan't be a moment, but here's the paper."

Miss Prince put the *Daily Mail* on the small table beside his chair before bustling out of the room. Neil, horrified that she should turn her back on a strange woman who for all she knew could be a man in disguise, had to force himself not to reprimand her. He would, of course, have the opportunity later, after Cathy had relayed to him what she, no doubt in his feminine presence, would relay to Cathy . . .

"What a blessing I was here, Miss Bartlett," said Miss Prince, very quickly returning with a tray on which was the familiar flower-patterned tea service and the no less familiar ginger biscuits. "I'm sure Miss McVeigh—oh, dear me, Mrs. Carter, that is to say, Cathy—I'm sure she would have been disappointed to miss you. Have you come far? Do you take milk? Sugar?"

"A little milk, please. No sugar. I've come up for the day from Brighton, where I live. Cathy and I were at school together—"

"Really?" Miss Prince's sudden keen look told him he had made one mistake, at least: dressing as a woman had not narrowed the eight-year gap between him and his wife. But at least she wasn't asking him if he knew such and such a back-crack in Brighton.

"At the same school would be more accurate," he said, smiling. "She's younger than I am, of course, but we've known each other for ages through our families and she followed me in due course to St. Werburgh's . . . I got my appointments over quite quickly and just thought I'd call in on the off chance she might be at home, we hardly ever manage to see one another these days." He hesitated, then went irresistibly on. "You obviously know her quite well. How is she?"

"Oh dear . . ." Miss Prince in her perturbed excitement let her teaspoon clatter on to the tray. "I wouldn't say I knew her *well*, Miss Bartlett, that is to say, not—well, not intimately—but she *has* told me her little secret, perhaps she's told you too, it isn't a secret now, of course, or I wouldn't be telling you—"

"Telling me what, Miss . . . er . . . Prince, didn't I see on your door?" He had only just reined himself in in time, not to let her name trip off his tongue.

"Prince, yes, how observant of you . . . Telling you that Miss McVeigh—Cathy—is having a little one in the autumn. *Yes*"—as if he had been about to contradict her—"isn't it lovely news? I can tell you're surprised," said Miss Prince complacently.

"And delighted, of course." That she had correctly read an assumed emotion on an assumed face.

"Forgive me, I don't recall . . . I don't remember seeing you at the wedding, though obviously you must have been—"

"That was *such* a disappointment. I had to be away. My only contribution was a telegram, and I can hardly expect you to remember *that.*"

"No . . . But what a great pity, Miss Bartlett. It was a lovely day, Miss McVeigh looked really beautiful. You're sure you won't change your mind and have a little biscuit? No? Well then, another cup of tea."

"Thank you." His lipstick had made a noticeable arc on the rim of the delicate cup. "Yes, it was a pity."

"You've met Mr. Carter—Neil—though?"

Again the temptation refused to be denied.

"Actually I haven't. It seems absurd, but whenever Cathy and I have got together it's always been at lunch or tea-time—like this—and of course Neil has always been at work. I gather she's very happy, though."

"Oh, yes. Miss McVeigh's a happy person, isn't she? Oh dear"— Miss Prince choked over her biscuit—"I wasn't suggesting that Mr. Carter wouldn't make her happy, of course, they're very happy together, very happy indeed, and Mr. Carter is always so kind to me, so very kind . . ."

The lady protests too much, he suspected, remembering all those times he had looked at his watch with simulated urgency. But the old girl's unmerited loyalty warmed him as well as pricking his conscience. "I'm so glad . . . These are very nice flats," he said with quiet desperation. A clock painted like a daisy told him it was not yet half past three.

"Yes, aren't they? They're pre-war, you know, when builders still used good materials, but they were ahead of their time in having good-sized kitchens and bathrooms. Most thirties flats skimped on those essential offices, so we have the best of two worlds here, good building and a modicum of modern space."

When Miss Prince spoke to him as himself she was in a state, he ruefully realized, of permanent fluster, and this was the first time she had made it understandable to him that she had once been a school-teacher. Albeit with terrible problems of discipline.

"Yes, I see . . . And a nice balcony." He got up and threaded a sedate way between the little tables. "I don't suppose that was so usual before the war, either."

"No," said Miss Prince eagerly, jumping to her feet and reaching the window before him. She opened the patio door. "This door's new, of course, the owner before me had it put in. The Carters have a modern door, too, I think most of the flats do, now, but I confess a regret for the old french window."

"It's a nice balcony," said Neil, going out and leaning over to confirm his hope that there was no way Miss Prince could see the entrance to Westcote Gardens.

"Yes, it is nice." Miss Prince made another symbolic gesture, this time of shepherding her visitor in out of the chilly wind. "Of course, I face north, which wouldn't do for the youngsters—Mr. and Mrs. Carter face south and sit out a lot in the sun—but the sun's a bit much for me these days, and on a warm day it's very pleasant just to get the air—"

"I'm sure it must be." Neil stopped in the middle of the room, loath to sit down again.

"Mr. Carter lived in another flat on this landing," said Miss Prince excitedly. "That's how he and Miss McVeigh—Cathy—met. It was very romantic. There was another lady in the fourth flat . . . Quite a story, Miss Braithwaite, but too long to go into now and I was never sure . . . Anyway, Mr. Carter—Neil—realized it was Cathy he loved, and when they got married they moved into her flat—more sun, and she'd painted some pictures on the walls I gather they didn't want to leave behind, although what they'll do when they eventually buy a house . . . Which they might feel they want to do now, I suppose, with the baby . . ." Miss Prince, obviously realizing for the first time the possibility of his and Cathy's departure from Westcote Gardens, looked suddenly stricken, stirring his conscience anew.

"Oh, I don't imagine they'll be thinking about it for a while yet," he encouraged truthfully, "although I suppose eventually . . ."

"Yes," sighed Miss Prince. She felt under the tea cosy, disguised to look like a thatched cottage. "The tea's stewed, I think, but I'll make us another pot. You just look at the paper—"

"Thank you," said Neil, having to make an effort to moderate his usual firm tone at this point. "I've taken up quite enough of your time as it is—you've been really awfully kind—and I've just remembered there *is* one other call I ought to make while I'm in town. I'll go now, and come back in half an hour or so. If Cathy's still not home," he added, seeing the sudden hopelessness in her face, "I'll ring your bell again, if I may, and give you a note for her."

"Please don't *hesitate*, Miss Braithwaite . . . Barclay . . ."

"Bartlett," said Neil, after a moment's confusion.

He didn't get out under another ten minutes, having to look at the rest of Miss Prince's flat, and when in the public entrance hall he took his watch out of Cathy's handbag he found that it was a quarter past four. Cathy, he was fairly confident, wouldn't be a moment later than five, and maybe earlier, so there might not be very much more time to put in. While he was standing there, wondering just what he would do, the outer door swung briskly inwards to admit another householder, a man known to Neil because of his enthusiastic membership of the management committee and his unpopular unofficial role as the building's watchdog, in which he regularly and unsuccessfully attempted to recruit Neil's police persona to settle minor civil disagreements.

But for once, recalling the inadequacies of Miss Prince's eyesight, Neil was glad to see George Benson.

The hawk eyes were on him at once, of course, but merely in potentially aggressive curiosity and—he registered in amazement—reluctant attraction.

"Can I help you?"

"Thank you, no." Neil smiled, evoking a blink and a jerk of the adam's apple. "I've been visiting in the building, and was just wondering about my next appointment."

"Forgive me, I just thought . . ." Old Benson, insensitive as he was, had picked up the implied mild rebuke. But not, it seemed, any whiff of masculinity. He really had passed his own test, Neil thought elatedly as he went out through the door Benson was holding open for him, and could go on to the real thing.

He had thought of walking along to the small memorial garden where he had asked Cathy to marry him, but now it occurred to him that he would be wise to make himself known to her outside the range of Miss Prince's observation—if he was really as successfully disguised as he now believed, she would repudiate her old friend Rosemary Bartlett in view of Miss Prince's spyhole or, more probably, her open front door . . .

There was a seat just outside the entrance to Westcote Gardens, on the wide pavement and partly concealed by the long branches of the great horse-chestnut which was the pride and joy of the flat residents (except, of course, the inevitable minority which wanted it cut down or mutilated). The green fists of the new leaves were opening out and he could sit there in comparative obscurity, not causing too much comment that a well-groomed woman should choose to loiter on a cold windy day . . .

To his relief Cathy was driving between the gateposts only a few moments after he had sat down. He was so pleased to see her, he started striding after her car before remembering who he was and moderating to what he thought would be a long-legged female gait. He was standing by her door as she got out.

"Cathy . . ." He hadn't, of course, really passed his test until his wife failed to recognize him.

She was looking at him, puzzled. "Forgive me, I don't think I . . ."

"Don't you know me, Cathy? Rosemary Bartlett. I went up to your flat and when you weren't in I called on your neighbour Miss Prince, and she told me—Cathy!"

Oh, but he was an idiot, he had sent her stumbling back against the car, her hand on her heart.

"It's Neil, it's Neil!" he said urgently. "Oh, darling, I'm an oaf, forgive me. I got so swelled-headed managing to deceive Miss Prince, and then that fool Benson, I couldn't resist seeing if *you* . . ."

"It was your voice, grafted on to . . . No, I didn't recognize you, Neil. Even now . . ."

"Cathy, I'm so *sorry*. But I promise you there's a method in my madness. I'm going to investigate your Mrs. Willoughby's murder privately and I wanted a disguise so that I could approach the lesbian lady and the actress. It works."

"Yes, but Neil . . ."

"Are you all right?" He was holding her hands, chafing them as if it were midwinter. "Do you forgive me?"

"I'm all right, and I forgive you. I'm only taking my hands away because, dressed like that, you'll look better without them."

"For a moment I forgot about the baby, I was so carried away by my own cleverness." Once he would not have said such a thing, not even allowed himself to think it. There was no doubt Cathy had made him a slightly nicer person. "Miss Prince gave me tea—of course—but I just couldn't face two hours of her. I was stupid enough to come out of the flat at three and then of course I couldn't go back in in case she was watching. I told her I had something else to do and then would come back and try you again. However cross with me you are, hold it until we're inside because she's bound to be glued to her spyhole and dash

out to tell you a whole lot of nothing about the arrival at her door of
this friend of yours. We've just met now in the car-park—"

"Which we've just done. All right. I'll just get my gear out of the
boot."

Cathy was still looking for her key when Miss Prince's door opened.

"Ah, there you are, Cathy, and there's your friend, isn't that lucky?
She came about three, one of her rare visits from Brighton, she told
me, on the off chance of finding you in . . ."

"Go and change," said Cathy, the moment she was able to shut the
front door with them both behind it, "and then we'll talk."

In the event she confined her strictures to the crumpled state of the
spare-room bedspread, but her instinct was to mistrust the idea of him
amateurly sleuthing.

"It'll be all right, Neil, they'll have the book tomorrow, and they'll
visit everyone in it."

"I don't like the idea of your being a suspect for that filthy murder. I
won't have it, in fact. And Rosemary Bartlett will get far more out of
them than the police as the police. No, not Rosemary Bartlett, I
thought I'd be your cousin."

"My *what?*"

"Your cousin. One of the ones who, like Rosemary, couldn't make
the wedding. But one to whom you've always been especially close. I'll
model myself on sister Angela, she's more like me than like you, thin
and dark and sharpish features. I couldn't be like Penelope—"

"Why be like either of them, for heaven's sake?"

"Because I want to be as convincing as possible when I tell the
women I'm worried about my cousin, expecting a baby and having
found Mrs. Willoughby . . . I'll be a solicitor like Angela. Solid and
informed."

"That doesn't make *you* solid and informed."

"It'll seem to," he said eagerly, more and more convinced in the face
of her reluctance that this was a charade he must play.

"Can't you just be a friend?"

"Only if I want doors shut in my face. Try to understand, love . . ."
He put his arms around her. "I've got a unique opportunity and I want
to exploit it. For you, and for the truth, and to get some maniac shut
away before he does it again. It's almost as if I was meant to get
suspended at this particular moment—if I'd been at work in the usual
way I couldn't have done anything at all, but now . . ."

She sighed. "I can see, Neil, I can see. I can't object, but I don't exactly relish it."

"You'll be back at school tomorrow," he urged, "so you'll be far too busy to be wondering what I'm up to. Well, I obviously won't be able to see your Miss Littlewood until the evening, with her spending the day in an office, but the other one, the actress, I shall have to visit her in the morning or the afternoon. First thing tomorrow I'll try and get a dark wig, and a jumper and skirt at Marks. Now, I want you to tell me every least thing you can about those two women . . ."

When, at bedtime, he was putting the milk bottle holder out, Miss Prince's door opened.

"Good evening, Mr. Carter, Neil, I was just going to ring and give you or your wife my key. I'm going away first thing in the morning for a little holiday." She crossed the landing and put the key into his hand—reluctant, he thought, to concede the gesture as the alternative to ringing his bell. "Wasn't it nice your wife having an old friend so unexpectedly? When she arrived Cathy was out and so I asked her in to tea. It really worked out very well."

"That was kind of you, Miss Prince, very kind." For the first time in their acquaintanceship he allowed a silence between them, a tacit invitation to her to fill it, and was somehow chagrined that she said merely, as she slowly retreated backwards towards her own door, "Well, good night, Neil," forcing him to speak quickly to prevent her closing her door before he could deliver her a fierce but friendly lecture on the folly of inviting strangers into her home.

CHAPTER SEVEN

As soon as Cathy had left for school he went on the tube to Marble Arch and Marks and Spencer, where he bought a brown bat-wing jumper and the longest short skirt he could find. For the wig he chose the anonymity of a large store which his resourceful wife had observed was promoting a new department, and told the assistant he wanted it for some amateur theatricals, smiling his confidence that she would appreciate his preference for the privacy of a fitting-room.

The second one of the stack she brought him was as good as he was likely to find. The flash of understanding of men who dressed up as women for no reason beyond their own satisfaction was unwelcome, even though he knew at the same time that this would never be for him . . . The shoes he already had would do—the only other thing he bought was a second pair of tights.

Back in the empty morning flat, the sound of a vacuum cleaner wailing in the distance, he was assailed by a sense of disorientation and defeat, an overwhelming awareness of being separated from his energy source, and sat a long time over a coffee at the kitchen table before he could fight it off. The assumption of his female persona wasn't the fun it had been the day before, but in the moment of pulling on the dark wig his optimism returned. He had little doubt he would be unquestioningly accepted as Cathy Carter's concerned older married cousin. Married . . . Fool, he had forgotten the wedding ring.

His annoyance with himself—and his slight anxiety that he might have forgotten another vital thing—shook him out of the last of his low spirits. And it was probably as well to go to Woolworth's as a woman before presenting himself at Sandra Fane's flat—by the time he'd walked from the tube, bought a gold-coloured ring, and travelled by bus to Maida Vale, he wasn't having to think so precisely about each step he took.

The block of flats was good-looking, the same vintage as Westcote Gardens and also set back from the road in a generous parking area edged with plants and bushes. A notice on the wall of the lobby obligingly indicated the allocation of the flats—number 9 was on the first of the two upper floors.

His own temperament would have had him taking the stairs two at a time, but he forced himself to ring for the lift and stand in apparent patience awaiting its descent from the top of the building. When he heard the outside door open behind him he turned round in pleased anticipation of another encounter.

Coming into the building were two men, one of whom almost stopped his heart before flooding him with a knee-weakening gratitude. He didn't know Detective Inspector Gerald Capstick particularly well, but thank heaven he knew him well enough to be warned that here were two policemen on an official visit. Now they were beside him, he recognized the sergeant too, although if he'd seen him on his own he would merely have been puzzled, wondering if the man had once served him in a shop.

"Nice morning," observed the detective inspector.

"Very nice. Yes." Neil gave an involuntary shudder of relief that he had encountered the detectives while he still had the chance of taking the lift to the floor above Sandra Fane's flat. Unless, of course, this was a diabolical coincidence and the inspector and the sergeant were going up to the second floor as well—he had hardly expected his colleagues to have assimilated the contents of his anonymous package, which could only have reached them that morning, to the extent of already taking action on it. Unless, of course, Sandra Fane's name and address had featured elsewhere among Mrs. Willoughby's effects . . . He realized that part of his reaction to the two policemen was a disdainful surprise that they hadn't been prepared to walk up one flight of stairs.

Inside the lift the sergeant examined the buttons. "Which floor?" he asked Neil with an unnerving smile, after pressing the one for the first.

"Second, please." The breathiness in his voice wasn't assumed this time, it was his reaction to the further and even more horrible realization that he could already have been in Sandra Fane's flat when his colleagues arrived, or arrived himself to find them there. His satisfaction at being free to work on his own had made him absurdly over-confident . . . He could feel the sergeant's eyes on him, and turned to study the wall until he and the inspector got out of the lift. At the second floor he walked on tiptoe over the resonant tiles to the stairhead. Holding tight to the support rail, he began to creep down. Halfway he heard the two voices.

"Looks like there's nobody at home." He heard a bell faintly ring. "Better try a neighbour."

There was a shuffling of feet, followed by a double chime. A door opened.

"Yes?"

A woman's voice, already impatient.

"We're sorry to disturb you, madam." The inspector spoke ingratiatingly. "We're looking for Miss Sandra Fane, but she doesn't appear to be at home. We were wondering if you would be able to tell us where we could find her."

"And why should I?"

"We're police officers," came the inspector's voice again, more quickly. "Miss Fane was a witness to an accident recently and it would be helpful to us if we could have a word with her."

There was a pause, no doubt while credentials were being examined, and then the woman's voice in another mood, scarcely less aggressive.

"If Miss Fane's not at home she's at the theatre." The tone implied that this should be common knowledge.

"The theatre, madam?"

"The Touchstone. The new play," said the voice, as if addressing an imbecile.

"Oh, yes," said the sergeant. "I thought the name was familiar in some way. There's been quite a bit about the play—*The Horseshoe* or something like that—in the press."

"All right?" asked the female voice. "So you know where to find Sandra Fane."

"Thank you," said the inspector with dignity, and a door sharply closed.

"Straight there, Governor?" asked the sergeant warily. His Sergeant Hughes, Neil reflected, sometimes spoke to him in that tone of voice when he suspected his superior's ego might have been bruised.

Cursing the encounter he'd begun by welcoming, Neil cautiously descended the rest of the top flight of stairs, approving the sound of heavy feet in parallel below him—the other two policemen were at least relying on their legs for the downward journey. He waited until the creak of the swing door heralded silence, then carefully negotiated the lower flight. He felt exhausted as he left the building, and went into a small cafe along the road for a Welsh rarebit and a cup of coffee, gradually reassembling his optimism for the second time that day. When Detective Inspector Capstick and his sidekick got no joy from Miss Littlewood's they would knock up a neighbour and find out where she, too, spent her weekday hours. Then they'd go along to see her at her office—it wasn't the sort of matter which could be left until she got home from work. Miss Fane couldn't be back at her flat until late that night, but he'd go along to see Miss Littlewood during the evening.

The idea of spending the afternoon as a woman to save himself the business of so soon dressing up again was quickly routed by the idea of getting home as speedily as he could in order to return himself to normal. On the tube he started to wonder whether Miss Prince would have left for her holiday. If not, and she opened her door upon him opening his, the only explanation he could think up was that he really was Cathy's cousin, letting herself in with the spare key Cathy had given her. And sporting the same face and figure as Cathy's friend Rosemary.

He really had underestimated the pitfalls of what he had undertaken as a foolproof exercise. Safely back in the flat with the knowledge that all Miss Prince could have seen was the back of a dark female head, he tore off everything he was wearing and doused his face with soapy water until it smarted. When Cathy came in he was lying on the sofa listening to Brahms and in need of care and attention.

He had thought he would conceal the elements of near miss in his morning's activities, but found himself telling her about them. To his relief her immediate reactions of alarm, distaste and incipient "I told you so" suddenly disappeared in a yelp of laughter. He joined in, less and less inhibitedly and with each chortle seeing it more clearly as a farce.

"It *is* funny, isn't it?" he asked her, when sheer weakness had quietened them.

"Of course it is, although it could have been anything but."

"I know, I know. That's why I'm not going back to those flats today. It'll be all right tomorrow, and Miss Littlewood will be all right later on tonight."

"Tonight . . ."

"Darling, I *can't* wait until Saturday, and by nine o'clock, say, there won't be any risk of meeting Inspector Capstick or any other members of the official force. It's only a quarter to five, by the way . . ." He tried to backtrack on the invitation in his face as he remembered the significance of the day so far as his wife was concerned. "How was the beginning of term?"

"The usual chaos. Special interest and attention, of course, from the staff. The news hasn't penetrated downwards yet, but I don't suppose it will take long. Did you say it was only a quarter to five?"

He woke from a sleep so deep and peaceful he thought it was morning. Cathy got out of bed first to cook an easy meal, and after they'd eaten kept out of the way while he got himself ready. Although he could see she was steeling herself to look at him as he came into the sitting-room before leaving, she saw him off cheerfully enough. He took her car, and when he had found Miss Littlewood's semi-detached house a little way short of Kew he drove round the neighbouring streets and discovered that the orderly suburb ended just behind the houses opposite. He parked there and set off on foot round the corner, walking as unobtrusively as he could while trying to walk like a woman. It was difficult, but at least he was confident of being able to deal with a mugger.

The plain dark van he had noticed while in the car was still parked on the stretch of road linking the road he had left to the one into which he was turning. As the row of houses which contained Miss Littlewood's came into sight he saw a man leaving one of them and walking quickly to the gate. A man in a peaked cap which, with the suit he was wearing, could add up to a uniform. Dark grey? Under the sodium street light he couldn't be sure, but as the man passed him he noted the luxuriant moustache and remembered his conversation at his own front door with the man from the private postal service. The same man? The same moustache, but he wouldn't have expected to see such a service in operation in this area of London, nor quite so late. A coincidence? He couldn't be absolutely sure it was Miss Littlewood's house the man had come out of . . .

Her tiny front garden was paved and plain. The single shrill note of the bell was quickly answered. Neil was accustomed to doors on chains and a face at the crack inquiring who he was, but Miss Littlewood pulled her door immediately wide, her angry stare moderating as she took him in. Anger at being disturbed, or at being disturbed a second time? There seemed nothing from Cathy's impressionistic description which didn't fit, except that the heavy-duty shoes had been replaced by unbecoming slippers.

"Miss Littlewood?" Was it his imagination that her breathing was unnaturally agitated?

"Yes."

"Please forgive me," said Neil politely, "for calling on you like this without any warning. I'm Cathy Carter's cousin Josephine Webster." He'd thought the name up while Cathy was getting supper. "I don't know if you'll remember Cathy, she's—she was—a client of Mrs. Willoughby's." The face had darkened, suspicion had entered the small, deep-set eyes. "In fact she was the person who found Mrs. Willoughby —dead—and she's been very upset and worried that the police may think she had something to do with her quite awful murder." Neil paused for thought, and because he didn't much like stating his complex business outside on the path.

"I really don't see what it has to do with me," observed Miss Littlewood. There was no doubt a caution had entered her manner which had been absent when she had opened the door.

"Of course not," said Neil quickly. "It was only . . . Well, I was so worried about Cathy—she's having a baby, and finding that poor woman in the state she was—you'll have read about it—I just thought I'd ask you if you knew anything about Mrs. Willoughby which might give some clue as to why it happened. Cathy's mentioned another person she met at Mrs. Willoughby's as well," he went on hastily, in the face of the furious silent protest, "a Miss Fane, I shall be going to see her, too. Cathy's no idea I've come to see you, of course, but however crazy I just felt I had to try and do something for her . . ."

"You'd better come in." The fury had yielded to the lack of expression with which Miss Littlewood had registered his presence. She stood silently aside and he preceded her into the small hall, carpeted in a shade of purple he particularly disliked and almost bare of adornment. "Come in here."

The purple carpet extended into the small high sitting-room, but there were a few photographs, and a large pale water-colour of an Isadora Duncan-style figure dancing in a maze of outflung scarves.

"Sit down . . ."

"Mrs. Webster. Josephine Webster."

"Josephine. My name's Amanda. Coffee?"

"Thank you," said Neil, taken aback and suddenly, instinctively, uncomfortable. "That's very kind."

"Shan't be a moment."

While Miss Littlewood was out of the room he thought of getting up and having a closer look at the photographs, but felt bolted into his seat. She was soon back—when she came in he realized he had been wishing it was Miss Prince he was expecting—carrying a tray on which were two thick pottery mugs and a pottery plate containing health-store biscuits.

"I'm sorry for Mrs. Carter," she said brusquely as she set the tray down, "but I'm sure I don't know anything more about Mrs. Willoughby than she does."

"She doesn't know anything," said Neil, and was aware of a darting glance. "They met on a bus, of all things, and when they were talking Mrs. Willoughby mentioned her dressmaking, and that she altered things as well. My cousin"—by what generous gesture of providence had he been enabled to turn the word "wife" into the word "cousin" without stumbling?—"wanted a few things let out and some maternity clothes, and it seemed like a lucky encounter. Also my cousin is an artist, and thought Mrs. Willoughby had the sort of face she would like to paint." Instead of feeling sorry for himself that afternoon he should have gone to see Jim Grayson; he had the excuse of collecting Cathy's gear, for goodness' sake. He'd go in the morning.

"My connection with Mrs. Willoughby was purely business," snapped Miss Littlewood, suddenly fixing him with a direct gaze which she held to his face like a searchlight. Glad of the protection of the make-up, Neil steadily and smilingly returned it until his hostess, shaking herself in a way which reminded him of a shaggy dog, turned her attention to the tray and her mug of coffee.

"Of course," said Neil. "I'm only clutching at straws."

"And if I did have anything to say I'd have said it to the police. They came to see me at work today. I wasn't surprised, Mrs. Willoughby had a book in her wardrobe where she marked off payments. Her clients' addresses were probably there as well as their names, but even if they weren't my name isn't exactly common and Miss Fane has a certain recent notoriety." Miss Littlewood's tone was suddenly sarcastic, and Neil wondered if the two women had coincided in Mrs. Willoughby's front room, the younger making plain her indifference to the older.

"Of course you'd tell the police all you could," said Neil quickly. "As my cousin did. But it isn't always the facts which offer the solution . . . I'm a solicitor, by the way, although I haven't practised since I had the children. It may be part of the reason why poor Cathy's talking to me so much. She wanted to talk to you and Miss Fane, see if between you you could find some clue to what happened, but she just hasn't been up to taking the step of getting in touch with you. It was easier for me . . . There's a young man living downstairs in the house, isn't there?"

Miss Littlewood snorted. Neil found his glance caught by her right hand, red and ringless and lying on her plump knee. The hand which could have delivered that piercing thrust . . . The crime was so terrible, he would be wrapping himself in a cocoon of reserve with every possible suspect. "Jim Grayson, private eye. The apple of Mrs. Willoughby's eye—and the collector of Miss Fane's affections too, I gather. Mrs. Willoughby wasn't too keen on that, but I hardly think it would have given rise to murder."

"Of course not, and anyway Mrs. Willoughby could have opened the door to someone who was neither a friend nor a client . . . Did you know any of her other clients, Miss Littlewood?"

She was regarding him thoughtfully and his discomfort was increasing.

"I've coincided with the pallid creature who was run over. Mrs. Willoughby advertised in newsagents' windows, she may have had the odd one-off client for her powers of clairvoyance."

There was no mistaking the scorn in Miss Littlewood's voice, but Neil was unable to let the reference go. "Forgive me, it's none of my business, but did you ever avail yourself of her—"

"It isn't any of your business, no, but of course I didn't. Do I look the kind of person to be taken in by that sort of tomfoolery?"

"Probably not," said Neil, wishing it wasn't the sort of disclaimer which needed to be accompanied by a smile. "But some people take it very seriously."

"No doubt." She was staring at him again. "It's good of you, though, to be concerned for your cousin." Reluctantly he recognized a change of attitude from disdain to comparative friendliness. "But the police haven't shown any particular interest in her, have they?"

"Goodness, no." The exclamation was Cathy's, but might be Josephine's, too. "It's just that she feels they'll be bound to consider her in connection with what happened, and at the moment it isn't good for her."

"She has no reason to think"—the searchlight was on again—"that someone might have wanted to kill Mrs. W?"

"I'm sure she hasn't. Have you?"

"Why should I have?" The aggression was back, to his relief.

"Why should Cathy? It was your question."

"It was, yes. I'm sorry."

He tried not to think that Miss Littlewood's conciliatory attitude might be attributable to her reaction to Josephine Webster. It was taking him all his time, now, to go on acting as a woman. "That's all right. But as we're all obviously concerned that Mrs. Willoughby's murderer is brought to justice, perhaps you'll consider answering it."

"What nonsense," said Miss Littlewood, but mildly. She picked up her mug and drained it. "Of course I can't think of any reason why anyone would want to kill that old woman."

The voice was brusque and decisive again, but Neil was certain there was fear in the eyes which were now not quite meeting his. Perhaps it was his glimpse of this unexpected emotion, coupled with the instinct developed from years of asking questions, which was making him believe that Miss Littlewood was lying.

"Thank you." His visit had been worth while, and it was time it ended. He got to his feet.

"Do have another coffee before you go!"

Miss Littlewood had followed suit so quickly, she was already standing close beside him, the hand which could have wielded Mrs. Willoughby's scissors urgent on his shoulder.

Pity eased his repugnance. What loneliness, what despair perhaps, to clutch at the straw of a married woman with children who had shown no interest. Unless, of course, the mere act of being self-consciously a woman was to be provocative.

"Forgive me," he said, aghast. "My husband's waiting—"

"Round the corner? Afraid of encountering the police, of course."

The hand had dropped and Miss Littlewood had moved away from him. Her eyes were contemptuous, but he thought he saw disappointment drowning in the scorn.

"Of course." He tried to sound humorously rueful as he walked towards the hall. "We know very well I shouldn't be here."

"You realize it's my duty to tell the police you have been?"

"But I don't think you will," said Neil through stiff lips. He should have realized, oh, he should, that he could be doing his wife harm rather than good. "You know why I came." That part of him at least was honest, and he tried to show it in his eyes. "Misguided, perhaps, but with the best of intentions." Misguided without a doubt, but he still wouldn't be leaving it there.

"How did you find me?" It was all right, she wasn't going to shop him, but she couldn't retreat without trying to put him on a smaller spot.

He had his explanation ready. "Mrs. Willoughby told my cousin your name was Amanda. Very sensibly you're merely 'Littlewood, A,' in the telephone book, so I looked in the Electoral Register for the Littlewoods with the initial *A*. You're the only Amanda."

He thought he saw a flash of respect. "You really felt it was worth coming here, didn't you? I'm sorry you've wasted your time. But I won't say anything to the police, no." Her voice sounded tired, and he fancied her large square body had slightly sagged. Pity, now, with the front door open, was his exclusive emotion.

"Thank you. And for bearing with me. Let's just hope this whole awful thing will soon be cleared up."

"Oh, it will be. Good night."

"Good night." He had intended commenting, at the last moment, on the late service afforded by the man in the peaked cap, but if the man's visit had not been in the course of business the threat of Miss Littlewood's hostility returning with an intensity he was this time unable to deflect was too serious for him to take the risk.

He was getting into the car as he took in the last thing she had said. She was confident the murder would be solved, and she didn't talk off the top of her head. Perhaps this was yet another pointer to the dishonesty of her answer to the question she had asked him first, the question whether someone could have had a reason for wanting Mrs. Willoughby dead.

CHAPTER EIGHT

Waking from a nightmare in which a minuscule lift carrying Detective Inspector Capstick, an enormous leery-eyed detective sergeant and his androgynous self had stuck between floors, Neil decided it would be practical as well as prudent to delay his second visit to Sandra Fane until the afternoon. Not only had just one day garnered him a pile of evidence as to the vulnerability of his female persona, he had also learned that Miss Fane had morning rehearsals. She could well have afternoon ones as well, of course, to say nothing of matinees, and he had no intention of following his colleagues to the theatre, but she must surely have some time to draw breath between rehearsal and performance. To his satisfaction, he discovered from the paper over breakfast that *The Magic Horseshoe* gave its matinee performance on a Thursday. He would return to the flat in Maida Vale after lunch.

He could, though, still manage to postpone the task of rubbing down an old chest of drawers recently purchased by Cathy, which he had earmarked as a slightly less depressing activity to accompany the noise of neighbouring vacuum cleaners than continued fruitless puzzling over the little group of letters beside his wife's name transcribed from Mrs. Willoughby's second black notebook. He could go and see Jim Grayson to negotiate the return of Cathy's easel, paints and canvas.

Soon after she left for school he took the tube to Holborn and Grayson's office, savouring a hitherto unrecognized pleasure in being himself (despite an unnerving second in which he found his hand wandering to his hip in one of the limited range of gestures he was cultivating as Josephine), and in doing something which even his superiors would be unable to find less than exemplary.

The office was in a marble-paved pedestrian lane not far from the tube station, its door between a florist and an establishment which might have intrigued him with its announcement of tin-making "on the premises," had he been less blinkeredly intent. Cathy had told him Jim Grayson seemed pleased with his office accommodation, and from the outside at least it was easy to see why. A brass plaque indicated GRAYSON & EARNSHAW, INQUIRY AGENTS, on the one upper floor. The door didn't open but there was a bell.

"Yes?" It was a woman's voice.

"Mr. Grayson?"

"Who is it?"

"Neil Carter. Husband of Cathy. I think he'll see me."

"Of course, Mr. Carter." The pause had been brief. "Please push the door."

The stairs went up immediately in front of him, like the stairs Cathy had described but uncarpeted marble and clean and light. The door at the top repeated the firm's name in gilded letters on glass, and opened as he turned the brass knob.

A severe-looking elderly woman was behind a typewriter. When she smiled she was at once mild and friendly. "Please go straight in, Mr. Carter." There was a door to each side of her and she waved at the one on the right. "Mr. Grayson is free and would like to see you."

Why was his heart beating so uncomfortably?

There was only time to register that it was. The man behind the desk had got up and come round to meet him, was taking his hand in a firm grip.

"Unofficial meets official," he said, smiling. But Neil's first impression was of strain, with physical resources stretched to meet it. Jim Grayson was thin and pale, his short pale hair lifeless and untidy, his jeans and open-necked shirt geared for observation in undistinguished surroundings. Neil thought he looked forty and was probably thirty-five. He liked the wide-spaced, steady and intelligent eyes, despite a reluctance to admit it—a reluctance which he recognized with amazement and shame as jealousy.

Not jealousy alone, though—he had a job to keep his eyes away from Grayson's pale, long-fingered right hand and suppress the speculations which had assailed him when he had looked at Miss Littlewood's pudgy red one.

"This is a wretched business," he heard himself saying.

"It's devastated me." Grayson looked through his visitor at the horror Neil was unable to share with Cathy. "I can't take it in. How anyone . . ."

"Not so nice, either, for you or my wife, to be considered as possible violent killers. Forgive me, but I hardly imagine I'm putting a thought into your head."

"Of course not. It's obvious to me that I must be a prime suspect. I've no way of proving I was out when your wife arrived. Or that I hadn't been in."

"On the other hand, the people Mrs. Willoughby could have opened the door to are legion."

Grayson's gaze shortened to take in Neil, but his face remained expressionless. "In which case it's possible the mystery will never be solved, and your wife and I will never be quite comfortable again." Neil's face must have shown some reaction, because Grayson hurried on. "Excuse such miserable pessimism, I'm still punch-drunk, as I said. And it's just occurred to me that you could be here professionally. My first reaction was that you'd come about your wife's things."

"I have. And I can't go anywhere professionally at the moment." There was no way Grayson could have heard about his suspension, but it was still a relief to know that he hadn't. Neil told him what had happened at the local station.

"Good for you!" It was the first sign of animation. "You couldn't have done anything else."

"As my wife and other people tell me. But I've earned myself a punishing frustration—all day in which to wish I was part of the investigating team. I wouldn't have been anyway, of course, with Cathy being involved, but at least if I was able to work I'd have my own affairs to take up my time and my energy." That was how he would have felt if he hadn't started his own business.

"I can see, yes."

Something had flashed across Grayson's face, and Neil said on impulse, "Trying something yourself?"

"I'm as tempted as you must be, natch." There was a hint of amusement in the eyes which so openly met his. "But I think I'm best keeping my head down. The police don't like private eyes who try to be clever, particularly when they're in trouble." It was an attractive smile, transforming Grayson's face. "And my situation being as it is, I could get other people into trouble just by going to see them."

"Sandra Fane?"

He had decided to risk the impertinence of it, in order to observe the reaction. But Grayson merely said, sighing, "No, not Sandra, thank

God. I made no secret before—before Ma's death that I can hardly bear her out of my sight."

"Must be a bit difficult, you keeping office hours and she on the stage every night." He might just earn himself information about where Grayson was likely to be that afternoon.

"I don't keep office hours, and the theatre comes out at ten-thirty."

"Yes, of course." If Josephine Webster did coincide with Grayson at Miss Fane's it wouldn't matter. So long as Grayson didn't mention it to the police. He'd already decided, warned by Miss Littlewood's hostility, to ask Sandra Fane to keep Josephine's visit to herself, and he couldn't envisage any difficulty or danger in extending the request to Grayson. Like himself, though, Grayson was trained to observe. "Going back to black Saturday . . . You implied just now that you haven't an alibi." He had been naive to imagine himself able to refrain from asking questions, direct or oblique.

"I shouldn't think I have. I was doing some sleuthing near the Oval, but as the object of the exercise was to be as unobtrusive as possible I hardly expect the police to come up with someone to confirm my story. I can't even prove I wasn't at home, as I said. And obviously my dabs were all over the place."

"In the best bedroom?"

"They didn't need to be. The doorknob and the scissors would have been wiped clean." Grayson closed his eyes.

"The doorknob would have had Cathy's dabs on it by the time it was looked at." The mutual pre-emptions, thought Neil, were rather like a ritual fencing with foils on, each succeeding comment should have been accompanied by a side-step. Yet in a sense they were feeling their way together. "But whoever it was would probably have been blood-stained."

"I suppose so." Grayson stared at him. "And somewhat simpler for me to have got rid of it than for your wife. Well, impossible for her, I would have thought." They were trying to make it easier for one another, for heaven's sake, and Grayson was actually being generous—anyone in the position in which he'd found Cathy could have been over to the sink in the other room to wash, and come back. "I'll bet your colleagues were longing to have a look in my bathroom and kitchen." The sudden snort of laughter made Neil jump. "The sergeant did look in the bathroom, of course. But I'd swear it was for a true call of nature, he could hardly have assumed his sick green look at will.

Though if he did remember his duty after he'd thrown up he probably just thought I could have used the kitchen."

"What about the old fellow opposite? The police will have talked to him."

"Oh, yes. They brought me back from the station because they wanted a word with Bolshaw. Not so old, actually, just one-off. It took him an age as usual to open the door, and then he was only peering through a crack and had to be persuaded to let them in. They asked me to help, but I couldn't. In the end they tried laying the situation before him and appealing to his common sense. I rather admired the inspector's patience and initiative, and it paid off. Of course I don't know what happened when they got inside. I tried to make some comment to Bolshaw when I saw him this morning, but he just went 'M-m-m, m-m-m' and scuttled behind his door. It's awful, Neil, but I keep thinking that if he'd had a brainstorm on Saturday at lunchtime . . . He spends most of the day in the library, but he comes home for lunch."

"Have you got a reason for thinking that? I mean, did he and Mrs. Willoughby—"

"No reason at all, beyond the fact that he's paranoiacally unable to make contact beyond saying good morning. Ma and I used to puzzle over him sometimes. I'm sure she never had any more to do with him than anyone else did—that is, they passed the statutory time of day. That's why I said brainstorm."

"Have the police been in touch with you again?"

"Yes. But I got the impression their chief concern this time was to learn the routine of the house—if you can call the various things that go on there a routine. And they wanted to know about Ma's appointments, how regular they were and so on." Jim Grayson paused. "Cathy," he said diffidently. "Have they seen her again?"

"Not yet."

They stared at one another, until Grayson looked with an over-elaborate gesture at his watch. "Coffee time. Do stay and join us. And meet my partner. If we happen both to be in the office mid-morning we have coffee together. In his room," said Grayson, smiling again. "It's more elegant."

"Nothing wrong with this."

"It suits me. Oh, we have the same basic shape, but he's done things with his. Come and see?"

"Thanks, I'd like to . . . Just before we go, what was Mrs. Willoughby like?"

"Your wife must have told you." It was the first trace of reserve.

"Of course, yes, as far as she could. But she didn't *know* her."

Something he was unable to define crossed Jim Grayson's face. "And you assume I did. That's true of course, up to a point. She was a secretive old thing, kept her life in separate compartments. I mean— she was fond of me, I'm sure of that." Grayson paused while his adam's apple jerked up and down. "And she seemed to like Sandra, although we both knew she wasn't really pleased about our getting together in a relationship which excluded her. It was almost as if it wasn't fair play, *she* had discovered us both, showed us off to each other . . . Oh, I'm making too much of so little. But her secretiveness . . . One thing the police told me—and didn't tell me to keep to myself—was the truth about that son of hers. They wanted to know what she'd said to me about him, and she hadn't said anything, she always answered so curtly when anyone mentioned him, and she always just said he was abroad. The police told me they've found out he's in an institution in Kent and that he's a hopeless and intermittently violent idiot. Congenital. The institution's private and pricey, no wonder she lived so meanly for herself." The voice broke and Grayson walked to the window, where he stood looking out. Neil waited. "Poor Ma," said Grayson eventually, in his normal voice but without turning round. "She'd come back from the country with all those carrier bags, and say she'd been collecting work. Perhaps she had, but I know now that most of the stuff was his dirty washing, of which there was rather more than there is for most of us. Apparently she always insisted on doing it herself. I often found her locked in that little bathroom when I went up to see her, and now I think of it, I've never been inside it. I wish I'd known. Dear God, I wish I'd known!" At the tap on the door he spun round. "All right, Mrs. Baxter, I'm just coming. Add a cup, will you, please, Mr. Carter will be sitting in on the morning conference." Only a pink tinge to the whites of his eyes betrayed his brief loss of control. "I think the police found it hard to believe I hadn't known about Ma's son."

"Cathy asked her, too, and got the same answer." Neil was following Grayson past Mrs. Baxter's typewriter into a mirror image of Grayson's room. He realized from the relationship of door and windows and ceiling that it was a mirror image, but the impact was entirely different. Where Grayson's desk was functional and his other furniture restricted to two metal filing cabinets and two plastic chairs, Dave Earnshaw had a large eighteenth-century kneehole desk topped with tooled leather and a silver-gilt writing set. The sides of his brass-knobbed wooden filing cabinets were almost invisible under the trailing leaves of the plants arrayed on top, and there were four Impressionist paintings (unfamiliar to Neil, but surely not original?) and two showy abstracts, to contrast with Jim Grayson's bank calendar hanging askew and already dog-eared. It amused Neil to think of Mrs. Baxter's connecting office, with its reproductions of Shotter Boys' London and vase of spring flowers, as a linking device to lessen the cultural shock.

"Neil, meet my partner Dave Earnshaw. This is Neil Carter, Dave. You met his wife at my place—"

"Yes, of course. Please sit down, Neil." Earnshaw indicated one of the yellow velvet chairs. "Coffee? I was sorry to hear about your wife going to see Mrs. Willoughby just when she did. Milk? Sugar?"

"Neither, thanks." The contrast between the two partners was as dramatic as the contrast between their offices. Earnshaw, with his conventionally handsome features, neatly cut hair and immaculate suit, would not have been amiss in an early Ellery Queen movie, except that his voice was quintessentially English. And his smile as dazzlingly exclusive to Neil as Cathy had told him it had been to her. In the field, as in their offices, the partners would be able to reassure the gamut of a clientele.

As if in response to his thoughts Jim Grayson said, laughing, straddling the only basic chair in the room and leaning his arms on the back of it, "We cater for all comers, you see. Dave takes care of the classy end."

"And I can black up, and Jim can dress up, if required. It suits our personalities this way, but it's not an inflexible arrangement." Dave Earnshaw shook his head in mock reproof at his partner's stance, placing Grayson's coffee carefully on a coaster at the edge of the desk closest to his folded arms before sitting down neatly in the other velvet chair. Watching him and the precise way he moved, Neil thought he was reminded of a particular pre-war film star, but couldn't quite nail the original. The sense of familiarity could, though, come from the composite image of the heroes of the old black and white films he watched as often as he could on television.

"This is a dreadful business," Earnshaw was saying.

"Did you know Mrs. Willoughby?"

"I met her a few times at Jim's place. As a shape hovering above stairs, except when Jim gave a party."

"A few times is just about it," said Grayson. "Number 2 Pleasant Street isn't exactly Dave's spiritual home."

"I had a chat with her once at one of your parties," said Earnshaw, after another mock-reproachful glance. The two men complemented each other so well Neil was reminded of a high-class cabaret act. "Or rather, she had a chat with me. All about her spiritual capacities, I found it a bit hairy. Oh, Jim, I'm sorry." Sorrow came as powerfully out of Earnshaw's face as good humour. "I know how fond you were of the old lady, I didn't mean—"

"That's all right, Dave, I'm afraid I used to laugh at her sometimes myself."

"No, you didn't. For goodness' sake, don't start reproaching yourself, you were her good deed in a naughty world, and you know it. I say, steady on!" Grayson had blundered to his feet and gone to stand looking out of another window. "He's taken it very hard," murmured Earnshaw to Neil.

Warm, handsome, understanding, thought Neil, Earnshaw must be hardly able to move for would-be girl-friends. He was interested, and reassured, to find no evidence in himself of the sexual jealousy which would have obtruded on him despite himself in the days before he had found Cathy . . .

Jim Grayson was coming to sit down again, less exuberantly, and a bell was ringing on Earnshaw's desk, drawing attention to the golden daffodil which was the telephone. Lazily Earnshaw reached for it.

"Yes, Mrs. Baxter? Ah, yes." He held the receiver out to Jim Grayson, who leaped to his feet to hurl a few monosyllables into the gilded trumpet.

"Afraid I'll have to leave you," he said to Neil, handing the receiver to Earnshaw after a couple of abortive attempts to rehang it. "Forgive me, but something rather urgent has cropped up. The Davies business," he said to Earnshaw.

"Of course," said Neil. "Just tell me when to come for Cathy's things. And perhaps you can also tell me how to go about getting hold of the two dresses Mrs. Willoughby had ready for her. She says they've got her name on."

"The police are dispersing Ma's work-load, but I can be your agent.

I'll tell them I'm bringing your wife's painting gear round to you and I shouldn't think there'll be any difficulty."

"That's fine, I'll be grateful, but there's no reason why you should bring them, in fact. I'll come and collect them."

"And see the house, eh? Of course, come for a drink. Bring Cathy. Oh, no, she wouldn't . . . Just give me time to get on to the police about the dresses. Unless Cathy's waiting for them."

"No." He looked every day, but he couldn't see any change yet in the beloved shape. "Give me a ring when you've squared it. I'll come down with you—"

"You'll finish your coffee, Neil," said Earnshaw, as Neil pushed his card into Grayson's hand. "Don't bother about him, he only ever drinks halfway. Take care, Jim."

With a quick smile at them each in turn, Jim Grayson charged out of the room. Earnshaw picked up his coffee cup and saucer and leaned back in his chair. "Poor old Jim," he said. "He lost his grandfather a week or so ago, and now this. And *finding* her. Your poor wife found her first, though, didn't she? And being . . . Forgive me, Jim told me she was having a baby. Is she all right?"

"I think so. She says so. And I've watched her pretty closely and not seen anything to alarm me. I just keep hoping it won't crop up later."

"I know what you mean. It's a bit the same with Jim, he's highly strung at the best of times."

"You're on the outside," said Neil. "Well, slightly more than I am. But at the same time you're a bit closer to the situation. What's your reaction?"

Earnshaw leaned over to deposit his coffee cup on the tray. "My bet's on a casual nutter, maybe someone who saw the old woman's card in a newsagent's window, came for psychic guidance and didn't like what he or she heard. Although in that case one would scarcely have expected to find her lying down on her spare-room bed, she should have been slumped over the table beside her crystal, or tarot cards or what have you."

"She could have completed a consultation," said Neil, working it out as he went, "then seen whoever it was go down the stairs and appear to let themselves out. My wife told me she never went down the stairs with her clients, I suppose because of her heart condition, she got very breathless even without exertion. Then she could have gone into her spare room to lie down and the person could have crept back upstairs again. He or she might even have picked up the scissors in readiness."

"Yes . . ." Earnshaw looked thoughtful. "But from what Jim tells me Mrs. Willoughby always clicked her locks . . . Oh, I don't know. Of course one would prefer to think it was the work of a psychopath off the street, but if it was, then the case will never be solved and Jim— and your wife perhaps—will always feel they're being looked at askance—"

"That's what Jim said." He could feel anger tightening inside him. "That's why I'm so frustrated." As he got to his feet he told Earnshaw his situation, receiving the commendation which he was coming to expect but which had no mollifying effect on his fury.

"It's very tough on you," said Earnshaw sympathetically. "Anyway, I'm sure I speak for Jim as well when I say that if any information comes our way we'll share it with you. Not that it's likely to, but you never know, with Jim living in that fearsome house."

"Thanks. Now, I mustn't take up any more of your time."

"My pleasure, Neil."

If Earnshaw had a visible fault, it was perhaps that he was a shade too agreeable. Unless that was just his, Neil's, churlish reaction, and jealousy was still lurking somewhere. It would be interesting to see what he was like with women—in his experience, men who were fulsome with their fellows tended to be hard on women. His sudden realization that he had established the means of finding out was followed by a sense of disappointment that it was unlikely he would ever encounter Earnshaw in his female persona.

His enterprise was fantastic enough as it was.

It was still only eleven o'clock when he found himself back in the street, and he mooched the short way to Lincoln's Inn Fields with thoughts of the women's netball he'd watched there years ago when- ever he could, while on a job in the area. But that had been at lunch- time, not during office hours . . . It was cold and windy, sending pink and white blossom whirling to the ground and himself back to the tube, although for the first time since he had moved into Cathy's flat he didn't relish the thought of it. At least, though, he didn't have to go through his usual procedure of getting his front-door key ready to plunge into the lock before himself plunging from the lift across the landing—there would be no one behind Miss Prince's spyhole on the alert for the sound of the lift gates. And at least domestic cleaning time was just about over; on his way into the building he had passed a couple of women who looked like dailies.

Until he was actually in the sitting-room he had intended to start work on the chest of drawers, but he found himself getting the transcripts from Mrs. Willoughby's notebook out of the drawer where he and Cathy had agreed to keep them hidden, and sitting down with them at the desk.

Mrs Cathy Carter, 36 Westcote Gardens, Westcote Road,
N.W.8.
T OWGTF CWTRG.

Several lines of letters beside the other names in the book—Sandra Fane, Amanda Littlewood, Stella Lawrence and the three women who had been crossed out—but only those three words (if it was three words) beside Cathy's. If the *T* was an *A*, then there was an *A* in each of the longer words. There were two *G*s, and *E* was the most common letter in the English language . . .

A freak flame? A bleak grace?
A great shame?
The *T*, of course, could be an *I* . . .

There was no way he could get any further, except into the depression which seemed to hover over the letters, but he puzzled at them for so long, he found himself with time only to dash down a banana and a few scoops of cottage cheese before getting ready to call on Miss Fane by the early afternoon.

He had enjoyed his second transformation less than his first, and this third one he found almost distasteful. He wanted to be spared, now, having to show his female paces, and he opted for the bus rather than the tube, as offering a comparative anonymity in its seating arrangements by providing a prospect of backs of heads rather than faces.

By the time he was approaching the flats in Maida Vale for the second time his repugnance—which he had decided was due to his demonstrated success as a woman—was under firm enough control for him to feel confident of making proper use of both his working and his acting skills.

The lift was already at the ground floor, and the lobby was deserted. His reluctant memories of the audible dialogue between Detective Inspector Capstick and his sergeant took him straight to Miss Fane's door, the closest to the lift. He didn't know whether he was glad or sorry when he heard feet approaching.

"Miss Sandra Fane?"

He was astonished to find how much information there had been in Cathy's verbal sketch. The only thing which didn't accord was the hair, which had a fragile cloudy prettiness, probably indicating it had very recently been washed. The smile, the sense of life and warmth, were so heady he found himself considering—academically, to his relief—his degree of devastation if he had been free.

"Yes." He was a stranger as well as a fraud, but there was no noticeable reserve. "Can I help you?"

"It would be a miracle, I suppose, if you could. Forgive me, I don't really know why I'm here." It was easier for a woman, he decided, to be self-deprecating. "I'm Cathy Carter's cousin Josephine Webster. I think you met Cathy at—at Mrs. Willoughby's—"

"Yes, oh, yes!" Still as spontaneous, reminding him by sheer contrast of Miss Littlewood, Sandra Fane stood back from her doorway, smiling sadly. "Please come in."

"Thank you."

The room into which he followed her seemed to be full of photographs and flower-patterned chairs and sofas. "Do sit down."

"Thank you," he said again. "You really are very kind."

"How is Cathy?" Sandra Fane took the chair opposite and leaned towards him.

"She's all right. I suppose Jim Grayson told you—what happened."

"Yes. And that she's having a baby."

"Mrs. Willoughby didn't tell you that?"

"Oh, no. Mrs. Willoughby was—secretive." That word again. Sandra Fane used it diffidently, as if it reproached the dead. Or more likely, thought Neil, watching the warm bright face, because she couldn't bear to criticize anyone, however obliquely. "How can I help you—Josephine, you said?"

"Yes. Look, I might as well admit that I'm here simply because Cathy's devastated, and I felt I wanted to be doing something for her. Of course there isn't anything I *can* do, but I thought if I came to see you you might just be able to think of some small thing which could help get to the truth of this awful business, and lift the suspicion Cathy feels is over her. I know you'll have spoken to the police and told them all you could, but perhaps thinking aloud to another woman . . . I'm a solicitor, by the way, although I haven't practised since I had my children, so perhaps that's what got me here. Cathy's no idea I've come, by the way . . ."

He tailed off, his attention draining from what he was saying as it was caught by the strange look in Sandra Fane's face—an eager look, a look which said, *Yes, yes, fine as far as it goes, only take the next, the real step, please* . . .

"What is it?" he asked. "You have got something to tell me, haven't you?"

"I think you have something to tell *me.*" In such a woman, even a gentle hauteur was harsh.

"Not that I know of." His heart was banging.

"I think Cathy has the same worry I have. And wants to know what I've done about it. I'm sorry you weren't frank with me, but I'll be frank with you. I didn't tell the police all I could have done. Any more than she did."

"Miss Fane . . . Sandra . . ." Neil spread his arms, conscious too late of their length and size. "I honestly don't understand what you're saying. Cathy's my best friend as well as my cousin and she didn't keep anything back from the police. I'd stake my professional reputation on it." He would. His heart now was so unruly he could hardly speak without revealing his agitation. "What else could she have told them?"

Sandra Fane leaned even nearer to him, and he felt the power of her wide eyes as a physical probe. "Nothing," she said at last, in a whisper. "You're telling me the truth." She sank back in her chair, her eyes closed, her chest rising and falling in a highly erotic way. "I'm glad," she murmured. "When I saw how young and sweet she was, I was unhappy. As for me"—her eyes shot open—"I'll tell you what I held back—what a fool I was to hold back, what I'm going to ask your advice on now you're here." Sandra Fane sat upright, raising the delicate right hand in which he could not prevent himself imagining a pair of scissors. "Mrs. Willoughby was a blackmailer."

CHAPTER NINE

A freak flame . . . A bleak grace . . . A cheap shade . . .
The phrases paraded menacingly past his mind's eye.
A great shame?
But Sandra Fane believed him because he had been telling Cathy's truth.

"A blackmailer?" he repeated stupidly.

"Yes. Nice, cosy, reassuring Mrs. Willoughby."

"Cathy thinks she was all those things."

"Oh, she was." With a sudden sharp gesture Sandra Fane broke off a loose thread from the cover on the arm of her chair. "Even when I was made to see where all her interest and concern was leading, I still thought so." Her laugh had the edge Neil was unable to find in her face. "She wasn't greedy, she set a modest sum and never upped it. With me, at any rate, despite the improvement in my finances. And she behaved just the same as she did when the subject was dressmaking. Well, it was all business, of course—she should have had BLACKMAIL across one of the corners of her card the way she had DRESSMAKING and CLAIRVOYANCE. And it was her three activities, I suppose, which added up to her livelihood. 'I've got a nice little business, dearie,' she used to say to me." For an uncanny instant Sandra Fane fleshed out another of Cathy's sketches. "She was quite unembarrassed about it. I don't know how many other blackmail clients she had, although I should think that big Lesbian must have been one of them."

"I'm so sorry . . ."

"Don't be. Be glad Cathy wasn't part of it. I think it was marvellous of you to come." He really was glad Cathy had granted him immunity to that smile. "And as far as I'm concerned as well. It's been such a relief to tell someone what I've had to keep to myself for so long."

"You mean you haven't told *anyone?*"

"Not a soul."

Which must mean not even Jim Grayson. He hadn't expected to find that out so easily.

The smile was sad again, as Cathy had described it. "Blackmail. Remember. It's a threat to tell a shameful secret. If you could do the telling yourself you wouldn't be vulnerable."

"Forgive me." Neil felt Cathy's bracelet jangle under the excited jerk of his hand. "Not knowing the reason for what Mrs. Willoughby was doing to you, I was assuming it was the law you were afraid of."

Sandra Fane shook her head. One thing Cathy had omitted to tell him was how gracefully it surmounted her neck. "Not the law. It isn't anything I've done. It's what I am."

The smile now was heart-rending, and it wasn't the effort he would have expected to lean towards her and urge her not to say anything more.

"Thank you, Josephine." In her turn Sandra Fane was leaning forward, stretching out that suspect hand to touch his, leaving a tingling awareness where her finger tips had rested. "But you've made me realize I wanted to tell someone, and it's easier talking to a stranger. Not that I feel you're a stranger, although that must sound ridiculous when we've known each other about ten minutes. I've never had a 'best friend,' I suppose I'm what's known as a man's woman, although in fact I like *people* and hate categories and won't accept that every reaction one has to another person is tinged with sex."

"I think I know what you mean." At least he could see to it that Sandra Fane, believing she was at last reaching out to a woman, never discovered she was once more reacting to a man. So that now, if at no other time in his increasingly complex charade, he had to act his part inwardly as well. He tried to smile unprovocatively, wishing he had a sister so that he wouldn't be so totally unpractised, feeling shocked *en passant* to realize that except for his wife he'd never had a female friend. (There was another small shock, part pleasure, part disquiet, in the original thought that this might be why Cathy was the only woman he had ever contemplated marrying . . . He couldn't pursue that now.) "I've been lucky to be so close to Cathy, but otherwise my close people, too, have all been men. Boy-friends, and then husband, and then sons." He had plunged back into fantasy, and in his concentration on the astonishingly clear mental picture of two non-existent school-boys complete with old-fashioned school caps he had put a hand up to his face, a gesture he had forbidden himself, and felt incipient beard under the make-up. He should have shaved again at lunch-time. But he had no need to prolong things now, it was already clear that his first visit to Sandra Fane had secured him a series if he wanted it, if Mrs. Willoughby's murder remained unsolved. Although when Miss Fane was content to leave the theme of friendship he would be unable to resist asking a few more questions then and there . . . "I'm a solicitor, by the way." The further credential, so vital for the mistrustful Miss Littlewood, scarcely seemed necessary here, but Josephine Webster had already acquired for him that particular and indivisible truth which attaches to characters in fiction, and as such she was a lawyer. Besides, even with the complaisant Miss Fane the profession would have its uses, offering Mrs. Webster something of the authority Neil Carter was accustomed to deploy as a detective inspector . . . "I suppose that's an extra reason why I've felt anxious for Cathy—I know quite well they may come back to her if the investigation bogs down, and that's something she can do without just now . . . You said you hadn't told the police about the blackmail?"

"I said I hadn't told anyone." Sandra Fane leaned forward again. "Oh, Josephine"—there were freckles sprinkled across the bridge of her nose—"I think I should have told the police. I knew about the murder right away from my friend Jim Grayson, who lives on the ground floor of Mrs. Willoughby's house—Cathy may have mentioned him to you—and so I had a couple of days to think what I was going to do. I'd just about decided to tell them, but when they were suddenly in my dressing-room asking me if they were right in assuming I was a client of Mrs. Willoughby's, it didn't seem so easy. When I said I was they asked me of course what I'd been doing on Saturday afternoon. I told them I'd been at home and that no, there wasn't anyone to vouch for me that I had. Perhaps that's why when they said she was dead and asked me if I thought there might be a reason for someone wanting to kill her I heard myself saying that so far as I knew there wasn't. The next minute they were showing me my name in that black book of hers she always kept in the wardrobe. That was just all right—why not a list of clients?—but there were groups of letters beside my name which didn't appear to make sense. To me or to the police, but I knew they must be to do with the blackmail and the police are hardly likely to write them off as doodles."

"A black book?" Sandra Fane, of course, if she was what she seemed, hadn't handled either book and was assuming that the two were one.

"She made a note in it when you brought her money. For clothes and the other. As soon as I saw that page I wished I'd told them the truth but somehow I couldn't unsay what I'd said so I just—I just hoped for some luck and that everyone else involved would be as cagey. And that they'd never be able to decipher those letters." Sandra Fane flopped back in her chair and for the first time, as the light went out of her face, Neil saw the signs of strain.

"They will decipher them, and I think you should go back to the police, tell them before they find out." Even if the computer didn't break the code, those little groups of unintelligible letters—he sped through Cathy's yet again—were suspicious as they stood, and surely some victim, sometime, would confess. "I'm sorry," he said, as he saw her face. "But that really is good professional advice."

"I know, I know. It's just that I'm cravenly, sickeningly frightened. That they'll think I killed her because I lied and because I haven't got an alibi and because I'm in her book with those letters by my name."

"Other people will be in the same position. And Cathy was *there.*"

The lightning change from fear to concern had a clear reflection in her face. "Oh, God, poor Cathy. I'm not usually so horribly self-absorbed. But at least she hasn't got her name in the book."

"They haven't shown it to her, certainly." Because when the police had confronted Cathy the book had been in her handbag. Now, though . . .

"Oh, Josephine, isn't it all a terrible mess?"

She was leaning towards him again, and he knew Cathy would have responded with her arms. He, though, before he could offer comfort, had to convey the information that Josephine Webster was not demonstrative.

"I'm very sorry for you," he said calmly. "And for Mr. Grayson. And I understand why you reacted to the police questions the way you did. Most people would have done the same, it's the instinct for self-preservation. I just think it could work against you in this case. Go to the police before they come back to you, and they'll understand your reaction, too. And you've told me you're not afraid of them so far as—"

"My mother died in an institution for the criminally insane."

He had to look away from her, his glance lighting inappropriately on the porcelain figure of a young girl dancing.

"I can understand why you paid up," he murmured to it. Then turned sharply to face her. "And how you must have hated Mrs. Wil-

loughby," he added harshly. It was one of the shots in his detective
armoury, and he had used it on a reflex. If he had stopped to think he
would have refrained—as Sandra Fane's new friend Josephine, he had
more to lose than to gain from such shock tactics. And she was looking
puzzled as well as bruised. He must be vigilant, or he would lose the
ground he had so easily and perhaps so dangerously gained. "I'm sorry,
Sandra," he said gently, reaching out a wary hand to touch her arm. "I
think I was wanting to make you admit you hated her. You've been
going on as if you didn't, and I think you should, you must."

She shook her head, trust back in her eyes, half smiling. "I didn't
hate her. It *is* strange, I suppose. I hated what she was doing, and
especially when she was threatening me over something which wasn't
my fault, but I never hated *her*. Perhaps because she didn't hate herself." She showed surprise. "I've just realized she didn't despise herself
for what she was doing, she was making use of a sort of talent she had
—for getting people to talk about themselves—and she was being reasonable about it, not putting people into impossible situations—"

"One of her clients probably committed suicide."

"Perhaps she was on the brink. Oh, I'm not saying it was anything
but wicked. But she had a son . . ."

He listened in silence to what Jim Grayson had told him that morning. Sandra Fane, while offering the story as the probable explanation
of Mrs. Willoughby's unpublicized activities, was not affected by it as
Grayson had been.

"And I didn't *have* to tell her," she said finally, smiling her sad smile.
"Yes, I did tell someone."

"You told *her?* I assumed she'd ferreted it out." Via the man in the
grey uniform, who had come to see if he could ferret something out
about Cathy? And who had some connection with Miss Littlewood . . .

"No. I told her. She coaxed it from me over the crystal. Claiming to
see something which was troubling me." It was Cathy, of course, who
had made this sound familiar. And with Cathy, Mrs. Willoughby
hadn't got any further than trying. *Had she?* "It just happened, I
suppose, that she caught me at a vulnerable time. I'd met Jim and I
was wanting to tell him, it was near the surface. So I told *her.*"

"Cosy and kind and motherly. And right away—"

"Oh, no. It was on my next but one visit. She had to check it out, of
course, but I don't think she was ever in a hurry. She just said in her

usual homespun way that she was quite sure I'd want the unfortunate fact about my mother to remain a secret between her and me and not appear in the popular press now that I'd started to do so well, and if I could see my way to letting her have a regular ten pounds a week in addition to what I paid her for dressmaking, then I wouldn't have to worry. She was quite concerned when I went faint—that was because she was looking and sounding just as she always did, I thought I was out of my mind. She brought me a tot of brandy and made me sit down. When I'd recovered enough to leave I asked her if Jim was involved and that was the one time she showed some emotion, she said certainly not as if *I'd* made the obscene suggestion. Her reaction seemed genuine, but of course I felt wary of Jim the next time I saw him. I couldn't come out with it and ask him if he knew the truth about his dear Ma, so I just had to watch and hint and . . . and . . . I think that was as bad as anything else. You see, I love him."

"But you came to the conclusion that he wasn't involved with her?"

"Yes! That he didn't even know."

"Will you consider, now, telling him your secret? If you don't and it comes out . . . If you really feel you still can't tell him about your mother, you should at least be able to persuade him that what you're hiding isn't to do with yourself. If you believe in his innocence without having any way of proving it, he'll surely believe in yours."

"Oh, Josephine, you were sent to me today, you really were, darling."

"I'm very glad indeed if you feel I've helped." He was aware of a growing apprehension which had a very different root from the apprehension he had felt at Miss Littlewood's. "I can't pretend I came with anything but selfish motives."

"But you *understand* so perfectly!" Sandra Fane jumped to her feet. "And now let's have some tea, I should have made it ages ago."

Neil was upstanding, too. "I'm afraid I have to go." The carriage clock on the Adam mantel said nearly four o'clock. "I have an appointment at half past four. Another time?"

"Oh, please. Will you give me your telephone number?"

"I'll give you Cathy's. I'm there a lot of the time at the moment, and my husband doesn't know I've involved myself in her trouble." It was another reflex, he hadn't thought about what would have seemed, before his visit to Sandra Fane, her most unlikely request.

"Here's mine." She took a card from the tiny top drawer of a tiny inlaid table. "And please write Cathy's on here. There's another thing," she said, as Neil reluctantly inscribed his telephone number on a black pad with its attached gilt pen, together with his wife's name and the name Josephine Webster in brackets. "If the police find out what it was Mrs. Willoughby was blackmailing me over they're bound to feel I'm half programmed for murder. The genes for the job as well as motive and opportunity and no alibi."

"Don't think like that!" As he had been thinking. "You mustn't. And I'm sure the police—"

"You must have had the same sort of worry about Cathy, to have come to see me. And as far as Cathy's concerned it's only that she was there. No motive."

"No motive, no." If Cathy had had a motive, she would have told him . . .

"But it's specially awful for her just now, with the baby." Her face shone with compassion. "How is she? Really?"

"All right, I think."

"If I ring and she answers, I'll just ask for you? Will that be all right? You can tell her you've given her number to one or two of your friends . . ." The elegant right hand, the hand which could have killed Mrs. Willoughby, was round his wrist.

"Goodness, I hadn't thought of that aspect of things." Because of not having thought, in his wildest flights of imagination, that Sandra Fane would ever want to get in touch with Josephine Webster. He tried hastily to imagine himself into a position of having to hide from Cathy the fact that her non-existent cousin was in touch with a fellow client of Mrs. Willoughby's. "Yes, that will be fine." The hand felt like a fetter. "Despite being close, we've always lived our separate lives. And another female voice will hardly arouse her curiosity." He gave himself high marks for tormented ingenuity on that one. "Perhaps I should just mention, though, that Cathy thought you had a distinctive voice— could you alter it a bit?" He was almost amused to find himself refining on a situation already so convoluted.

"Nothing easier!" Animation was there again, in contemplation of her skills. The hand squeezed. "I do hope you'll stay for tea next time. Any day but Thursday as a rule, although we do occasionally have afternoon rehearsals . . . Now I know I've got to let you go. Thank you for helping me. You really have."

"I'm glad."

Gently he disengaged his hand and, as with Miss Littlewood, led the way to the front door, opening it before turning to say goodbye.

"Goodbye, Josephine."

And yes, of course, Sandra Fane's arms were round him, her cheek was against his. She had whirled away as rapidly as she had whirled against him and he was walking to the lift, his body aware of its contact with her but nothing in his head beyond the knowledge of that involuntary response. When he had vowed exclusive loyalty to Cathy he had added in his mind that he would do his best, and his best was still good enough. He had been slightly afraid, but he had discovered he had no need to fear Sandra Fane.

He was whistling as he closed the front door behind him.

"*You* sound cheerful."

Cathy called from the sitting-room but didn't run out to greet him in her usual way, reminding him of what he had just forgotten—that his return home hadn't transformed him back into himself.

"See you in a minute," he shouted back, plunging into the spare bedroom. He took off everything he was wearing, put it away, and got into a pair of trousers and his own shoes and socks before charging across to the bathroom with a jar of cold cream. The only unusual thing about him when he went into the sitting-room was a slight rosiness about the jowls, but he was aware at once of a constraint, despite Cathy's bright smile, and that he was about to contribute to it.

"All right?" he asked as he flopped down on the chair which faced the sofa where she was spread out. "You're home early."

"And you're home late." The words didn't go with that smile.

"I don't think I mentioned any particular time. What sort of a day?"

"The usual sort and, yes, I'm all right." She made a movement of getting more comfortable. "How did you get on?"

"I learned a few things." Why hadn't he gone at once, as he always did, to kiss her before sitting down? To do it now would be to acknowledge the tension.

"Yes?" She was looking at him only in short glances, each accompanied by a burst of smile.

"I went to Grayson's office this morning, as you know. Had a chat with him and his partner Dave Earnshaw." He made an effort. "I found out what you meant about Earnshaw's smile." She accorded him another one herself, perhaps not quite so wide and empty. "It was great to be going about as myself again." Cathy now smiled a conspiratorial smile at her lap, and he felt a twitch of irritation. "They've got quite an impressive set of offices, Grayson's is as different from Earnshaw's as they're different from one another."

"Goodness!" The irritation was now demanding outlet, but before he could express it she said, keeping her eyes down, "And how was Miss Fane?"

"Miss Fane told me Mrs. Willoughby was blackmailing her. With the fact that her mother died in an institution for the criminally insane." He wanted to stop there, but he couldn't. "Cathy, if she'd tried to blackmail you, you'd have told me, wouldn't you?"

Her face was reddening, he thought with anger, and then it was breaking up like a baby's into tears. He flung himself across the small space on to the sofa beside her, taking her in his arms. To his enormous relief she didn't resist him.

"Oh, darling, forgive me. You didn't tell me about the crystal and that upset me. And it just made me think—when Miss Fane told me what Mrs. Willoughby had been doing to her—that perhaps she had tried with you and you hadn't told me for the same reason you hadn't told me about the crystal, that you thought I wouldn't take you seriously. So I'm blaming myself, don't you see?"

"You mustn't, it's me . . . The crystal was nothing, but even so I was wrong not to tell you about it, I was condemning you without knowing what your reaction would be. And I was horrid when you came in. It was just that I felt all resentful, sort of hating the thought of you being . . . like that . . . and then feeling ridiculously jealous of you being with Sandra Fane, imagining you perhaps feeling . . . perhaps she feeling . . . Oh, Neil, it must be something to do with how I am at the moment, I honestly would never—"

"It's all right, darling. And I've no intention of keeping anything of my contact with Sandra Fane secret from you. I think she *did* feel something. It was almost tragicomic, the way she told me she was a man's woman without wanting to be and how marvellous it was at last to be establishing a rapport with a *woman*."

"But that's dreadful, poor Sandra!"

"She'll never know, I'll see to that. And I shan't be seeing her often enough—"

"I know, I know. Forgive me, Neil."

"And you forgive me." He must conduct the dispersal of their first incipiently serious quarrel the way he intended to conduct it in the future. "Just for a moment it crossed my mind that Mrs. Willoughby might have got some sort of hold over you and that you might be keeping it from me the way Sandra Fane's keeping her secret from Jim Grayson."

She didn't even flinch, making it one of the best moments of their marriage. "That line of letters in the book. I can see. And just for a moment it crossed my mind that you might find the extraordinary Miss Fane irresistible."

He held her against him. "She embraced me as I was leaving and I was aware of it. As I'd have been aware if I'd walked into the expanse of plate glass on the way out of her flats. Can you understand that as well?"

"Yes." She drew away from him to look into his face, and slowly the gravity in them both gave way.

To be replaced, in Cathy's, by horror.

"Mrs. Willoughby blackmailing Sandra Fane! You did say that, didn't you, Neil?"

"Yes."

"I can't take it in. She was so—what Mummy would call wholesome. You don't think Sandra was acting in another play?"

"No. She thought at first I was holding back the truth about you, but eventually she believed me. I believed her."

"Neil . . . Miss Littlewood. Mrs. Lawrence. Things are coming clear . . . Mrs. Willoughby must have been *trying* to find something out about me. I remember now I said some stupid thing about deceiving you by going to see Dr. Kelly without telling you, and she obviously held on to the word 'deceive' and hoped it really meant what it said, because she brought it up again later and I can see now that she was disappointed when I told her all it was. And then when she kept saying she could see in the crystal that something was troubling me and why didn't I tell her about it . . ." He felt her shiver. "All that performance makes me even more sure that eventually she *did* see something."

"It was a performance which marked Sandra Fane's downfall. She had something to tell and she told. But although Mrs. W did so well for herself, I think she had some help. You remember—or perhaps you don't, it was just incidental at the time—when you came back from your first visit to her, or somewhere round about then, I was here doing some paper work and I told you a man in a grey uniform had called, trying to deliver a parcel to 36 Westcote Road? I'm almost certain I saw that same man coming away from Miss Littlewood's house just as I turned the corner into her road. There was a plain dark van parked nearby which might have been grey to match—I couldn't be sure by the street light—and I'd bet a big sum the man got into it. He could have been collecting from Miss Littlewood. Keeping the business going. Or Miss Littlewood could have been part of it, too."

"No way of finding out."

"N-o-o . . ." She gave him a look. "That notebook holds evidence of blackmail," he went on quickly. "And if none of us busts the code and they come back to you, I'll let the Chief and Co. know somehow."

"Neil, not Sandra. You couldn't."

"Not Sandra. Not anyone. Just an extra piece of the truth for them to apply to the situation as they think fit." It hurt him to say "they" instead of "we," all the more so because it was becoming easier. "But I can't believe that not one of Mrs. Willoughby's victims, past or present, will spill the beans."

"So far as we know there weren't many. Victims, I mean."

"There were enough. And if there weren't, as I said . . ."

"Yes." She let out a long sigh and relaxed against him. "I see that you'll have to. But let's have another go at the code together this evening. It would be much better if you could let them have chapter and verse. Now, I'm going to do a few things in the kitchen."

Watching her flit out of the room—the way she moved hadn't begun yet to alter—he decided he was dog-tired. Heaving his legs up on to the sofa, he felt something under his feet and made a groaning chore of leaning forward to retrieve the booklet which was halfway down the side of the cushion. When he leaned back with it in his hand he saw that it was *The Month with St. Barnabus.* He knew that within minutes he could be asleep and he read on as a soporific, scarcely registering.

St. Barnabus Parish Magazine, Vol. 10, No. 2. April . . .

He'd already had a silly little dream in which he'd tripped over the leg of a chair and jerked awake. But he hadn't been to sleep . . .

Thought for the month. The great promises of St. John. Verily, verily, I say unto you, Whatsoever ye shall ask the Father in my name, he will give it to you . . .

A big claim . . . He had jerked awake again.

All that the Father giveth me shall come to me: and him that cometh

*to me I will in no wise cast out. Ye shall know the truth and the truth
shall make you free (AV)* . . .

Cathy came tearing across the hall in response to his shouting.

"What is it, Neil? Oh, darling, are you all right?"

"I forgot! I forgot you shouldn't have shocks. I am the most awful—"

"Just tell me what it is."

"It's this church booklet you must have picked up on Sunday. There
are some passages from the Bible and then in brackets . . .
Look . . ." He pulled her down beside him and put his finger under
the two letters. "Authorized Version. Even I know that. Version of a
text. Cathy darling, come across. 1C13 . . ."

"I said chapter and verse, didn't I?" she whispered, turning to look
at him. "One Corinthians 13. The most famous words of St. Paul.
Apart, I suppose, from it being better to marry than to burn. *Though I
speak with the tongues of men and of angels and have not charity* . . ."

CHAPTER TEN

Cathy wrote the letters of the alphabet in a row, and underneath them Neil wrote the opening letters of the thirteenth chapter of St. Paul's First Epistle to the Corinthians, leaving out those which had already occurred until only *X, Y* and *Z* were unpaired, and only *Q, X* and *Z* hadn't appeared in the text.

In the next moment they found out what had been written in Mrs. Willoughby's book beside Cathy's name.

A clean slate.

"I'd worked out the vowels for the simplest solution," he said, to cover his emotion. "And that's what it's turned out to be. There were so many possible combinations, but I kept saying *A freak grace."* What he had kept saying was *A great shame.* "So far as Ma Willoughby was concerned, it was a great shame." He had to exorcise his lack of faith.

"I know I disappointed her, but she must have had more failures than successes. I mean, I can't imagine any of my friends being blackmailable, I think she was lucky to get the few she did."

"I expect she was always trying. Just as she would always be trying for clients as far as her dressmaking and clairvoyance were concerned. And her victims would stick with her for the dressmaking too, for cover as well as convenience. Sandra Fane said she was as matter-of-fact about it as she was about everything else. That was what made it such a shock when it came."

"Yes. Let's see what she said about Sandra."

Neil wrote as he read.

Daughter of Rose Alice Jenner, convicted 1971 of murder of Anne Wells and Rosemary Henson. History of mental illness, developed into persecution complex where she believed victims were plotting to kill her. Invited them to tea and poisoned food. Found unfit to plead. Died 1977 in Broadmoor. Daughter changed name and established unconnected life.

"Neil, how wicked."

"And yet Sandra Fane doesn't hate Mrs. Willoughby. Or so she said. And I must admit that while she was telling me I believed her."

"She's an actress. But I could understand it, somehow, if she didn't."

"She said Mrs. W was so reasonable—not greedy or threatening. Oh, that sounds absurd, but when Miss Fane was speaking—"

"She does dazzle," said Cathy, without overtones. "But if she knows about the son . . ."

"Grayson told her. Or maybe the police. But I still think it's unlikely she could feel so forbearing."

"Unless she killed her, and just pretends to be. I gather she didn't say anything to the police."

"No. I'm pretty sure Miss Littlewood didn't, either."

"Miss Littlewood! Why are we waiting?"

Amanda Littlewood. Convicted Liverpool 1972 of sexual offences against female minor. Served nine months. Name changed by deed poll and job secured in London through good offices of a relative. Moved 1979, with references, to present post.

"Someone with the temperament could kill to preserve that, Neil. Her whole way of life threatened. References null and void."

"I think she'd have the stomach for it. I think Sandra Fane might, too."

"And both of them might have strong moral and/or religious principles. We don't know—"

"We don't know *anything*." He flung himself irritably about the sofa.

"You know more than you'd know if you were still at work," said Cathy, to accompany an intimately restraining hand.

"I know different things." He fought off the temptation to be distracted. "Let's look at Mrs. Lawrence."

Arrested after domestic incident in which her husband died. Convicted of manslaughter. Suspended sentence. Reverted to maiden name and moved to London. Companion to the Hon. Mrs. Cecily Shelmerdine.

"And desperately anxious not to rock the pleasure boat. Which this coming out undoubtedly would do. I should think it was the situation which killed Mrs. Lawrence, rather than lack of a modest weekly sum. She couldn't live with it."

"It really is wicked."

"And efficient. I'm certain Mrs. Willoughby had someone working for her. Her dear Jim, for instance. I mean, this is specialist stuff."

"Could he be your man in grey?"

"I've tried to fit his face under the cap and behind the moustache. I can do it. But I can do it with just about any man of roughly the same height and shape. Unfortunately when the man in grey was here I wasn't really noticing him, I was just thinking about getting rid of him and back to my paper work. Why are you smiling?"

"Thinking about the baby. Could it be a woman?"

"I don't know. I assumed it was a man because that was what the moustache indicated." As the female wigs indicated a contralto rather than a tenor voice. "But I just don't have a good enough memory of the encounter for it to be of any real use."

"It couldn't be Miss Littlewood, if you saw him coming out of her house and then spoke to her the next moment."

"I'd say it couldn't be Sandra Fane, but I've seen little bits of her acting. I'm not getting anywhere, am I?"

"Considering the situation you're in, I think you've got an extraordinarily long way."

"I'd like now to try and—"

"Even if Mrs. Willoughby had this mystery man in the grey uniform to help her, Neil, remember her talents." Cathy's face, as severe as she could make it when she wasn't angry, was trying to tell him the extraordinarily long way was far enough. "Everything we've read in that book could have been told her by her victims of their own free will. She just had that special way with her. Think of me, spilling the beans about the baby five minutes after I'd met her. I know I'm supposed to be artless and outgoing and all that, but even so . . ."

"Yes, I accept that, although it's hard to imagine Miss Littlewood being disarmed by any woman who wasn't young and feminine."

"Perhaps Miss Littlewood was the exception who proves the rule. Or part of the set-up. I know she was rude to Mrs. Willoughby, but that could have been a cover-up or her natural bad manners."

"There's an idea. And I've now got two possible reasons for her visit from the man in the grey uniform. Even with only one it's on the cards that he'll visit her again. I could—"

"Let's have a look at the names which were crossed off."

All three were of women who had turned out to be as unsatisfactory as Cathy, but via dead ends which, unlike Cathy's "deception" of Neil, had been considered hopeful enough to merit detailing. When they'd read the three entries Neil put all the bits of paper involved back into the folder he'd found for them, and the folder at the back of one of the desk drawers. Such care, he suspected sourly as he closed the drawer and locked it, was an expression of his constant wishful thinking that the Chief might present himself again.

They had had their supper and were drinking coffee when the front doorbell rang. Remembering that Miss Prince was away, he jumped to his feet. Then sat down again, weak with apprehension of a disappointment to his ridiculous half hope. Or a fulfilment of his fear that they would come back to Cathy . . .

"I'll go," she said, after a glance at his face.

While she was out of the room he sat rigid as if rooted to the sofa, acknowledging for the first time the fierceness of his ache for contact with his colleagues. And his expectation that eventually two of them would come officially . . . When he recognized the voice in the hall his delight was so dizzying it sent his head briefly between his knees. Then when he was once more on his feet he was tense again, in case Detective Inspector Peter Cummings was followed by a sergeant.

"Peter!" Cathy had pushed the sitting-room door to, there was no one else. Neil crossed the room to take the outstretched hand. "Am I glad to see you!"

"I've wanted to see you, Neil." Peter Cummings, large and fair and half smiling in his usual restrained way, was a joy to behold. "How are you?"

"I'm all right. Apart from being disorientated and very easily bored. Ever been suspended?"

"No. Thanks," he said to Cathy, as she pointed to a mug. "Two sugars."

"I hardly dared hope anyone would come," said Neil, as Cathy disappeared. "How's the Chief?"

"Growling well. This business has really got to him. You having to be done without, I mean."

"Good."

"Not so much because of the work-load, although of course there's a steady flow of routine grumbling. He actually seems to feel you've had a raw deal over something which—well, he doesn't really see how you could have handled it less drastically than you did."

"The Chief said that?" He felt as if he was waking from a long sleep full of nightmares.

"Not in so many words. But the message was clear."

"Thanks for telling me, Peter, I appreciate it."

"I've decided to tell you more . . ."

Cathy tapped on the door before slipping in with Peter's coffee, and out again.

"More?" His throat was tightening.

"I'm on the case." Peter stared at him expressionlessly through the steam rising from the mug at his lips, and wariness weakened Neil's excitement. "I've decided to put you in the picture in certain areas. Even to ask your help."

"I can't imagine . . ." He didn't have to imagine, he knew.

"Strictly off the record, you'll appreciate I could get into trouble, with your wife being involved. I mean, Neil," amended Peter Cummings hastily, "with her having discovered the body. I feel you've had a bad break, we all do, that's another thing I wanted you to know. And anyway I owe you one."

"I'd forgotten," said Neil truthfully. Purely by chance he'd been able to tip Peter off the year before about one of the people involved in a case of his.

"I hadn't. I owe you my promotion. But this isn't just for your benefit. I could do with your help."

"How on earth can I help you?" He tried to look puzzled and intrigued, knowing as he spoke that Peter would reach into his briefcase and bring out another transcript from Mrs. Willoughby's black book.

"Yesterday the officers in charge of the Willoughby case received a notebook by post, containing certain names and addresses." Peter's eyes slid away, but it was easier not to meet them at that point. "There are letters beside each of the names, in unintelligible groups. The computer's had a go at them, but the only things it can make suggestions on so far are the vowels. There must be a key text, but the clue to it's somewhat slender. Here . . ."

"Come and sit on the sofa," invited Neil, trying to swallow on his impatience.

Peter showed him the key, and the entry from beside one of the crossed-off names. So it was obvious at once that he wasn't prepared to offer very much.

"If you could just bring your great brain to bear. And it'll be something to do . . ."

"Yes. Thanks, Peter, I'll try. Where did the book come from?"

"It came anonymously, and that's as much of a puzzle as anything. The writing in it's the work of the old woman, that's for sure. If the murderer found it at her place and took it away with him, he—or she— would hardly have sent it on to us later. Unless whoever it was decided it might help in implicating someone else. And who else could it have come from?"

Peter's eyes were meeting his now, the question must be innocently rhetorical.

"Yes, it's a mystery within a mystery. No fingerprints?" He felt uncomfortable, the more so following the qualified generosity.

"Wiped clean."

"Um. Can I ask how the investigation's going?"

"It isn't, Neil, honestly, but we've learned something interesting from the lab which has narrowed the field pretty dramatically. Off the record, it's not being made public, but when the old lady was skewered she was already dying from a massive dose of Digoxin."

He had jerked, and Peter had turned to look at him.

"That explains something Cathy said which puzzled me. She said the eyes and mouth were closed and the face looked peaceful. I couldn't understand it."

"There's your answer. She took the drug for a heart condition. One a day was the dose—two would have been dangerous—but she was in process of digesting eight. They were mixed with Mogadon, which would have made the Digoxin more palatable whatever she took it in. And, more relevantly perhaps, it would have ensured that death was just like falling asleep."

"Did you find any traces?"

"A mug on the draining-board in the other room had strong tea dregs laced with the mixture. No doubt how it was administered. She could have put herself to bed after drinking the tea, and composed herself to die, as it were. She was lying sort of neatly, with her hands together on her chest. What we're tending to think at the moment is that someone came on her there, already in a coma, and took advantage of what he or she had found." Peter paused, his eyes again veering away from Neil. "There's one major implication, as you'll see."

"Narrowing the field. You just said."

"Yes. If anyone had rung the house bell she couldn't have let them in. Well, your wife was let in by Mrs. Monkton." Peter was making himself meet Neil's gaze. "Path tell us she took the mixture about half an hour before she was stabbed, so whoever stabbed her was either in the house already, or was let in by someone in the house, or had a key."

"I agree it cuts out every Tom, Dick and Harriet." He could feel the anger growing inside him, mixed now with apprehension. "But I can't believe it was beyond the ingenuity of any of Mrs. Willoughby's regular visitors—clients or otherwise—to have got access to a house key—even maybe the key to her own doors—for the length of time it takes to make an impression." He continued in his head. *Sandra Fane could have got her hands on Jim Grayson's. And Jim Grayson . . .*

"True."

"And by all accounts—by Mrs. W's account to my wife—the brood upstairs wasn't exactly well disposed to her."

"There are a mother and child upstairs, that's all. And a nutter on the ground floor, one Cyril Bolshaw, a teacher who had a nervous breakdown which left him pathologically shy and unable to work—even earned him a disability pension. His record's blameless and he didn't seem to have anything to do with Mrs. Willoughby—none of his dabs in that room, not that there were any of *anyone's*—but he was in that house at that time . . ." Peter Cummings looked away again. "Not much blood, of course, with all the old woman's processes on the wind-down. Just that one thin trail across the wall and on the front of her dress. Whoever wielded the scissors had a lucky break there. If she hadn't been dying already there'd have been one hell of a mess."

"Yes." No pointer to innocence, then, in being free of blood stains. "You'll be wanting to talk to Cathy again, won't you? To ask her if she saw that teacup?" He watched the embarrassment turn into gratitude. But Peter had been a bit more generous to him than had been necessary to secure his assistance.

"Thanks, Neil, yes." The embarrassment was still there. "I'm afraid . . . In view of—one or two other developments—I'm going to have to ask your wife for a further statement. Sergeant Williams is meeting me here in"—Detective Inspector Cummings glanced down at his watch—"ten minutes."

"Not just a question, then, of clearing up a few points, as we say?" *A clean slate!*

The phrase was so insistent in his head, he almost felt indignant that

Peter Cummings wasn't taking account of it. He'd do that in the morning, though, when Neil rang to tell him he'd solved the code. The only way to contain the anger now was to keep reminding himself of Peter's ignorance, how things must look in the light of it.

"We do feel we need a further statement. Not only from your wife . . . Until Sergeant Williams arrives I'm still unofficial, Neil."

"I appreciate that." He appreciated, too, that by not telling him at once how his visit was to develop Peter Cummings had ensured his maximum cooperation. Or thought he had. If Cathy's name hadn't been in the book he'd have been tempted to take his time in solving its mystery.

The telephone, shrill beside the sofa, made Peter jump as well.

It was Jim Grayson.

"Just ringing about your wife's two lots of gear. Her painting things and those dresses. I told the police you were coming round to collect the easel and so on, and they released the dresses to me. Can you come tomorrow?"

"You know me at the moment. I can come any time." He turned and grimaced into Peter's eyes before they had a chance to shift.

"I'm tied up for most of the morning," said Grayson. "But if you'd like to make it for a snack lunch, I've got biscuits and cheese and fruit."

"That would be fine." The stab of pleasure was out of all proportion to the arrangement he had just made, and irrelevantly he wondered if that was how young married women had felt before the days of women's lib, getting an invitation to interrupt the cosy flow of days spent keeping house. "Time?"

"Oh, make it twelve-thirty if you can."

"I can. Goodbye. That was Jim Grayson," Neil said slowly and clearly to Peter Cummings as he replaced the receiver. "Cathy left her painting equipment in his flat the day she found the old lady. Which no doubt you know. Grayson's asked me round to collect it at lunchtime tomorrow—I'd already offered—and the couple of dresses Mrs. Willoughby made for my wife. Your team have released them to him. Don't tell me you'll arrange to have them delivered, will you, Peter? I'd like to go once inside that house."

"Of course not, Neil, that's fine," said Peter heartily.

"Anything else you feel you can tell me?" asked Neil, as the other detective inspector looked again at his watch. He wondered if he could elicit a hint, at least, of Cathy's connection with the notebook.

"One or two points are likely to emerge while I'm talking to your wife." Peter appeared to have entered a transitional phase preparatory to becoming official. He cleared his throat. Neil tried to force himself to appreciate how awkward it was for him, that he couldn't really be behaving any other way. "She'll tell you, no doubt."

"I expect she will. No objection to my calling her in here and letting her know you want another statement?" No point, any longer, in hoping to learn more.

"None at all!" Peter was almost manically expansive, but Neil knew from his own experience how hard it was, when there were no major concessions possible, not to make too much of the minor ones.

He went over to the door and called her. She came out of their bedroom.

"Will you come in, Cathy?"

"I suppose it's my turn now," she said to Peter, as soon as she was in the room. Again embarrassment gave place to gratitude, if even more briefly.

"We'd very much appreciate a further statement, Mrs. Carter. My sergeant will be here in . . ." He consulted his watch again. It was the one recurrent action of the evening which Neil knew was fuelling his rage. "Three minutes."

"Give or take the traffic," contributed Neil.

"Of course." Peter had begun to sound slightly pompous. "When he arrives," he continued, to Cathy, "I'll tell you your rights—"

"Neil!"

"Just official stuff," he responded reassuringly, further annoyed to hear the false brightness of his own voice. "You'll have had it the first time, but you were probably too shocked to notice. The law is very strict with the police these days."

It was a relief to hear the doorbell. When he had let the sergeant into the flat and into the sitting-room Neil went into the kitchen and made himself another coffee which he drank at the kitchen table, trying to quell the unruly mixture of panic and rage which was churning inside him. When the kitchen clock had crawled three quarters of an hour Peter came to find him.

"We're off now, Neil." He was his natural self. "Your wife has answered a few more questions and given us a further statement. If you can come up with something helpful on those letters and figures . . ."

"I'll try." He didn't suggest more coffee, or a mug for the sergeant,

whom he knew by sight. When he'd shut the front door on them he
sped into the sitting-room where Cathy was sitting, for once conventionally, in an armchair. He dropped down by her feet.

"All right?"

"Yes. They asked me if I could think of any reason why my name
should appear in a notebook sent anonymously through the post, and
why there should be some unintelligible groups of letters beside it."

"What did you say?" He cradled her legs, aware through his anxiety
of his pleasure at the shape of them under his eyes and hands.

"Just that I could only think it must be some sort of register of
clients, and that perhaps the letters were measurements." There was a
glimmer of amusement in her eyes, which he clutched at, as she
stopped staring into space and looked down at him. "Neil, can we have
solved the code by the morning? I know it's ridiculously quick but I'd
like them to understand my bit as soon as possible, and you can say I
was reading a church magazine and you saw—"

"I'd already decided. First thing. Peter gave me a selected item, too.
A crossed-off one, of course. Did he actually show you the book?"

"Just a photostat of the page with my name. It was a bit difficult
making myself seem surprised and then upset, when what I really felt
was relief that it had happened at last."

"You were expecting it, weren't you?" He laid his head in her lap.

"Of course. Weren't you?"

"Yes. They went straight to Sandra Fane and Amanda Littlewood on
the strength of those entries, they were bound to come back to you.
I'm surprised in a way they didn't come sooner, but I suppose Mesdames Fane and Littlewood dissembled well enough to make it seem a
real possibility that the book was innocent. And they'd had one bite at
you, as it were." He hesitated. "Did Peter tell you Mrs. Willoughby'd
taken an overdose of her heart medicine before—before the attack?"

"An overdose?" Her hand kneaded his shoulder.

"He didn't tell you. Well, he was by the book, I suppose, and he
knew I'd . . . Cathy, when Mrs. Willoughby was killed she was already dying from eight times the prescribed dose of her heart drug
Digoxin."

He hadn't expected relief, but he was glad to see it.

"Oh, Neil! I said she looked peaceful and asleep. That must mean
she didn't know anything about the attack. It must, mustn't it?"

"I think that's one assumption we can make. She'd taken the lethal dose at least half an hour before she was attacked."

"I'm so glad. Whatever she did . . . *No one* should know they're going to die like that. And it means she wanted to die, the murderer only did what she wanted. Neil, though . . ." He got up and moved to the sofa and she followed him, curling into his arm. "She was so awfully down to earth. *Sensible.* I just can't imagine her deciding to commit suicide, waste part of her life . . ." Cathy shot upright, and he feasted on the renewed animation of her face. "That day, though, when she saw something in the crystal . . . And then Mrs. Lawrence was run over. When I was leaving I was sure I could see her just the other side of her curtain, standing like a statue. I suppose she could have been shocked into remorse. I mean, it must be awful to find yourself responsible for someone's death. If you're not a murderer, that is, and I'm sure Mrs. Willoughby wasn't *that.*" She flung back against him. "Unless the murderer gave her the drug. But then he—or she—wouldn't have had to—to do that other awful thing, would they?"

"I tend to think that whoever wielded those scissors hadn't made any plans in advance. But that's only my instinct from years of seeing how people react. I don't *know.* I only know that I'm getting more and more angry."

"I'm . . ."

"What?"

"Nothing."

"You were going to say that you're getting more and more frightened."

Her eyes dropped. "Perhaps."

"That's why I'm angry. But I can't think what more I can do."

"There isn't anything more," she said firmly, smiling at him. With all his experience, he couldn't say whether the smile was spontaneous or induced. "And as I didn't kill Mrs. Willoughby I shan't be charged with her murder."

Memories of various celebrated miscarriages of justice passed through his mind, but he didn't voice them. "What else did Peter want?"

"The history of my acquaintance with Mrs. Willoughby. To ask me if I might possibly have seen the notebook that day. I had to look them in the eyes and lie. I got on as quickly as I could to telling him about the times I'd seen her bring the other book out of the wardrobe. Of course I acted as if I assumed it was the same book . . . Then he asked if I'd noticed anything in the way of used crockery and so on on her draining-board. I told them I'd noticed a mug with what looked like tea dregs after I'd been sick at the sink, but I couldn't think why they were interested in that, of course."

He tightened his arms round her. "It was Jim Grayson on the telephone while Peter was with me, to ask me to go round at lunch-time tomorrow to collect your painting things. And those dresses." He felt her shudder. "The police have been back to him as well, he told me this morning. They'll be back to Sandra Fane and Miss Littlewood too, and they don't have *A Clean Slate* written beside their names." He wouldn't say anything about the lack of blood.

"Jim Grayson isn't in the book at all." She pulled free of him. "Nor Mrs. Monkton nor the funny man on the ground floor."

"Peter told me a bit about him." In an effort to distract her he passed it on. "He's got a blameless record but I think they find him a tempting prospect. They'll be less interested, of course, when I give them the key to the code. Although of course it's just possible the murder hadn't anything to do with the blackmail after all, in which case it could have been Bolshaw's mental injuries taking a new turn. I wanted to ask Peter what size and shape of man he is, but I decided it would be less obtrusive and probably more informative to ask Grayson tomorrow."

"That uniform again."

"Yes . . . On second thoughts, though, having seen it emerge from Miss Littlewood's, I'm inclined to think that it wasn't worn by Bolshaw."

"Having thought you might have seen it emerge—"

"It's not beyond the doggedness of a Miss Littlewood," he interrupted, "nor the wit of a Miss Fane, to have laid hands on a key to that house for long enough to take an impression. And Sandra could have used Jim Grayson's key. In collusion or out of it. And if Mrs. W was in process of committing suicide she could quite well have left her room doors open, don't you feel? A conscious or unconscious escape route—"

The telephone rang, and his arm was nearer. It was Sandra Fane.

"Josephine?" She hadn't been quite sure. "I'm just in from the theatre."

"Yes, it's Josephine." Anxiously he made a face at Cathy, and rejoiced at her response.

"All right to talk?"

"Not really."

"I understand. Anyway, I was just testing."

"That I'd given you the right number?" It was a strange sensation, to be aware of hurt in a telephone silence. "I'm sorry, I was only joking, of course I know you weren't—"

"I was just making sure I didn't dream your visit this afternoon." He had a close-up vision of her poignant smile.

"You didn't."

"I know. You can't *think* what a relief . . . a comfort . . . I'll go now. It won't be too difficult—you won't mind?—if I ring again?"

"Of course not. And if you remember anything . . ."

"If I do, I'll tell you first, Josephine."

He didn't tell her her duty. Lowering his voice as if an ignorant Cathy was within earshot, he asked her if she had been to the police.

"No," she said, after a fractional pause. "Still thinking. Still gathering courage, if I'm honest."

Was she honest?

"I hope you'll gather enough. I must go now. Good night. Try not to worry."

"I'll try. Good night, Josephine."

"She's setting a bit of a pace, isn't she?" said Cathy as he put the receiver down.

"As I told you, first rapport with a woman. Oh, darling, no man is an island."

"I'm not complaining, so long as you told her not tonight, Josephine."

"Why didn't I call myself Pat, or Di?"

They got ready for bed through hysteria-edged giggles, but Cathy woke them both just before dawn, screaming out the climax of a nightmare.

CHAPTER ELEVEN

He was glad the house where Mrs. Willoughby had lived was not at all like his recurrent dream of it with Cathy on the doorstep. In the dream he was always trying to stop her going in, and as he studied the vertical line of bells he had the sudden relieved conviction that his own entry would bring to an end the nightly re-enaction he was beginning to dread.

Even on a mild spring day there was a wind on this spot which funnelled through him, making him glad of the warm knowledge that his colleagues now had the key to the code in the black notebook, together with a dutiful translation of the one dead entry Peter Cummings had vouchsafed him.

"Cor, mister, you going in *there?*"

"You don't want to go in *there,* mister!"

Two small boys were scuffling about behind him. A woman with a basket on her arm gave the house a malevolent glance as she went by, then Neil a suspicious one before quickening her step.

Number three of the four bells had an empty space beside it. Beside number 2 was the name GRAYSON.

Neil pressed the bell, and thought he heard it faintly ring. The boys, jostling one another, ran off as a crackling sound heralded the distorted voice.

"Yes?"

"Neil Carter."

"Push hard, Neil."

Grayson was waiting for him by a half-open door to the right of the immediate steep staircase. The door to the left was even more dilapidated.

"Come in quickly," said Grayson. "It's pretty sordid out here. I know I ought to move but I never seem to have time . . . Did you have to run the gauntlet?" He shut his front door on them.

"Only a very small one. Actually," said Neil, looking round the large light room where Grayson had led him, "you make more of this than your posh office."

"I don't intend to," said Grayson gloomily. "But when I'm in the office I'm nothing but a workaholic. And Dave went so far ahead it seemed chic not even to start trying to catch him up." The grin transformed the anxious face, but it faded as Grayson turned to the table against the wall. "It's all here. Including the dresses. The police handed them over very tidily in this plastic bag."

"Thanks." He tried to banish his surge of distaste as he saw the fabrics through the sheath. He wanted to persuade Cathy to wear the dresses.

"Do sit down. And have a drink. What would you like?"

"Ale, if you have it."

"I have. In the fridge. Excuse me a moment."

As Grayson left the room Neil got up from the chair he had obediently taken and strolled to one of the windows. Judging by Cathy's lyrical description of the view from the back of the house, he must be directly below Mrs. Willoughby's best room. As he looked irresistibly up at the cracked white ceiling he remembered how little blood there had been . . .

"Here we are." Grayson was carrying two froth-topped tankards. As Neil sat down again he flopped on to the sofa. "Cheers."

"Cheers," said Neil, taking him in. "Something on your mind? Apart from our mutual misery, that is."

Admiration flashed across the anxiety. "Yes. As a matter of fact I was going to ask your advice. The woman upstairs . . . Mrs. Monkton . . ."

"Yes?" His finger tips were tingling, a phenomenon which tended to be a reliable indicator of incipient revelation. "The woman who let Cathy in that day? My colleagues told me there isn't a big family—"

"Ma exaggerated the Monktons." Neil saw Grayson's hands clench on his knees. "There were only ever husband, wife and child, although relations of the husband did tend to visit, and stay on. Not any more, Mr. Monkton walked out a week or so before Ma—died."

"And didn't come back?"

"I've never seen him. I didn't know he'd gone until the police told me, and then I realized he hadn't been around."

"You were going to ask me . . ." prompted Neil softly.

"Yes. Mrs. Monkton came down last night to see me. I could hardly believe the sight of her at my door, she's never been down before. She told me she'd remembered something about that day. At least, she'd suddenly started to think that something which had seemed quite ordinary at the time might have a bearing . . ."

"Yes?"

"She told me she'd shouted to Daphne that lunch—she called it dinner—was ready, and when the child didn't answer she came downstairs to the first landing to look for her and found her sitting on the bottom step—I've seen her there myself when I've been up to visit Ma." Grayson flinched. "She grabbed the child's hand and started hauling her upstairs, and she says it was then that she was aware of the back of a man in uniform on his way down the first half of the stairs to the ground floor. Unfortunately she didn't wait to see his profile as he turned for the second flight. I gather she saw him without registering him, because subconsciously she thought he was the gas or electricity meter man or someone like that, and she told me she forgot all about him when the police were asking her questions. Of course she didn't say all this as clearly and straightforwardly as I hope I'm saying it now, I had to—"

"A man in uniform? She was sure he was wearing uniform?" He dug his finger tips into his palms, trying to subdue their uneasiness now it had proved itself.

"Well, she was sure of the hard cap, and the dark suit, and they added up for her to a uniform. Neither she nor I had visits from any meter men that day, though, and they weren't due. It's odd, isn't it? One might have thought of a bus driver, say, just off duty and nipping in for a quick reading, only Ma wasn't in a state to open any doors." Grayson flinched again. "The police told me. She'd taken an overdose of her heart drug. Did you know?"

"A colleague told me that much, yes."

"Ma was the last person I could have imagined committing suicide. She was always so cheerful and down to earth." Grayson took a long draught of beer. "But there was the son, I suppose." *And Mrs. Lawrence's death.* "And perhaps it was a bit like those bright, jolly girls in Catholic families who become nuns, the last girls one would imagine . . . None of us can ever really know what goes on behind other people's facades. I still can't take it in, though. To do—that, and then to be murdered."

"At least we can assume she wanted to die." As so often, Cathy had got to the heart of it.

Grayson stared at him, his eyes filling with tears which quickly spilled over. "Thank God she didn't know, Neil." He made no attempt to wipe his cheeks and collar. "About the attack. She just—had another afternoon nap."

"That was Cathy's reaction." He got up and went back to the window, where he stood staring out but no longer seeing the view. "So it couldn't have been a casual off the streets," he said, after a few moments during which he heard Grayson blow his nose. "It had to be someone with a key." He turned round. "Mrs. Monkton must go to the police."

"Of course." The tears had gone and Grayson's voice was normal. "But that's the trouble. She has a morbid fear of anything to do with Authority. It was bad enough having the police come to *her*, but to go of her own free will to *them* . . . She knows she ought to, but I don't think she's likely to—"

"And you're wondering if you should do it for her."

"Yes."

"You should, no doubt about it," said Neil reluctantly. For Jim Grayson to go to the police with Mrs. Monkton's piece of information would be for him, Neil, to lose his one advantage over his colleagues—his knowledge of the man in the grey uniform.

"Thanks." At a stroke Grayson had shed at least his outer layer of anxiety. "I thought that's what you'd say. I'll go this afternoon. And I'm pretty sure Mrs. Monkton would like to get it off her chest, really, it's just that she can't take the initiative." He hesitated. "I just wondered . . . Would you like to have a word with her?"

"Of course I would. Thanks for the suggestion. But I won't. My future rather depends on my playing it by the book." While playing it under cover. "But I wouldn't mind a casual word with the old fellow opposite. You said he spends most of the day in the library, so that would be the place, wouldn't it? If I just knew what he looked like . . ."

"That's easy. It's very much of a branch library—left out of the house door, by the way, and down the next side street but one—but historically it's been housed in a large old building which up to now it's retained—pure local authority oversight, no doubt. Anyway, this old building allows it a reading-room area with the newspapers on sloping stands—you know the sort of thing—and old Bolshaw always sits in the innermost corner, or as near to it as he can get. He's quite striking-looking—a good head of grey-white hair, tall, good physique, rather disconcerting blue eyes. Not, I think, that you'll be able to do more than sit and look at him. I suggest you do that first—drink him in so that when you speak to him and, having said good morning, he takes himself off, at least it won't have been an entirely fruitless exercise."

"Thanks, Jim." And perhaps Bolshaw would react somewhat differently to an overture from a woman. The murder victim had been one. "Another thing, to abuse your good nature. Any chance of having a look round upstairs?"

"That was taken for granted." Grinning again, Grayson got to his feet. "Lunch first, though. I warned you it was basic."

But he wheeled in a trolley attractively laid with cold meats and salad, a choice of cheeses and a bowl of fruit.

By tacit consent they talked of other things while they ate. Question and answer about the amateur and professional approach to surveillance was absorbing enough, but Neil was still aware of his finger tips, and despite the ease and interest of the conversation it was a relief when Grayson pushed the trolley away and suggested they go upstairs.

"We can't get into either of Ma's rooms, of course, but you can see a bit of the bed and the window of her best bedroom through the keyhole, it's worn big like the one to the bathroom."

"My wife looked through the bathroom keyhole."

"She told me."

"I should have thanked you," said Neil, in sudden ashamed realization, "for twice looking after her. Perhaps for saving our baby."

"Nonsense." Grayson turned from him in embarrassment, leading the way out of the room. "Anyone would have done what I did. I'm just glad I was there."

Was he, the second time? Neil had no doubt, at least, that his instinct was to like Grayson, if not to trust him. But he couldn't trust anyone who had had the opportunity of driving those scissors home.

"Ma always stood at the top when she was expecting you up." Grayson had dropped his voice to the respectful undertone of a man looking round a church. "I can almost see her now."

"Perhaps you'd really rather not—"

"Come on!" Grayson quickened his pace up the steep narrow stairs.

"Hello, Daphne," he said loudly and cheerfully when he was almost at the top.

There was no response, but a little girl in a brightly coloured cotton dress was sitting huddled up on the first of the linoleum-covered steps up to the second floor.

"Daphne?" persisted Grayson. "Shouldn't you be having your dinner? Where's Mummy?"

The child stared at them wide-eyed, her chin on her knees, her hands interlocked to hug her legs to her. As Neil followed Grayson across the dismal landing he saw that her whole body was trembling.

"Daphne," said Grayson more gently, squatting down in front of the child and attempting to take her hand. "What's the matter? Have you been a naughty girl?"

Still the wide eyes fixed them unblinking. Grayson was unable to detach the rigid fingers.

"She's in shock," said Neil, going on his knees beside Grayson. "Something's frightened her." The forehead under the untidy hair was cold and moist to his touch. Even his hand in front of the child's eyes hadn't brought a reaction.

"Mrs. Monkton!" Grayson got to his feet and squeezed a few steps up past the child. "Mrs. Monkton!"

There was no response.

"Better go and see, Neil?"

"Yes." His finger tips were alive again, but this time he was afraid of their message. "If there's anything . . . We'd better leave her here as she is, it won't make any difference for a few minutes, then we can take her down to you if—"

"Of course. Come on!"

The staircase, like the lower carpeted one, had two short flights, and there was a broken-down chair with the sagging remains of a cane seat in the corner of the turn which impressed itself on him with the clarity he tended to find in objects peripheral to a serious crime.

But the serious crime had been committed on the floor below and it was his wife who had indelibly learned its details . . .

"There isn't a front door," Grayson was saying. "Well, no one but the tenants of the place ever need to go up. I don't think I've been up more than a couple of times in the six years since the Monktons— Neil!"

Grayson had been walking in front of him across a tiny hall as bleak and grimy as the two below, and stopped abruptly on the threshold of the room with wide-open door opposite the stairhead. All Neil could see as he cannoned into him was a cheap and shabby settee, then, as Grayson ran forward and he followed him into the room, the legs protruding beyond it—one foot in a high-heeled shoe, one bare. On the floor round the feet was a profusion of yellow and white petals.

"Dear God . . ." Grayson pulled back against the wall as Neil knelt down. It could be, though, that when you were able to select your cases you got by for years, maybe a working lifetime, without ever seeing a body done to death . . .

The woman lay on her stomach, her head to one side between her raised arms, a dark stain spreading in a faint glimmer from beneath her breast on to the dingy carpet. He put his hand on her wrist.

"Is she . . ." whispered Grayson.

"She's dead, yes," said Neil shortly, straightening up. "And I should say from a shot to the heart. Is it Mrs. Monkton?"

"It must be. The hair . . . figure . . . And I think I recognize the dress."

"I'm sorry, but try to make an effort and look at the face. There's a profile for you to go on."

"Of course, Neil. Forgive me."

Grayson came slowly forward and dropped to his knees. "It's Mrs. Monkton," he said.

"Thanks. There's nothing we can do for her. Better see to the child. Are you all right?"

Grayson had clutched at the settee as he stumbled to his feet, and Neil had to fling himself on to the seat to prevent its flimsy weight toppling backwards on to the dead woman.

"I'm all right. I'm sorry, Neil. How long would you say?"

"This morning, before I came. Rigor mortis is spreading from the jaw."

"If I'd been in I'd have heard—"

He had pulled Grayson over to the door and now rounded on him, all his professional reflexes back in action despite his aching awareness that he was without authority. "Did you tell anyone what Mrs. Monkton told you last night?"

"Of course not."

"Not even Sandra Fane?"

"That's enough, Neil!" Anger gave Grayson strength to move away from what had become the support of Neil's arm. "It was a professional matter."

"Sorry. It just struck me that perhaps it wasn't. I mean, Mrs. Monkton could have come down to you because you were the man about the house as much as because you're a private eye, and you could have seen it that way. Anyway, you didn't tell anyone. Let's go down to the child."

Daphne Monkton was still sitting on the bottom step. As they came behind her Neil's scalp crawled at the soft tuneless monotone. Her eyes, when he and Grayson had passed her heedless body, were still fixed on space. He bent down and gathered her unresisting into his arms.

"Lead on," he said to Grayson.

The child seemed scarcely to weigh, and lay motionless but at least now silent. Neil followed Grayson back into his flat and set her down on the couch.

At once she stirred, turning on her side to face the windows.

"'Ad a flat 'at on," she said distinctly, then put her thumb in her mouth and at last veiled those unnerving eyes.

"Neil . . ."

"I'll ring the police."

"I was just going to suggest it. You won't need to dial 999, will you? Wait a minute!" said Grayson sharply, as Neil put out his hand.

"Well?" It was unfair to be so curt with Grayson, who seemed scarcely less shocked than the child, but it was the one outlet for his anger.

"It's just occurred to me . . . Neil, if you'd like to go . . . I mean, there's no need for you to be mixed up in this. I can say I went upstairs because I heard the child cry out, or something like that, and that I discovered the body on my own. If you think you touched anything printable you could run up and see to it. Then when the police come I can tell them . . . But what Mrs. Monkton told me won't have any value now, will it?"

"Not much. But you've all the more reason for passing it on."

"Of course. Yes," said Grayson miserably.

"And I won't go, although thanks. I wouldn't run away, even if I hadn't told a colleague I was lunching with you today. Detective Inspector Peter Cummings was with me when you telephoned last night." Grayson stared at him. "Better sit down a minute," advised

Neil, taking his arm again. His body was as inert as the child's, and it was easy to steer him to a chair. "I rather think I've had more experience of violent death."

Grayson didn't contradict him. Neil went back to the telephone, rang the Yard and asked for the Chief, a list of alternative CIs forming hopefully in his mind as he waited. The Chief was there.

"It's Neil Carter, Governor. I'm at Jim Grayson's, the house on Pleasant Street, came to collect my wife's painting gear and the dresses the dead woman had made for her. Peter Cummings knows, he was at my place last night when Grayson rang to ask me over." His anger grew as he decided he was protesting too much. "We found the child of the woman in the top flat in shock on the stairs, and when we went up we discovered Mrs. Monkton shot dead."

"I'll be along, Carter." Neil had to admire the resilience which had needed only seconds to come up with so restrained and expressionless a response, particularly in the light of the Chief's short temper.

"Right you are, Governor. They won't be long," he said to Grayson, going to kneel by the child. He put his hand on her forehead and she opened her eyes and took her thumb out of her mouth.

" 'Ad a flat 'at on," she again informed the windows.

"Independent corroboration of the mother's story, at least," said Neil. His effortful smile was lost on Grayson, whose head was in his hands. Crushed by contemplation of the evil still at large under his roof, or of his own further deed?

"Let me get you some brandy," suggested Neil, briefly remorseful at the turn his thoughts had taken. It was absurd to imagine this devastated man putting on a uniform and slipping upstairs. And Grayson, if he had killed Mrs. Monkton, would hardly himself have mentioned the man in grey . . .

Unless that *wasn't* what Mrs. Monkton had said about him. Unless she had said something far more compromising, such as that she hadn't heard the street door close after him. In which case what Grayson had done was to render the uniform harmless to himself, separate himself from it, turn it, even, into a red herring—not, of course, intending to use it again anywhere near Pleasant Street. If Grayson had gone upstairs that morning to Mrs. Monkton, there would be no flat cap, no dark grey jacket and trousers, in his flat now.

"Thanks, Neil, that helps." He had handed Grayson a generous tot of brandy, and taken one for himself. "It wasn't the body that got to me, I've seen bodies before, and one or two of them in pretty horrendous condition. It was knowing Mrs. Monkton after a fashion, and having talked to her last night . . . And another dreadful thing in this house . . . While I was out on a job again on which I'd have failed if anyone had been aware of me. No alibi for the second time, Neil, and this time the only other adult occupant of the house apart from old Bolshaw."

He'd have been squeamish in the circumstances, too.

"No one saw you go out? Come in?"

"Bolshaw would probably have been at the library. And if Mrs. Monkton saw me go, that's not much help, is it?"

"Her husband! He left her, you said. Why should her death have anything to do with the death of Mrs. Willoughby?"

Grayson appeared to be uncheered. "It's too much of a coincidence. She tells me something which could mean danger for someone, and she dies."

"But you didn't tell anyone, so how could that have a bearing on her death?" *Unless you killed her yourself.* Grayson was either pathetically ingenuous, or disingenuous to a rarefied degree. Neil couldn't remember ever before being faced with so disparate a choice of terms in which to define one man.

A flash of panic animated the weary face. "It isn't all that difficult, Neil. Mrs. Monkton must have told someone else as well."

"That's possible, of course."

Of course it was. And it was possible Mr. Monkton wouldn't be able to account for his movements . . . And Bolshaw . . .

"Did Mrs. Monkton come into your flat to talk to you? I mean, she didn't say what she had to say on your doorstep?"

"Of course not. Oh, before I asked her in she did say she had something worrying her about the day Mrs. Willoughby was killed. Well, naturally, or I might have thought she'd come down to seduce me, or something."

"Right. Did you notice if Bolshaw's door was shut?"

"I didn't notice it at all. But if he'd had his ear to it I suppose he might have heard . . . And if he didn't go to the library this morning . . ."

It was a relief to hear the doorbell, even though he wasn't exactly looking forward to seeing the Chief. "I'll go."

On the step was the Superintendent. So the Chief had played it by the book and received the reward of virtue. Unless, of course, the Super had been with him when he took Neil's call, and he hadn't had a choice. Neil experienced an unprecedented pang of pity for his immediate superior.

"Come in, sir." He knew the sergeant, and the WPC. "Chief Inspector Larkin told you—"

"I know why you're here, Neil. You'd better lead the way."

He took them as far as the first landing, came downstairs to find the forensic team filing in, conducted them up to the same spot, and came down again to Grayson's flat, where the WPC was cuddling the child on her lap. "Big buncha flowers," the child was saying. "And then Mummy. And then Mummy. And then Mummy." It was like a record with the stylus stuck in a groove. But at least the presence of a woman seemed to be breaking into the shock.

The Super and the sergeant were soon with them.

"We'll take your statement, Neil, and you can go. If Mr. Grayson would be good enough to wait in another room."

The sergeant escorted Grayson out.

"Where did you find the child?" asked the Super, when the sergeant was back.

He resisted the lure of an easy lie. And anyway, he hadn't agreed anything with Grayson. "At the foot of the stairs up to the second floor, sir. We'd had lunch and before I left I couldn't resist just going up to the landing where my wife—"

"Of course, Neil. You're human." It mightn't have been so simple with the Chief.

The child had stopped saying " 'Ad a flat 'at on," and he had to repeat the words several times before the sergeant got them right. The Super asked him if they had any significance for him, and that was the moment in which to cite his own experience of the man in the grey uniform (now, in his mind's eye, carrying an elaborate arrangement of flowers). But with only a few seconds' hesitation he let it pass, merely saying he thought Mr. Grayson would be able to give a helpful answer.

"He told me something, sir, which he was going to tell—the police —this afternoon." The Super's large, deceptively gentle face grew kindly, and Neil knew his hesitation had been observed. "As it's only hearsay as far as I'm concerned, I think I should leave it to him."

"All right, Neil. Read and sign and then be on your way."

There was of course a small crowd outside the house, but he had been ready for it and plunged through with his head down. At least his one quick glance hadn't recognized any reporters, and no one followed him. Cathy had said she would be back early, and striding towards the car-park, his burdens under his arms, he was filled with a joy and a relief that he was going home to her which flooded out all other emotions. She was in the kitchen, the front of her apron covered with flour, so that he had two reasons to seize her gently.

"Oh, darling."

"What is it, Neil?"

"Can you leave all that? Bring tea into the sitting-room? Yes, there is something, but not to do with you or me."

"I'll be with you by the time you've rung Peter Cummings. He rang to tell me what the words were beside my name in that book. That was nice of him."

"It was. He didn't tell you anything else?"

"No. Neil . . . ?"

"It's all right. I'll talk to you when I've rung him."

Peter hardly waited to be thanked for what Neil called the good news. "I knew you were going to see Grayson today, so it wasn't the surprise it would have been. But it's extraordinary . . ." That the wife had discovered the first body and the husband the second. But this time Cathy had been at school, and he hadn't been alone in the house . . . On a surge of belated relief he realized that Mrs. Monkton's death had put Cathy in the clear. Not that this would incline him to leave things alone. "How is the Chief?" he asked cheerfully.

"Indescribable. Be glad you're not here just now. I must go, if he catches me he just won't believe I rang you about the notebook and nothing else. And anyway, that's another sore spot—just before this latest news broke I'd told him in confidence that it was you who solved the code, appealing to his sporting instinct." Peter gave a mirthless laugh. "Then I told him I hadn't told him, that officially we'd worked it out through a concerted middle-ranking office effort. My hope was that it would persuade him to some activity on your behalf . . . Well, perhaps it still will when he gets over today's big frustration."

"Another form of blackmail. I'm more grateful than I can say." It wasn't lack of self-confidence, then, which made Peter stick to the book—he'd have to have plenty of it to admit, however unofficially, that he'd confided details of a case he was on to an outsider. (The word hurt in his mind.) And it was only because he'd been so quick off the mark that he'd been able to do it at all, it would be days, now, before anyone dared offer the Chief anything but profound respect. And although the Chief couldn't have Peter disciplined for what he would deny, there were many day-to-day ways in which he could show his displeasure . . .

"We want to see you back."

"I'll never forget this, Peter. How's the sergeant?"

"Broken jaw. Loose tooth. Subdued. Mainly, I suspect, because when he looked for sympathy it wasn't forthcoming. He's all right, Neil."

He put the painting gear and the dresses in the spare room, then went to change his jacket for a pullover, savouring the elusive scent of his wife which he was always aware of during his first moments in their bedroom. He wished he didn't have to tell her about Mrs. Monkton. *Nothing to do with you or me.* To do with him though, of course: he'd kept his secret and the one chance of finding the man in the grey uniform was still his.

He got Cathy through the story as gently as possible, but afterwards neither of them was hungry and they went very early to bed. They'd just replaced the receiver when the telephone rang. It was on Neil's side, but Cathy had ended up over there, and answered it.

"It isn't, actually," said Cathy, after listening. "But she's here. I'll just get her."

"Sandra Fane," said Neil, as Cathy put her hand over the mouthpiece. "I'm sorry, darling, but she was bound to ring—she'll have had another police visit to confront her with the decoded notebook as well as to check her alibi for this morning." He kissed her nose as he scrambled across her to take the receiver. "Josephine Webster here." Let Sandra Fane think there were other people who rang Mrs. Webster at the Carters'.

"Josephine! Oh, thank goodness I've found you! It's Sandra. Forgive me ringing so late, but I had to speak to you. A terrible thing happened at Jim's place today. Well, Cathy's husband will have told you, he was there."

"He told us, yes. It's dreadful . . ." He took Cathy into the curve of his arm.

"The police came to see me again. They wanted to know where I was and what I was doing this morning. And they've worked out the code in that book, they know what Mrs. Willoughby was doing and about me . . . The only good thing is that I told them before they showed me what she'd written by my name."

"I'm glad you did that. Where were you this morning?"

"At home. Shopping. I didn't use the telephone and there was nothing out of the ordinary at the shops. In other words, no alibi. If you could come tomorrow. Sometime—any time—in the afternoon. I really need to see you, I'm scared out of my mind. For Jim as well . . ."

"I'll come." He took one of Cathy's breasts in his free hand.

"Oh, thank you, darling, thank you. What are you doing now?"

"Getting ready to go home, you just caught me. We all feel a bit subdued." It was harder to get the voice right when he could see the hair on his chest and feel Cathy's nipple between his fingers. "Try not to worry. I'll see you sometime tomorrow afternoon."

And tomorrow evening he would start looking for the man in the grey uniform.

CHAPTER TWELVE

It was, of course, as he had feared: even the quality papers made much of the fact of Mrs. Monkton's murder having taken place in the same house as Mrs. Willoughby's, and the tabloid headlines ranged from *House of Death* to *Murder Mansion*. Readers were reminded, mercifully *en passant*, that the first body had been discovered by one of the victim's clients, but no information was offered as to the identity of the discoverer of the second—his colleagues, now, had really got their act together. Neil felt sorry for Jim Grayson and alarmed for Bolshaw. Neither was mentioned but it could only be a matter of time, and there was always the danger that Bolshaw's eccentric refusal to speak could turn him into a media monster.

He had decided to tell Cathy about his pursuit of Bolshaw some time after the event, and didn't correct her assumption that he would spend the morning on the chest of drawers. When she had whirled off to school he sat over the papers and the remains of breakfast—which he had insisted she leave to him—long enough to allow for the possibility of her bursting back in for a forgotten book or paintbrush, then cleared the kitchen and got ready.

Turning into Josephine now was merely preparation for a job of work. The day was chilly and windy, hostile to the wig, and his body felt coldly vulnerable as he crossed the forecourt in Josephine's fine wool skirt and thin jacket over the bat-wing jumper. But he was learning to project the unaware, distant gaze assumed by so many young women alone in London, and both on foot and on the tube it was enough to keep male interest in check.

He went first to the house on Pleasant Street—a few people were hanging about outside—then on beyond it to the second narrow road off, which he saw before he had properly turned the corner was dominated by the curly red facade of the branch library.

Its imposing doors took him from cold to warmth, and it was easy to imagine an unsociable solitary man finding instant haven in the ornate solidity of the circular vestibule lined with temporary display cases and shelves of worn-out books for sale, the impersonal smiles of the ladies beyond the inner doors, the book-lined series of almost cosy interconnecting rooms.

The largest and farthest was set with two rows of sloping tables, as Grayson had described it, each laid out with daily newspapers and current periodicals. There was the expected contingent of unremarkable old and middle-aged men engaged predominantly with the tabloids and the sporting publications, which impinged on him as an overall effect rather than a number of individuals, and one man at the far end of the row nearer the wall whom he would have seen above the ruck even if he hadn't come to look for him. Bolshaw did indeed have a fine head of grey-white hair. He also had a neat straightness of body as he delicately turned the pages of the *Daily Telegraph* and, thought Neil, something else indefinable which prevented him from merging with the general pattern of quiet dun-coloured activity in this corner of a public library.

An aura of madness?

Even the most normal of men would have been disturbed by a second and no doubt even more probing session with the police, and it could simply be that Bolshaw was an outstandingly handsome man— certainly he was the easiest among the possibilities to imagine inside the dark grey uniform . . .

Next to the *Daily Telegraph* was *The Times,* a publication according well with Josephine Webster's profession and appearance.

Shaking himself out of the constant temptation to think of Mrs. Webster as though she existed (he had never, though, considered her husband), Neil noted with satisfaction that *The Times* was available, and slid into the seat in front of it.

"Good morning," he murmured as he bent over the front page. There was no one on the seat to his right which gave access to the *Financial Times,* so he had turned very slightly towards Bolshaw.

"Good morning."

Neil was unable to resist turning fully under the impact of the polite normality of Bolshaw's response. In time to see a look of eager hopefulness fade out of the bright blue eyes, which at once dropped to the pages of the *Daily Telegraph.*

Hope of having discovered another potential victim?

But there was no series of murders currently under investigation in

London. Unless to wipe out the female population of one house could be considered a start.

Hope, more likely, of at last summoning up courage to go on to the next exchange.

"Chilly, isn't it?" continued Mrs. Webster. "You'd never think it was early May."

"I . . . Mmmm. Mmmm."

Neil had turned back to his own paper, but felt the draught from the agitated pages of the *Telegraph*. Really, it was a pity the desks weren't ranged opposite each other, so that he could look at Bolshaw without having to accost him. He forced himself to read the first inch or so of the items on the front page of *The Times*, then opened Josephine's bag, brought out a notebook, went back to the bag and began to fumble.

"Excuse me," he said eventually, when it was clear Bolshaw would not respond to so oblique an approach. "I seem to have left my pen at home and I want to make a note. Do you have one I could borrow for a moment?"

Bolshaw gasped. "I . . . I . . ."

"Not to worry," said Josephine cheerfully. "Perhaps you haven't got one." He remembered what Grayson had said about the logic successfully employed by his fellow inspector. "It's just that if you have I'd very much appreciate the loan of it. A Biro."

"A—Biro!" It was as if he had wrenched the word out of Bolshaw, and a Biro from a pocket of the shabby but elegant jacket. Bolshaw put it on the ledge between the two newspapers and snatched his hand away.

"Thank you so much." Neil picked up the pen, resisting the temptation to look at Bolshaw as he did so, opened his notebook and started making notes at random on one of the front-page articles under his eye.

"That's it!" he said after a few lines, turning slightly and holding out the Biro. "Thank you."

Bolshaw's well-manicured right hand moved spasmodically at the edge of his paper but failed to rise, and Neil, as if noticing nothing out of the ordinary, put the pen back on the ledge between them. As he went through the motions of returning to his paper he saw out of the corner of his eye Bolshaw's hand sidling the short distance necessary to retrieve the pen and then back as unobtrusively on to his own paper, as if to move openly was to court an ambush.

Bolshaw, without a doubt, had severe psychological problems.
But—homicidal tendencies?

"I haven't been here before," Neil said quietly, turning openly now
to his neighbour with what he hoped was a friendly smile. "It's pleasant, isn't it? Do you come regularly?"

The hope was there again, but it didn't survive speech. "I . . .
I . . ." panicked Bolshaw, struggling to his feet.

"Please don't move, I'm just going."

The thin arm seemed to creep away from his reassuring hand, but
Neil thought both gratitude and regret flashed across the eyes. Bolshaw, perhaps, was sorry for being as he had become, which included
recoiling from touch. He had retained his looks, and maybe Mrs.
Monkton had reached out a hand. But she'd have to have got him up
two flights of stairs first . . .

And he wasn't in Mrs. Willoughby's notebook any more than Jim
Grayson was.

So far as her third occupation was concerned, had Mrs. Willoughby
had only female clients? Or had there perhaps been a separate book for
men, which a male murderer had destroyed?

Apart from asking himself questions there was only one thing, now,
for him to try and do.

Smiling vaguely towards Bolshaw, who had returned with apparent
absorption to the *Daily Telegraph*, Neil left the library and went home.
A vacuum cleaner was whining somewhere and he was aware of the
chest of drawers awaiting attention. He wished Cathy was there so that
he could sort out his ideas on her, but it was essential for his telephone
calls that he should be alone. He made half a dozen short ones to the
same pattern, then dialled again and asked the male voice who answered if Moses was there.

"I'll just see, squire."

He waited, tense, playing with the beads round Josephine's throat.

"Moses here," came guardedly, when he'd almost lost hope.

"Neil Carter here."

"Blimey, Governor! I had something for you, they said you was in
trouble."

"I'm suspended for damaging a sergeant who insulted my wife. I
hope you got hold of Sergeant Hughes."

"In the end. Blimey, Governor, I could hardly—"

"Something for you to do for me, Moses. Hire a small car—whatever way you like, so long as it can't connect with me—and pick up a woman at the dead end of Oliver Road, second turning past my place off Westcote Road, at eight o'clock this evening. You can park there and wait if necessary. She knows you, she'll come up to the car and say your name." He hesitated, and described the shiny blue dress he'd worn for the police revue. "She's tall with a good figure and shoulder-length blonde hair." *Autres temps, autres cheveux.* Miss Littlewood had met Josephine Webster, and the man in the grey uniform had seen her, too.

"What then, Governor?" asked the voice at the other end of the telephone, on a heavy statutory sigh of patient endurance.

"She'll tell you. Don't expect much excitement. It's a surveillance job, and more than likely it'll turn out not to have a subject. Eight o'clock. And eight o'clock tomorrow and the night after and the night after that if you draw blank."

"Blank on what, Mr. Carter?"

"You'll see." It occurred to him on a cold pang that Moses might not feel the same loyalty to a policeman unbacked by an establishment which recognized the unique value of the personal contact. "You can manage it, Moses? The usual remuneration, maybe stepped up a bit."

"Course I can manage it, Mr. Carter. For *you.* But shan't I be seeing you?"

"Sooner than you think. Now just tell me what you're going to do . . ."

At least he no longer had the code to puzzle over. After he'd cleaned his face and got into old clothes he was attracted by the idea of being the active cause of a vacuum cleaner making a noise, and took Cathy's through the flat . . . He then worked for an hour flat out on the chest of drawers, making a noticeable beginning to its rehabilitation, before going for a brisk, unseeing walk while he wrestled with his ideas on the two murders. As he realized he was almost back at the flats he thought wistfully of his favourite local but instead turned into a pub he scarcely knew, not wanting comment on his freedom to be at home at weekday lunch-time. He had a pie and a pint, then went home to prepare for Josephine's second appearance of the day.

How long, he wondered, as if from somewhere far off, could he go on living like this?

It was impossible to side-step the tumultuous physical welcome. For a moment Neil was afraid the wig was in danger from Sandra Fane's eager arms, but at least his concern for it took precedence over other instinctive reactions.

"Josephine darling, I'm worried out of my mind. Come into the sitting-room." She was holding his arm with both of hers as she drew him across the hall. "I don't know if I'm more worried for Jim or for myself. He's so—so *unworldly*. I don't think he can conceive of wrongful arrest. He knows he had nothing to do with Mrs. Willoughby's death, or this other one, so he doesn't seem to realize how suspicious it looks for him. And for me." She laughed, heart-breakingly.

"I think—"

"Yes, darling?" asked Sandra Fane, as Neil stopped abruptly.

"I think he must realize it." He had been going to say that Grayson *did* realize it, before remembering that Josephine Webster had never met Grayson. "In his profession he's bound to have come across plenty of circumstantial evidence. You said he came round to see you last night?"

"Yes."

And did well to have hidden the anxiety which had been so evident to Neil. Unless it was anxiety of a different kind which he shared with Sandra, and she was now acting a part for the two of them . . .

While he was with people he would learn more if he took them at face value. Remembering his comment to Grayson that it might not be considered unprofessional to tell Sandra Fane what Mrs. Monkton had said to him, he wondered if he had done so—and if she had perhaps replied with a story of her own about the man in the grey uniform . . . His continuing desire to ask imprudent questions couldn't, today, turn into temptation—Josephine Webster wasn't in a position to frame them.

"Did Jim know Mrs. Monkton at all?" It was as near as he could get.

"Only to say good morning." Her face was as innocent as her words. And more frailly, spiritually beautiful than he had yet seen it. "Apparently her husband left her a week or so ago. It seems to me just as likely he killed her as the person who killed Mrs. Willoughby."

"The police should be able to find that out fairly easily."

"I suppose so." She leaned towards him with an elegant gesture of despair. "Josephine, the police know about me, now."

"At least you told them before they told you."

"Just." The old radiant smile was there, but glowing weakly behind the shade of her anxiety, and quickly fading. "But they probably thought I was trying to cut my losses."

"You did the wise thing. What was the reaction?"

"Muted. The inspector—chief inspector—just said, 'I see, madam,' or something like that, and then showed me the bit about myself they'd decoded."

"Did you say anything about why you hadn't told them at the beginning?"

"I said I'd panicked, and then felt I would be making things worse if I went back on my statement. I told them the *truth*. The chief inspector was very understanding. He was a big, red-faced man with hairs in his ears, I was a bit wary of him at first."

And would have done well to remain so. The Chief was never more dangerous than when he was being understanding. *Timeo Danaos* . . .

"And what was the reaction to your failure to come up with an alibi for this second murder?"

Carefully he crossed his legs, smoothing the full skirt over his knees with his braceleted hand.

"Still muted." Sandra Fane smiled sadly. "I think the chief inspector was trying to find out at the same time if I could give Jim one. I couldn't do that, either." Her eyes begged for consolation. "Oh, Josephine, isn't it a nightmare? What are we going to do?"

"The police are going to find the murderer, or murderers." He was still a policeman. "They are, Sandra."

"You make me feel so much better, darling, just by being here."

"Don't you think a pot of tea would make you feel better still?"

"So long as you'll stay and join me. Come into the kitchen!"

Sitting on a high stool as Sandra Fane flitted about, he was reminded with an almost painful surge of affection of Cathy in the old days when he used to cross the landing to look in on her and she tried to detain him with tea, sympathy and homemade biscuits . . .

"I can't tell you," said Sandra, with a transient dazzle in his direction as she flashed past, "what it's meant to me this past dreadful week to have found a real friend. I do hope when all this awful business is over we can meet properly, do things together—with your husband and Jim too," she added, he suspected as an afterthought. "And, please, I should like you to come to the play."

"Sandra . . ." He realized as he leaned towards her, smiling, that he had had what he was going to say in reserve from the beginning. "I'm

afraid I'm not going to be around for very much longer." He decided as
he spoke that he wasn't going to be around after that day. "John and I
have finally made arrangements to go and live in New Zealand." It was
positively Olympian, the things one could do with fictional characters.
"John's got family there, we had a holiday with them a couple of years
ago, and liked it so much we've been thinking of moving there ever
since. And now we've decided. We've hardly told a soul, we just
couldn't face the trauma of goodbyes, but we can't in all decency put
them off any longer, and I feel I should tell you."

"Oh, no." The full lips trembled, he found himself wondering academically what it would be like to kiss them, and then realized with a
sort of horror that the announcement of Josephine's departure was the
last straw to make Sandra Fane cry.

"Sandra, please don't." He had to hold himself in check not to run
out of the flat. He got off the stool and went and stood beside her,
putting his arm round her shoulder and feeling her body shake as she
began to weep. His instinct was to suggest that she cultivate Cathy as a
substitute, but he could hardly have put forward a more foolish proposi-
tion. "Sandra . . ." Miserably he pressed her against his side as the
sobs crescendoed and then began to die away.

"It's all right," said Sandra Fane, at the end of one of the longest
moments of his life. She moved away from him, blowing her nose. "It
was just one thing too many." It was a relief to see her wan smile. "And
it's not as if you're off this minute."

"No . . . But within the month. There's so much to do, uprooting
a lifetime . . . Cathy's not going to see so much of me now, I'm
afraid."

"So obviously I'm not, either." The smile was again brave. "Won't
you at least give me your own telephone number?"

"Oh, I'll be at Cathy's often enough for the next week or so," he
back-pedalled. "And if I'm not, she'll give me any message. It's a bit of
an unusual situation at home, as you'll appreciate, and my husband's on
a short fuse already."

To his relief and remorse she accepted it, gracefully bowing her head
on its long neck and spreading her expressive arms. "Forgive me, darling, I'm too demanding. I'll try not to bother you. It's just that it's
such a comfort . . ."

He allowed half an hour for the tea, including drying the few tea-
things, then got up to go.

"Thank you for coming, darling, and for all your wise advice." This time her arms were round him before he could open the front door. And this time, with an effort, he returned her pressure, rejoicing that there was no excitement in it.

"Oh, darling darling," he said to Cathy, when he had shed Josephine and flung himself down beside her on the sitting-room sofa. "If you only knew how marvellous it is to be *me* with *you.*"

"I do know. I hope you're not protesting too much." She grinned at him.

"I told Sandra Fane the Websters are emigrating to New Zealand next month."

"Neil . . ." She took his hand.

"But I did protest too much yesterday when I was telling the Chief why I was with Grayson. Ten years' buildup of confidence gone in a week." He got to his feet and started walking about the room. "Cathy, it's all beginning to get me down. That's an extra reason why I've got to do the thing only I can do to try and bring it to an end." He preferred to square it with her.

She sat forward, her hands twisting in her lap. "And if I told you I'd rather be a suspect in a terrible crime than worry about you being the victim in another one?"

"You couldn't have killed Mrs. Monkton, and I'm fairly confident no one official thinks you killed Mrs. Willoughby. I'm not doing this for you any more, darling, I'm doing it for the truth and for myself. Anyway, you don't know what it is."

"I can guess. Spying on Miss Littlewood until the man in the uniform calls on her again."

"Not bad," he said admiringly, sitting down again and reaching halfway for her hand, which she didn't give him.

"Then following him home or wherever he goes and trying to get evidence out of him. Or her. Neil, every stage of that could spring a booby trap."

"Not for Rosemary Bartlett."

She moved restlessly. "You're over-confident about that disguise. You told me yourself you hadn't realized how vulnerable it was—"

"That was when I was calling on people and being afraid of meeting —the police. The only person I shall call on now, if I get the chance, is the man in the uniform. And if things look like getting tough for

Rosemary, Neil will have a few surprises in store. Darling, I fooled *you.*"

"You daren't risk your car. Or mine."

"That's taken care of. I've appointed myself a minder. And the feeling I've had ever since I visited Miss Littlewood that there was something in my favour about the road where she lives resolved itself in my mind this morning into a For Sale notice on the house immediately opposite. I found the estate agent by trial and error, and the house is empty. All applications to view to be made to the agents."

"Do you really believe you're reassuring me?"

"I'm telling you it isn't a walk on the wild side." Her hand at last crept slightly towards his, and he took hold of it. "And it's all too likely to be a wild-goose chase. If Grayson's our man, I've an idea he'll have laid the uniform to rest. And even if he isn't, the visit of the man in uniform to Miss Littlewood could well have been a one-off event, particularly if he suspects the police may be watching her, and that will depend on whether she has an alibi for Mrs. Willoughby's murder—I wanted to ask Peter, but he's done superhuman things for me already and I didn't feel I could." He pulled her to him, meeting no resistance. "Darling, I just have to give this a go. Call it selfish, perhaps it is, but all my career means to me dictates that I make use of every bit of luck that comes my way."

"You'd be doing that if you told the Chief."

"The Chief has no substitute for Rosemary Bartlett." He ruffled her hair. "I'll be all right, I promise. If a very slender chance comes off, I won't go beyond what I know I can get away with."

"You'll be seen going into that empty house." At least, now, she was shooting at details.

"If we went in at the front, yes. When I visited Miss Littlewood I parked behind the houses opposite to hers—they back on to a lane. I remember thinking it was the place where the suburb took over from the country—it's not country now, of course, just a narrow breathing-space before the next suburb, or group of shops, or whatever. But the point is, there aren't any houses in it."

"And if you find the man in uniform, how will you tell—the police —that you're ahead of them? You're in trouble already, Neil, remember?"

"I do remember. But the forbidden thing I've already done—solving

that code—was on Peter's incentive and might even have been turned
to my account."

"Isn't it time you heard about the disciplinary hearing?"

"Early next week, I should say. Darling . . ."

"All right, Neil." The resignation of her sigh smote him without in
any way denting his resolve. "I know when I'm beaten. When does
your vigil begin?"

"Tonight. I'm being met just round the corner at eight o'clock. It'll
still be light. And I won't wait beyond ten."

They had a rather silent supper, early, and he said goodbye before
going to get ready. Cathy stayed in the sitting-room, exercising the
minor concession due to the loser by not pretending she didn't mind
seeing him in drag, and he called goodbye again without going back in
to her.

There was still no Miss Prince to get past, and he didn't see anyone
else in the public parts of the building. Walking round the corner was
to walk into the low gold remains of the sun under livid clouds, and he
was glad of Rosemary's dark glasses. There were three empty cars
parked at the dead end of Oliver Road and one Ford Fiesta with Moses
at the wheel, the whites of his eyes showing as he rolled them appre-
hensively across the street. By the time Neil had shimmied up to him
he was sitting hunched and inert, staring mournfully through the wind-
screen. Neil was amused to notice that he was freshly shaved, probably
the first time he had seen the long thin face in sharp outline.

"Moses Toosey?"

"The same, ma'am." Moses got out of the car and went round to
hold the passenger door open, making Neil wonder if he had been
telling the truth when he had once said he had been a chauffeur.

"Thank you." He could have told Moses on the telephone about
Rosemary Bartlett, but for Moses' own safety he wanted him to act as
if he was with a woman. And for him, Neil, it was a refresher course.

"Where to, ma'am?"

It was clear Moses was unsuspecting, even of the voice—his face
wore its usual look of slightly pessimistic serenity. Neil directed him
about two thirds of the way to Miss Littlewood's, then asked him to
stop under a sodium light in a street of small Edwardian villas.

"Moses."

"Yes, ma'am?" Slowly and distrustfully Moses turned to face him, fidgeting his legs as far away as possible from the area of the gears. His chief nark, Neil remembered, was reputed to be uxorious.

"Look at me, Moses."

The distrust visibly intensified, and Moses' pale eyes were as the eyes of the rabbit fixed despite itself on the stoat.

Nothing more.

"Aren't we meeting Mr. Carter?" asked Moses hoarsely.

"You've met him. Moses, it's me. Neil Carter. I'm not going to undress to prove it to you, but think about Mr. Carter and look again."

"Blimey, Governor!" Moses sprawled at ease in his seat. "And there was me thinking you was just about to make up to me. I don't mind telling you it's a relief. Not," he continued in hasty deference, "that you ain't a dainty dish, Governor, don't misunderstand me. But me and the wife—"

"It's all right, Moses, you don't have to be polite about an illusion. Now, left at the end of this road."

CHAPTER THIRTEEN

"What's the dolly bit for then, Mr. Carter?" asked Moses as they drew up two back gates short of the house opposite Miss Littlewood's. Hoping to avoid having to pinpoint the house from the front, Neil had gambled on the estate agent erecting a notice at the back as well—and there was one where he would have expected to find it.

"It's because I'm hoping someone I want to follow will come out of the house across the road, and if he does I want to follow him as a woman. It makes life safer for you too, Moses. Come on!"

When they had shut and locked the car and unsuccessfully assailed the latch of the gate, they separated to examine the wall for the best spot at which to scale it.

"It's all right, Governor." Moses' voice came faint and from a little distance, and Neil saw an arm beckoning from among the foliage of a small tree the other side of the gate from his own survey. Moses was already half-way into the back garden, snugly fitting a slit in the wall behind the tree.

"Them bricks has been knocked out and just stood back on one another," explained Moses when they were both the other side of the wall. He held Neil down behind some neglected shrubs and spoke in a stage whisper. "Someone else's already got in. Or been in. Better let me investigate."

"I'm the investigator," Neil whispered back, "but thanks, Moses." He disentangled a few hairs of the wig from a spiky shoot. "And for being so quick to spot the weak place. Indian file round the border, would you say that's wise?"

"It'd be wiser to give it up, Mr. Carter."

"I'm not giving it up. You can go and sit in the car."

"Mr. Carter!"

The back door was locked, but a low window beside it was easily pushed open. It must have been some time since the estate agent had shown anyone round. Moses climbed in first, disappeared, then returned to pronounce the immediate area clear and help the encumbered Neil over the sill.

"Someone here, though," hissed Moses, as they were looking round the kitchen.

"I'll go first," said Neil, on a flash of wild hope that the man in the grey uniform had also wanted to watch Miss Littlewood unobserved and had chosen this method. Anyway, if there was danger he ought to be the one in front.

The kitchen led into an empty hall where the yellow paint showed the shapes of departed furniture and pictures. Stairs went up beside them as they tiptoed into it, and opposite was the front door.

"On the left," murmured Moses, his nose crinkling. It wasn't the first time Neil had blessed his nark's ancillary attributes. "You got a gun, Mr. Carter?"

"No. Look, Moses, I may be going to play this cool. If you hear me saying I'm from the agency, just support me, will you?" If he hurled himself on the man in the grey uniform in this house rather than the man's own place his opportunity would be gone even if with Moses' help he subdued him. If he played subtle he might even be invited to call on him . . . The door to the left was ajar and slowly he pushed it wide open.

The tramp was lying on a grimy blanket in the bay window. He was raising a bottle to his mouth and when he saw Neil his face split into a delighted grin and he held it out.

"Och, it's a wee lassie! Ye'll be joining me for a dram?"

Moses, running past Neil waving his arms and growling, had the bottle dropping on to the blanket, and there was no more than token protest as they hauled him up and marched him, his feet just off the ground, to the window at the back. When they opened the window he went through without encouragement or assistance and was out of sight down the garden before they had any chance of sending his blanket and his bottle after him.

"I expect it's been his home for weeks, Mr. Carter," said Moses, his face registering a fastidious distaste which Neil considered overdone. But Moses had, after all, shaved for the occasion. "He won't be back, that's for sure. You won't much be liking the atmosphere in that room, though."

"We're going to be in the one over it. Easier to spot an arrival."

In the front room upstairs, too, there were grubby net curtains over the bay window. There were also a couple of large boxes to be dragged from a back room and used as seats high enough to see along the road to either side of Miss Littlewood's. Neil stationed himself to look in the direction the man in uniform had taken when he had left her house (he was no longer thinking it might not have been her house) the other time, placing Moses to look in the opposite direction. The possibility of a visit from his colleagues crossed his mind, but he was reassured by the thought that murder, again, would have warranted an immediate visit to Miss Littlewood's place of work. Unless, of course, she had an alibi for Mrs. Willoughby's murder and it was decided to leave her until the evening . . . He was prepared to take the risk.

It was half past eight, and at twenty to nine, in the rays of a sun which had decided to come out just as it was setting, Miss Littlewood emerged from the detached side of her house to spend ten minutes transferring several piles of weeds from the edges of her borders into a large cardboard box, with which she disappeared the way she had come. While she worked she didn't glance at the road or consult the large watch she wore on her wrist, and Neil was prepared for the disappointment of ten o'clock arriving without any further manifestation. There was, even, a slight sensation of relief in the prospect of escaping from Moses Toosey's restless, constantly impatient company.

"You satisfied now, Mr. Carter?" asked Moses on the way downstairs.

"You know I'm not, Moses. We'll try again tomorrow."

"Blimey, Mr. Carter!"

But back in the car, receiving the money for its hire and something on account for himself, Moses was seeing the enterprise as an adventure.

"Eight o'clock again tomorrow, then, Mr. Carter? Same time, same place?"

"That's it, Moses."

He was home at half past ten, to find Cathy in her dressing-gown but still up and with two mugs on a tray beside the steaming kettle. Every least event seemed to Neil of significance, as part of the creation of a new routine. It would help, the next frustrating night, and the next, to come home to tea and sympathy. Not that the sympathy was precisely in evidence, although he was prepared to define it as anything less than hostility or constraint, and Cathy seemed friendly enough—certainly the atmosphere was too good to jeopardize by telling her that evening of Josephine Webster's encounter with Bolshaw in the branch library. He did no more than peep at her round the kitchen door before going into the spare room and then the bathroom to restore himself and get ready for bed, and they sat fairly close together on the sitting-room sofa to drink their tea and watch an old black and white film. The film, of course, could not be guaranteed on subsequent nights, but Cathy's very slightly subdued normality was what really counted.

And it was an enormous relief, wakening to a Saturday, to be able to break the routine of the weekday—the solitude, the neighbouring vacuum cleaners, the chest of drawers. They went shopping together, stayed out for lunch and spent the windy, sunny afternoon on Hampstead Heath. They didn't talk about Neil's obsession, beyond a matter-of-fact practical reference by Cathy to the new evening ritual which had him squeezing her slightly responsive shoulders in gratitude.

Saturday evening in Acacia Road was even more uneventful than Friday. There was no tramp, no disturbance of Moses' memorized arrangement of the bottle and the blanket (carried out at arms' length on the Friday and with much facial contortion), and no appearance at all of Miss Littlewood or alteration to the uncurtained windows of her house—it seemed obvious she had gone out, and was still out when Neil and Moses abandoned their post at ten o'clock.

On Sunday morning he and Cathy found themselves ready to talk again about the two murders, beginning over breakfast in bed and the half dozen newspapers he had gone down to the road to buy. Two of them—one quality, one tabloid—offered features, as opposed to news items, on the Pleasant Street murders, but both in their different idioms were speculative pieces and it was clear his colleagues were still keeping the secrets of the blackmail and Mrs. Willoughby's alternative way of death.

"If the blackmail business got out," said Neil, as he threw the last paper on to the floor, "and the fact that Mrs. W was in process of committing suicide, "it would be the case of the decade. As it is, it's spectacular enough."

"None of it seems to have anything to do with my visits to her. I still keep feeling I'm going to wake up, then go and ring her bell and drink strong tea and get on with the portrait."

"Where is it?" He had wondered, since its disappearance from the spare room where he had put it.

"At the back of the other wardrobe, facing the wall with the sketch. Oh, Neil, thank goodness the papers didn't get hold of *that!*"

Or the fact of his suspension in connection with such a case. He had been half afraid the abused sergeant would have contrived to approach the media, and each time he left the flats in his own persona he was grateful for his continuing anonymity.

"Let's drive across Sunday London, Neil, and go to Kew Gardens. It's sunny again and not so windy on the balcony as it was yesterday." Cathy might be disapproving of his current conduct, but she, too, was seized with a sense of waiting which needed distraction where possible to ease its tension.

They took food and wandered about the Gardens nearly all day, and in the evening he met Moses as fruitlessly as on Friday and Saturday. On Monday morning, after the departure of Cathy to school, he found himself over the remains of breakfast in a state of utter dejection, his exclusion from the Yard become an almost physical pain.

The excitement of his private enterprise, which had cushioned him into exile, had waned to extinction. Josephine Webster was on the way out, and Rosemary Bartlett would be of no further use to him after Tuesday. Sitting rolling toast crumbs between fingers and thumb, Neil faced for the first time his gloomy conviction that if the man in the grey uniform didn't show up at Miss Littlewood's the next night, one week from his last appearance, he wouldn't show up at all.

As he worked on the chest of drawers he managed slowly to transform his despair into anger, at the height of which there was a telephone call from the Chief.

"How are you, Neil?"

Behind his self-pity and resentment was a mollified awareness that the Chief had waited in person for him to pick up his receiver.

"Governor!"

"Yes, well, of course, Neil, I know how you'll be feeling. Pretty inconvenient for me, too."

The mild grumble, indicating that the Chief had got over his inevitable anger at Peter's revelation about the code, reached him like a caress. He realized he had been worried about the Chief's reaction as the worry disappeared. "What's happening, Governor?"

"There's a meeting on Thursday." The Chief paused. Probably, to be fair, merely in order to find the best words. "It may be—I'm only saying it may be, Neil—there'll be a consensus of opinion that your punishment is already under way." The Chief would not, of course, refer to the solving of the code, but he had to believe that he owed the dangled possibility of a return to work without reprimand to the enlightened ingenuity of Peter Cummings.

"Thank you, Governor." Neil paused in his turn. "It's been a long week." Too late he realized the opening he had given.

"But I'm sure you'll have filled it constructively, Neil." The response, again, was uncharacteristically mild. But then, his constructiveness had been nothing to what it could—would—be if the man in the grey uniform called again on Miss Littlewood . . .

That evening she was already gardening when he and Moses took up their positions, stamping unattractively about her small domain and dealing roughly with the last few unwanted growths in the straight and narrow borders edging the square of paving.

"Blimey, Mr. Carter!" Cautiously Moses extended his thin neck towards the net curtain. "What d'you think a man could make of that?"

"Very little, Moses, and I speak from experience."

The head swivelled. "Governor, you never—"

"I was with Miss Littlewood for the length of a cup of coffee. I wore a dark female wig. I don't think she'd recognize me, but I wouldn't want to give her the chance."

And seemed unlikely to. Again Miss Littlewood showed no interest in her watch or the road, and disappeared down the side of her house half an hour before Neil and Moses left their post.

On Tuesday morning, sick with an inescapable sense of do or die, he had to get out of the flat and went to see Jim Grayson at his office, braced to learn the worst, in one direction, that his nightly failure was permitting.

Grayson looked ghastly, and the day before had had a long interview at the Yard.

"At least all my windows are on to the garden, Neil. Poor old Bolshaw has had one of his broken. He's even more scared, though, of going out than of staying in. There are nearly always a few people about outside, and he's even stopped going to the library. I don't much like running the gauntlet myself, although there's no doubt the police are keeping a particular eye on the house—even if it's as much to see that we don't abscond as to protect us. Anyway, I brought some extra food in on Saturday as an experiment, and Bolshaw took it from me readily enough."

"Why don't you go somewhere else? Sandra, for instance?"

"She's asked me, of course. But I'll stick it out."

Until when?

"It might be a long time," said Neil reluctantly. "It might be—"

"For ever. I know. But I'll stay on with the old boy for the time being."

It could be that Grayson was a particularly nice man. Or was keeping guard over some hiding place. A curious habit he had of occasionally jerking his head had become more frequent and pronounced.

Over coffee in Dave Earnshaw's office Grayson relaxed a little. Earnshaw kept trying to persuade him to move in with him, at least for a few days.

"No constraints, Jim, I've a nice little guest-room and you can come and go as you please. I tend anyway to meet my girl-friends at their places." Yes, Earnshaw would have girl-friends in the plural. Even, Neil thought, acknowledging the unfairness of the speculation, if he married one of them. "You really ought to get out of that atmosphere."

"Yes . . ." Jim Grayson looked bewilderedly round the elegant room. "I will of course, but I think for the time being I'll keep an eye on Bolshaw."

Earnshaw flung himself back impatiently in his chair. "The man could be a homicidal maniac, for heaven's sake. Bolshaw's a reason for you *not* to stay where you are."

"I'm not afraid of Bolshaw."

Because he knew he had no need to be?

"Look, Jim." Earnshaw now was leaning earnestly forward. "You didn't kill those women, but there was someone in the house on each occasion when they died whom no one could possibly describe as normal."

"I know it looks . . . But the police seem content for him to stay where he is."

"You saw him, didn't you?" Earnshaw had turned to Neil. "Jim told me you were going to have a look at him in the library."

"In the end I didn't. I just felt—well, I'm not on the case."

"Oh, I know it could be Bolshaw, Dave." Grayson rumpled his already untidy hair. "But I just somehow can't believe . . ."

Or just somehow couldn't go quite so far as to accuse another man of his own crimes? Whatever the truth of things, Grayson, wheeling nervously about Earnshaw's office and causing Earnshaw's elegant hand to drum on his desk top as he bumped against a table and set two china figurines chinking together, ought to be either taken in charge or released from unwarranted suspicion.

It started to rain just before he set out to meet Moses, and he took one of Cathy's umbrellas. Walking sedately down the road, he felt as weak and fluttery as he imagined a woman could feel, and when he got into the car he forced himself to brace the muscles through his body and remind them they might soon be in action.

It was hard to imagine. Acacia Road lay colourless and forlorn under the low grey sky and Miss Littlewood's garden was deserted. Half an hour went by devoid of all sign of life, save for a dog briefly at a neighbouring gatepost, before Neil saw a movement beyond the downstairs bay window.

"She's in," murmured Moses, whose usual ebullience the weather, or Neil's gloom, had mercifully damped down.

Miss Littlewood was in and pacing the room, according to the regular alternation of light and shadow. Preparing herself for a meeting with an opponent, or a partner? Neil felt the familiar tingle in his finger tips, and acknowledged with a lurch of the heart that it had never yet indicated wishful thinking.

Backwards and forwards, backwards and forwards the shadow swung, precise enough for Neil to measure his heartbeat by its movement. Halfway to the end of the road where his eyes kept turning, a woman in a mackintosh came out of a gateway with a very small white dog on a lead. She stood an indulgent moment, the lead slack, while the dog investigated a clump of grass just beyond her gate, then set off away from them, towards the blind corner where at that moment every hope of his life seemed pinned. When she disappeared smoothly out of sight he found himself disappointed and realized he had been expecting to see her jerk back to avoid a collision with the man coming the other way . . .

"I'll just take a turn round the room, Moses."

He had the shoes off and was testing his muscles again, perhaps in some primitive way willing the thing he was waiting for by deserting his post.

But he had been back at the window another twenty minutes before anyone turned the corner, and it was only the woman with the little dog, pausing again at her gate to allow it a final examination before persuading it, still reluctant, between the gateposts and out of sight behind some bushes.

Disappointment was coursing through him like a toxic fluid, and he was telling Moses that of course the person he was hoping to see would hold back a moment or so, to allow the woman time to get well ahead.

"You're quite right, Mr. Carter," said Moses admiringly. "He's timed it perfect."

Neil turned his eyes from the pacing shadow of Miss Littlewood to the man in the dark grey uniform walking quickly but relaxed along the road towards her house. It was so wonderfully extraordinary to be looking at him, a legend come to life, to be able to dwell on the details of the luxuriant moustache, the dark hair visible under the hard cap, the cut of the suit, the polished dark shoes, he was losing vital moments.

But he must, of course, see that it was Miss Littlewood's garden he was entering . . .

The shadow left her bay window as the figure turned in at her gate, and Neil, his shoes in his hand, was urging Moses to the door of the room and down the stairs.

"I'll drive now. What I want you to do eventually, when I leave the car, is to pull the high-tension lead out and then find your way home. I'm not expecting actually to have to bear out a story that my car's broken down—and if he lives in an upstairs flat it won't do anyway— but it's an easy enough way to nobble it and it's something which just could have happened unassisted. You can lock this car without the key, which I suggest you do as it'll complicate things if it's stolen."

Moses answered him when they were through the window. "I don't understand what you're talking about, Mr. Carter, but I'll see to the HT lead and I'll lock the car. Pity it's raining."

"A pity, yes," agreed Neil cheerfully. "Put a taxi down to expenses and ring me tomorrow." He felt as if he'd just taken a big shot of brandy, and wanted to go on talking. "There may well be a stop on the way, incidentally, where we'll both sit tight."

"On the way where, Mr. Carter?" asked Moses plaintively, as they got into the hired car.

"I don't know yet."

He reassured himself on his appearance in the car mirror, then drove slowly to the end of the lane, overshooting it just enough to see that the dark grey van was where it had been a week earlier.

"All right, Moses, you may think the next bit is the hardest." He eased round the corner until he was directly behind the van, but separated from it by the width of Miss Littlewood's road. No doubt the van had been parked where it was for maximum unobtrusiveness—a blank house wall to the left, a tangle of bushes across the road. The same setting as that for himself and Moses. For a couple in love.

"I'm sorry, Moses, but I want you to put your arm across the back of my seat, then put both arms round me the second the driver of that van reappears. Once he's inside you can slacken off." Neil had been glad to see the blind back of the van, the man in uniform could see behind him only through his outside mirror.

"Blimey, Mr. Carter."

"Just sort of lean towards me . . ." Neil paused, then forced himself to go on. "We'd better practise."

Moses' smell was dry, gritty, more of the clothes than the body, reminding Neil on an incongruous flash of a gardener he had followed worshipfully around when he was a child . . . When they had practised a couple of times they sat staring at the back of the van, Neil making himself relax, Moses squirming and sighing and releasing fresh small assaults of that early idyllic memory he would look at later . . .

"Here you are, Mr. Carter."

"Come on then, Moses. Come *on*. I'll do the looking."

Moses' far arm across his body and his face turned towards him left Neil space to see with one eye the man in the grey uniform pause with his hand at the driving door of the van, stare at them an excruciating moment (but not, he thought, at the number plate), then get into the van and start away. Straight on up the road bounding the succession of residential side roads identical to Miss Littlewood's, enabling Neil to begin his pursuit on an immediate acceleration as the van turned left on to the main road which bounded the suburban block.

He was lucky. Half past nine on a Tuesday night was supplying enough traffic to save them from being conspicuous, not enough to pose any real risk of losing the van. There were two cars between it and themselves when after a quarter of an hour of tortuous inner London driving, which seemed to have done no more than advance them a few miles west, the van turned right into a narrow road forming the far boundary of a small municipal car-park with which Neil and Moses were just drawing level.

There was no one behind him and he turned in at the entrance, passing the deserted pay booth and threading among the sprinkling of cars still parked, towards the top road into which the van had disappeared. He parked not quite precisely behind an estate car, so that again his right eye could see unimpeded ahead.

Facing them was a row of lock-up garages, and the van was parked just beyond the one furthest from the main road. The figure in uniform was already unlocking it, then disappearing briefly inside and backing out a red Porsche. Then going back to the van and driving it into the garage. The red and white notice on the garage door, which Neil spotted as the door was shut and locked, was no doubt the announcement of a burglar alarm in operation.

"Not bad, Moses. Stage your regular transformation scene opposite a car-park rather than a row of neighbours who start to notice an eccentric pattern, and to the people coming and going you're just someone else coming and going. It's taken some pretty clever planning to organize this set-up."

But he had known already that the figure in the uniform was a worthy opponent.

It was harder to keep up with the Porsche, as the style of driving had changed with the vehicle. They had been travelling for another fifteen minutes or so, in a steadily more salubrious direction, when Neil noticed that the silhouette in the Porsche had become hatless. His heart was beating so strongly he felt half suffocated, but the sensation could be partly due to the constriction of Rosemary's bra.

"Any moment now, Moses."

The Porsche was drawing up outside a row of modern town houses built in Regency style with small front gardens. Neil held well back as the figure in grey got out, locked the car, entered a gateway, walked up a path and faced a front door. He then drove quickly past and up the first side road.

"Blimey, Mr. Carter!" Moses mopped his forehead with a large dirty handkerchief, but there was no smell of sweat in the confined space and Neil took it as a gesture of protest.

"It's all right, Moses." They were safely out of sight and suspicion, in an upmarket version of their situation near Miss Littlewood's—what looked like a small park across the road, the wall beside them the windowless side wall of the house inside which must now be the man or woman in the dark grey uniform. "It's all over for you now. I'm glad it's a house, and an end house at that, it'll be natural to call for help at the first one I come to. Too easy for him to pop out and have a look, though . . . I'll see to the HT lead myself, you be on your way. Take a taxi and telephone me tomorrow morning. Go *on*, Moses. Straight ahead, if you don't mind."

Moses got out of the car with a wariness that had Neil itching to assist him, but gathered speed along the road in front and had soon disappeared. Neil saw to the temporary disablement of his car, then, after taking a look at himself in the mirror and pressing some of Cathy's powder over his nose, locked up and walked round the corner.

There was a light on in the hall of the end house, and in the room beside it light glowed through thin curtains. The next house was in darkness, and the house after that. Fate was approving of his mad enterprise, and he walked up the path and rang the bell.

The front door was opened quickly and sharply by Dave Earnshaw, whose frown cleared almost instantly to an assured smile.

"Well!" said Earnshaw. "Must be my lucky night."

With the removal of the cap, of course, the dark grey uniform had become an unremarkable dark grey suit.

CHAPTER FOURTEEN

"It's not *my* lucky night," said Neil, forcing himself to smile with what he hoped was refined provocation. "Please forgive me for disturbing you at this hour, but my car's stopped round the corner. If I could use your telephone . . ."

This, really, at the start of the encounter, was the crucial moment. His shock at finding Earnshaw was already tempered by an optimistic instinct that he was the type to be ignorant of the workings of the internal combustion engine or, if not, to be keen enough to detain a youngish woman by professing ignorance.

He was aware of hesitation, and of a very slight redness on Earnshaw's top lip.

"Of course. Please come in. I'd have a look myself, but I'm afraid it wouldn't do much good. Not exactly macho, being unable to fix one's car, but one gets by . . ." Earnshaw's smile implied other areas of richer endowment. He was already subjecting his visitor to a scrutiny which had Neil imagining the thought bubbles rising from Earnshaw's head with pictures of himself in impossible situations. Which he must approve rather than deplore. But the prospect of being met halfway made it harder to play his part.

"Thank you." He was in the hall, the door was closed behind him and he was smiling as ambiguously (again he hoped) as Earnshaw himself, whose hand was lightly on his shoulder.

"The telephone's just down the hall. I'll get you a drink while you're ringing, you must need it."

"I could use one. Thanks. I'll ask my boy-friend to come and rescue me."

"Look, I've just thought." Earnshaw had moved with silent speed to stand between him and the telephone. His gamble had paid off. "Why bring anybody out? The simplest thing is for me to run you home, and you can come back tomorrow with a garage man. This is a fairly respectable neighbourhood and your car won't come to any harm over one night." The speculative look intensified. "Particularly if it won't go."

"Well . . ." He tried to look tempted, not merely aware of the undoubted practicality of Earnshaw's suggestion.

"Come along," said Earnshaw, turning and leading the way through the doorway to the front room. Knowing, thought Neil, just when to show confidence. "What will you have?"

"Oh, gin and tonic, please. But I really think . . ."

"What do you really think?" Earnshaw turned round, his smile now of a brilliance to dazzle all but the strongest-minded of women. (How would it have affected an unattached Cathy?) "Look, it's settled. No trouble at all. In fact the contrary. Well, use your imagination, Mizz—I don't know your name, do I?"

"Rosemary Bartlett." Rosemary had been married when she visited Miss Prince, but he had decided to leave her wedding ring at home.

"Dave Earnshaw. At your service."

There could have been an emphasis on the last word. Earnshaw had moved over to a corner cupboard, where he was dispensing gin. His living-room was more quietly elegant than his office, with dull gold carpet and curtains and green velvet wing-chairs. There was a large knee-hole desk in the window which could have been partner to the desk in his office and had Neil's fingers tracing the shape of one particular appliance through the squashy leather of his handbag.

"Do sit down. That all right for you?"

He sipped, widening his eyes at Earnshaw with as generous a smile as he could conjure. "It's fine." He had seen the proportion of gin to tonic, and he could taste it. But he had a strong head, and he didn't reckon on the preliminaries running to a refill.

"Well, good." Earnshaw eased gracefully into a chair at right angles to Neil's, so that his hands were not far away from Rosemary's skirt. "Your health, Rosemary."

"Your health, Dave."

Earnshaw put his glass down on the small table beside his chair and started looking at Neil—so probingly it was an effort not to drop his eyes and he began to fear for the secret of his bosom. It could be, though, that the secret was already out and he was the object of a scrutiny whose motive was business rather than pleasure. In which case, in view of Earnshaw's record . . .

"Haven't we met somewhere before?" Earnshaw was asking softly.

It just might be the usual cliché, or a genuine recognition of the man Earnshaw had met twice, distorted by vanity as well as Neil's disguise.

Or, of course, a cat playing with a mouse.

"Have we? I don't recall." He tried to speak casually yet significantly, and, being careful not to touch the table, put his glass down too —because his hand was trembling, although the gesture suited the moment.

"I think perhaps you do. I think perhaps you recall we met at that dreary party in Chelsea last week. Has your car really broken down, Rosemary Bartlett?"

It would have been easier to believe Earnshaw had rumbled him than that his vanity was large enough to persuade him a potential party conquest had felt impelled to take events into her own hands. But a man who had done what Earnshaw had done must have a giant-sized ego.

On a courage-restoring wave of triumph Neil realized how the land lay. He shrugged, languorously. "It wasn't going when I got out of it, Dave."

"But you'd have asked a boy-friend to come here?"

He shrugged again, and was aware of a look of sexual antagonism flash across the handsome face. Earnshaw took a sharp breath and leaned towards him. "You knew, didn't you, that I'd put you off telephoning if you mentioned a boy-friend?"

Neil shrugged yet again. It was probably the last time his shoulders would be free for the gesture, and then . . .

"How did you find my address?" Earnshaw's hand was on his knee, lightly caressing.

"I asked our hostess." He had to clamp his foot to the carpet, not to pull away. "If you're not surprised at my coming here, you shouldn't be surprised at that."

"No. I'm not surprised." Because he knew he was the greatest . . . Earnshaw had absorbed his own sense of triumph and was ready to move on. The hand climbed to Neil's thigh, tightening. "And I like women who know what they want, they're more exciting to—explore."

"Subdue" was the word Earnshaw was more likely to have in mind. "I know what I want, too."

"I should think you do, Dave."

And you've had too obscenely much of it already, you bastard.

They rose on an instant, and Neil was inside Earnshaw's open arms.

Earnshaw's mouth was open too, bearing down on his. One of his hands was jerking at the back hair of the wig, which would have hurt like hell if it had been growing out of his head (he'd been right about Earnshaw and women) and was threatening to destroy Rosemary, so that there was no time to waste and now Earnshaw's mouth was wider still, gasping out the pain of Neil's knee to his groin, which was necessary for his anger if not his plan, and then his face had closed with the pressure to his neck and he was crumpled up on the carpet.

The first thing was to put on the gloves and wipe his glass and then, a bit clumsily, Neil sealed Earnshaw's mouth with sticking-plaster from his handbag, even though he didn't anticipate him coming round for some time, and dragged him out to the hall in order to padlock his wrist to the slim lower level of the cast-iron newel post at the foot of the stairs. There was one large bunch of keys on him, and he took it into the front room and opened the two locked drawers of the desk with one of the smaller keys. Each contained a stack of papers—the first a collection of pornographic magazines and the second a series of lists and statements which Neil didn't spend much time looking through because he saw on the top one the names he had hoped to see, and he locked both drawers and returned the keys to the pocket where he'd found them.

Then he went to the telephone, pleased that he didn't have to wipe it too, and rang Peter Cummings at home.

"Sorry to be so late, Peter, but a female amazon of my official acquaintance has just telephoned me the most amazing story of her evening's activities, and as I'm not in a position at the moment to do anything about it myself, I'm getting straight on to you. Can you find pen and paper?"

On the wall above Earnshaw's telephone was a photograph of an attractive smiling woman with her arms round two little boys, the better-looking of them obviously Earnshaw. Was it already determined, in those innocent days, what he would become?

"Right you are, Neil."

"Make a note of everything, Peter, it sounds important. The police should go to the home of Dave Earnshaw, 1 Montpellier Terrace, N.W.1. Yes, that's right," he answered the surprised grunt, "Jim Grayson's partner. They'll have to break in as Earnshaw isn't in a position to open the front door to them . . . I've no comment to make on the ethics of my lady's behaviour. There's a big bunch of keys in his trouser pocket—they'll have no difficulty getting access to it. One small one unlocks two drawers in the desk in the front room, and the papers in one of those drawers will speak for themselves." So would the papers in the other, now he thought about it. "The police should also go to a lock-up garage, one of a row facing a municipal car-park off Brunton Street, she's not sure of the postal district but it's West or North West. The end garage furthest from the main road, no doubt another key on Earnshaw's ring will open that. Another, I hope, will give access to the house where Mesdames Willoughby and Monkton were murdered."

"But, Neil . . ." came faintly.

"I think it would be wise to involve the Chief, Peter. And please impress on him that I asked you to—although, of course, you'd have done so anyway, et cetera, et cetera. It might just diffuse his wrath over the unconventional behaviour of my amazon. Who, incidentally, I will not be able to produce. This was her last inspired act on our behalf, undertaken on her own initiative following no more than the odd word with me from time to time and a strongly feminist concern with the Pleasant Street murder case. By tomorrow she'll have left London, and no forwarding address. Better get on with it right away, Peter."

"Yes, of course. Are you at home, Neil?"

He looked up the pretty hall, over Earnshaw's body slumped against the bottom stair.

"Yes. Did you get down all I said?"

"Yes. I'll—did you suggest I get in touch with the Chief *now?*"

"Right now. Don't be deterred by Amelia. I know my amazon, and I know this is important. And, Peter . . . If you want to leave me out of it and claim the amazon for yourself, that's all right by me. I didn't suggest it right away because of the inevitable flak. Play it as you prefer, but remember that if a man ever owed anyone anything I owe you. Just let me know what happens."

He took the gloves off as he walked round the corner. It was dark now, but a sodium street light helped him restore the HT lead, and it was a good moment as he drove away.

Cathy was in the kitchen and he tore past and into the bathroom where, as on the last four nights, he had left his pyjamas and dressing-gown.

"He came, didn't he?" she said, as he joined her in the sitting-room where she was pouring tea. She had given him only a glance.

"Yes." He went to pour himself a scotch to alternate with the tea. "It's over, darling. Finished. Done."

She looked up at him, smiling at his ill-concealed excitement.

"And who is the murderer?"

"Dave Earnshaw." He noted with satisfaction that she splashed tea into her saucer but didn't seem otherwise upset. "Well, he's the man in the grey uniform, so he's the man Mrs. Monkton saw twice—once after he'd killed Mrs. Willoughby, and once just before he killed *her*. Shooting her with a silenced pistol through an arrangement of flowers he was ostensibly delivering. They'll probably find petals on the floor of the van like the petals at Mrs. Monkton's. The arrangement must have been in an oasis rather than cellophane—"

"Neil. What happened with Earnshaw?"

His laugh sounded happy and light-hearted, even though there was still, for him at least, some way to go. "He recognized me—it's all *right* —he knew he'd seen me before, so his ego decided he'd met Rosemary at a party where she'd been so impressed she found out where he lived and called on him. His vanity was his downfall, darling, isn't it satisfying? Poetic justice." If he wasn't careful he'd be laughing too much. "When he—got hold of me, which he did pretty quickly, thank heaven, I knocked him senseless—rather more painfully than was strictly necessary—took his keys, opened a drawer in his desk—didn't need my bent wire—and found incriminating documents relating to Mrs. Willoughby, Miss Littlewood, Sandra Fane, et al."

"You mean . . . He was Mrs. Willoughby's assistant?"

"I think they assisted each other, but I didn't stop and work it out. I suppose she started to threaten *him* with blackmail, or perhaps he just felt he'd like her corner for himself. Anyway, I left him tied up and rang Peter Cummings on his telephone, telling him what was what and putting it all down to the activities of a female super-nark who's now left London."

"Which they'll believe?"

He shrugged, and this time Cathy's arm crept round his shoulders. "They won't have any evidence to the contrary, whatever they may suspect. That's my story and I'm sticking to it. Oh, darling, there's one thing, though . . ." He jumped up and began walking about the room. "I *enjoyed* it. I enjoyed being outside the law that for all my adult life I've been dedicated to upholding. I enjoyed being able to decide what to do simply on the basis of whether or not it would be effective, without having to think whether it was ethical, or befitting a police-man. Now I think about it, it almost frightens me. Some of my col-leagues over the years have called me ruthless—well, I confessed it to you—and I know now that I could have been a good—I mean a suc-cessful—criminal."

"I should think most good detectives could," said Cathy, reassuringly unimpressed. "I wonder if there's a key to Mrs. Willoughby's on that ring of Earnshaw's?"

"That's what I'm banking on."

"If there is, mightn't the police—the Chief and Co.—be suspicious that it was planted?"

"I've thought of that. With luck there'll be a bit of an Earnshaw fingerprint on the key, and certainly no one else's. And taken in con-junction with the papers and the van, I think that's the end of Gray-son's and Bolshaw's ordeals. And our bad dreams."

"Except about the overdose. I'm awfully afraid I shall always have bad dreams about that." But she was smiling at him. "At the same time, though, Neil, it does leave me still just able to understand why I liked her. I mean, it shows how desperately sorry she was for what she'd done."

"Try to remember that it saved her knowing about the scissors." He sat down again and put his arm round her. He was still suspended from the world he loved, his latest activity could as well work against him as in his favour, but he had hoisted himself from the abyss which had yawned on Monday morning, life was again worth living. He even thought of the solitary morning to come, the hours of waiting to hear from Peter, as exciting because of being part of being alive. And Cathy. And his child to be. Restored, he felt ashamed that these abiding facts had not been enough to repair him, that he'd needed the adrenalin of a job success.

"I've been a pretty lousy expectant father the past week or so, haven't I? Oh, darling, I'm sorry."

"Don't be ridiculous, Neil. You lost your job—temporarily—because of standing up for me, who started this whole business in the first place, and you've made the absolute best of not being allowed to work. That alone must have been so morale-shattering I'd have understood if you'd just sat and brooded."

"I tried that, but it made me feel worse than ever. And d'you realize that if I hadn't been suspended I couldn't have done anything about

Mrs. Willoughby, I'd have been too busy with my own cases? Not only that, I think I'd have considered myself—well, bound by the police ethic I've felt suspended from this past ten days as well as from my official work."

"Yes . . . I'm glad it's over. By the way, there's no film on to-night."

Wednesday morning was fine and he would like to have gone out, but Peter might ring at any time. At least there was the balcony, and he sat out there trying to read the biography of a famous forensic expert and get a few personal papers in order. He lunched on lager and an enormous salami sandwich, then fell asleep in the long chair in the warmest sun of the year. Cathy came home early and persuaded him to let her telephone-mind while he went for a brisk walk. Peter didn't ring while he was out, and it was an effort to do justice to the meal Cathy had ready. They were drinking coffee by the open balcony door, and the exhilaration of his renaissance was giving place moment by moment to anxiety, when he at last heard the telephone.

"Neil? Peter Cummings here. Convenient if I come round?"

"*Yes.* Have you—"

"There was a key for the Pleasant Street house. And those papers make it all pretty clear. Earnshaw has sung, as well. I think actually he's in a mild state of shock—one moment congratulating himself on his cleverness and an easy lay and the next chained to his own staircase with all his secrets laid bare. Well, I suppose it must have been like that."

"My amazon left some traces?"

"None. Beyond some traces of lipstick on a glass. But I can't imagine any other situation in which a man like Earnshaw would be off his guard. I thought I'd bring you a tape of the interview. Most of it was conducted by the Super, by the way."

"So once again the Chief isn't feeling happy."

"Not noticeably. And I didn't claim the amazon, Neil, so the flak's yours as well. Shall I come now?"

He was there in twenty minutes.

"What I don't understand," he said almost at once, as Cathy poured them all coffee, "is how your amazon got on to the man in uniform. Or was it that she knew Earnshaw as himself and heard him talking in his sleep or something?"

It was tempting, as it had been tempting to ring Peter anonymously, but he must admit to some connection. "It was through the uniform," he said carefully. "I told you I talked to her about the case once or twice. All that amounted to was a suggestion that she look out for a man in a dark grey uniform driving a dark grey van—Grayson had told me Mrs. Monkton claimed to have seen a man answering that description going down the stairs after Mrs. Willoughby was murdered—well, you know that, and you know what the child said when her mother was murdered too—and I suddenly remembered that what sounded like the same man had called on us one afternoon when I was at home, with a rigmarole about delivering a parcel, and I began to wonder if he was a henchman of Mrs. Willoughby's spying out the land so far as Cathy was concerned. It wasn't evidence, Peter, just a thought. I gave my amazon the name of Miss Littlewood's road, and she spotted him calling on her and managed to follow him home via his second garage."

"And you can't get in touch with her again." Peter was looking very casual, his head down as he stirred his coffee, but it could just be that the Chief had suggested he ask a few questions. Anyway, it was a good opportunity to rehearse what he would eventually have to tell the Chief face to face.

"Afraid not. She'd been intending to move on sooner, but as I told you, her imagination was caught by these crimes and she wanted to see if she could help." He decided on an artistic touch. "I think it would have broken her if it had turned out the murderer was a woman."

"Weren't you running a risk she might talk to the media?"

"Not with this one," said Neil firmly. He got up and brought his cassette player over. "May Cathy listen?"

"I've already bent the rules by taking the tape out of the office." He wouldn't press Peter to tell him if it was with the connivance of the Chief, and he would probably never know. "It isn't very nice listening, but please stay, Cathy, if you'd like to."

Earnshaw's voice contained neither the warm concern of his performance the couple of times Neil had met him in his office, nor the smooth confidence with which he'd chatted up Rosemary Bartlett, but it was relaxed and calm. Perhaps the man was in shock, as Peter had suggested. The Chief, and then the Super, had had no difficulty in getting him to talk.

". . . I met the old lady at one of Jim's parties. She put her hand on my arm as I was pushing through the crowd and asked me if I could get her a glass of water. She didn't seem to be able to get a breath and I helped her into a seat in a corner and fetched the water. I remember I was rather glad of the chance to reinforce the sympathetic-image bit, succouring the weak and helpless." Earnshaw laughed, a bitter, ironic sound. "I stayed talking to her. Nobody noticed us—I was kneeling by her chair and we were below waist level. A week or so later she telephoned me at home and asked me to meet her in some grotty cafe without telling Jim. Her voice was quite friendly and matter-of-fact, but there was something . . . Anyway I went, and she asked me if I would undertake some investigations for her—into various clients, I realized later. In the same voice, with the same pleasant smile on her face, she apologized for not being in a position to pay me, and said she was sure I would accept her undertaking to keep—something she knew —secret as payment enough. What she was saying was perfectly clear, but I remember I didn't take it in straight away because she went on being a friendly, slightly apologetic old lady . . . The thing she knew —I never found out how she knew, perhaps Jim told her he'd been puzzled at one time and she'd gone on from there—yes, it was to do with the firm's finances, but I expect I'll be giving you enough to save you bothering to go into that . . . Anyway, I didn't want anyone to know and so I agreed to work for her. That was about five years ago and the funny thing is that I've built up my own quite profitable clientele from her original suggestion. The van and the uniform were my idea and no one knew about them, though I used them on her jobs as well. Her bit of business grew more and more of a drag as my own expanded, and there was always the threat hanging over me that she might tell Jim or the police, but I hadn't really thought of killing her." From his tone of voice Earnshaw could have been saying that he hadn't really thought of inviting her to tea. "I used to visit her when we knew Jim was going to be out, but it wasn't too desperate if we got it wrong because I could always say she'd let me in and was entertaining me while I was waiting for him.

"That particular afternoon she was expecting me. Jim had told me she used to have a nap after lunch on her best bed, on top of that unspeakable orange satin cover—I once saw the shape of her body on it when she took me into that room—but of course I used to ring the bell and she used to let me in, so she was always waiting at the top of the stairs as I came up. That day she didn't answer the bell, so in the end I used my key."

"So she'd given you a key," commented the Super.

"Mrs. Willoughby give anyone a key? Oh, no. Jim's always leaving his keys lying around the office—he doesn't have an ordered mind— and right at the start of my association with her I'd taken an impression of his front door key, although I'd never used it and of course no one knew I'd got it."

"So you ran the risk of seeing Grayson there that day."

"No. He'd told me when we met in the office first thing that he wasn't going to get back to the house over lunch-time, as he sometimes did. He must have told you that as well, Superintendent." Earnshaw paused, and they heard what Neil thought might have been the creaking of the Super's chair. "I went upstairs and saw both her doors were open. I had a look in the front room and when I saw it was empty I remembered about her naps and I went across the landing and into the other room. She was lying on the bed fast asleep on her back—at least that's what I thought. I stood looking at her and hating her and then I looked round the room and saw the scissors on the dressing-table and suddenly had to be very quick to use them before she woke up." Earnshaw stopped again, out of breath, and this time there was no doubt a chair was grating on a hard floor. "She had a book where she kept all the gen about her clients. Not the book in the wardrobe in the front room where she ticked off their payments, there was nothing in that. She'd shown me them both, once, when she was in a good mood, and I knew she kept the significant one in a drawer of that dressing-table in the best bedroom. It was locked but the key was in another drawer—I used my handkerchief, I only ever touch printable things with my handkerchief when I'm in a place on my own business—and I got the book out and put it on the bed by her, I thought the police would suspect the people whose names were in it. I always carry the uniform hat and the moustache in my brief-case and I put them on—someone might remember seeing me leaving, and if Jim came back unexpectedly I thought it would be better for once for him to see a man in uniform rather than his partner . . . Then I started to go"—Earnshaw had begun to sound as if he had asthma—"and then I remembered my fingerprints on the scissors, and I went back and wiped the handles and the rest of what I could see . . . There wasn't much blood, I was lucky there wasn't much blood, there was none on me, I suppose because she was dying already, but I don't know anything about that, about what she'd done to herself. I'm just sorry she didn't know what I did to her."

"We'll have a break, I think." The Super's voice was only just recognizable. Cathy got up and went out on to the dark balcony, Neil could just see her leaning over the rail. Peter switched off, and they sat in silence.

"D'you want to go on?" asked Peter eventually, as he caught Neil's eye.

"Of course," said Cathy, coming in again. Neil was alarmed by her pallor, but she grinned in reassurance as she sat down by him and took his hand. Peter switched back on.

"What about Mrs. Monkton?" asked the Super, in a voice which had Neil imagining him with arm raised to ward off an attack.

"I didn't know Mrs. Monkton from Adam. But when Jim came into the office that morning he told me the woman on the top floor had been to see him with a story of a man in uniform going down the stairs."

"It was a professional matter." He could still see Jim Grayson's indignant face when he had suggested he might have told Sandra Fane. But Jim had a professional relationship with his partner and so he had told him and not thought of it as a telling.

"Nobody knew you as a man in uniform, Earnshaw." Neil had some idea of the effort it must have been for the Super to sound conversational. "Was Mrs. Monkton so much of a threat?"

"She was a risk!" Earnshaw sounded reproving, as if the Super ought to have known better. "She might have remembered more under police questioning—the police are clever. I started my career in the police force, Superintendent."

"Oh, no," groaned Peter softly.

"All right, Earnshaw. What happened then?"

"This time I was wearing the hat and moustache when I came. I rang her bell and when she answered I told her I had some flowers for her and she let me in and told me to come up with them, as I'd hoped she would. The flower arrangement was in an oasis, I had the flowers in my left hand and the gun in my right. She was in the sitting-room by the settee and I crossed the landing and went up to her and fired."

The Super said quietly, "But you didn't shoot the child."

"I didn't see it." Earnshaw sounded aggrieved. "I heard it sometimes when I went to see Mrs. Willoughby and I thought it would be at school. It must have been in another room."

"It was half-term," said the Super. "The child saw you. Weren't you afraid Jim Grayson might see you, too? Mrs. Willoughby wasn't there to give you an alibi."

"I got there at eleven. Jim wasn't coming home till noon or so, when he was expecting Inspector Carter for lunch.

"I suppose I was followed from Butch Littlewood's. I was a bit uneasy about going there; she had alibis for the murders but I knew there must be a chance her place would be watched." Again there was the creak of a chair. The Super acknowledging to himself a dereliction of duty? "But I couldn't resist keeping her going, the only one left from the Willoughby stable. I had to let Fane drop, of course, because of her connection with Jim. I should have dropped Littlewood too, and then there would have been nothing to link me. Caught by my greed, Superintendent," said Earnshaw, laughing. The laughter got louder and wilder, and Peter had his hand out towards the off switch when Earnshaw spoke again. "And then that policewoman . . ." The laughter turned into a snarling scream, there were the sounds of chairs and feet, and Peter's hand flicked up.

Your greed and then your vanity. He suddenly just had time to mumble an excuse to Cathy and Peter and get into the bathroom before being sick. When he came out Cathy was making fresh coffee. He put his arms round her, then took the tray and followed her back into the sitting-room. Peter came in from the balcony and they sat down and gradually and tentatively began to talk about it.

CHAPTER FIFTEEN

When the telephone rang mid-morning, he was so sure it was the Chief he left the chest of drawers at a run and threw himself, heart thudding, on the receiver.

"Neil Carter."

"Oh . . . I'm sorry to disturb you, Mr. Carter. It's Sandra Fane, you'll have heard of me perhaps through your wife." He had known she was modest. "I wanted rather urgently to talk to Cathy's cousin Mrs. Webster and I haven't got her telephone number. I haven't got Cathy's school number, either, or I wouldn't have bothered you. Please forgive me," begged Sandra Fane, in her most lyrical voice. "I wouldn't have rung if it wasn't very important."

"That's all right," he said, as deeply and abruptly as he could. "Josephine's coming to say goodbye to Cathy at lunch-time, Cathy's coming home specially"—how easy it had grown to toss off plausible lies—"and I'll give her a message. You'd like her to ring you?"

"I'd like her to come and see me." He'd managed it, she wasn't puzzled. He saw his strained face in Cathy's Art Nouveau mirror as he wiped his temple with the side of his hand. "I know it's asking an awful lot, I know she's just about to go away, but if you could possibly tell her it truly is urgent, I think she'd fit it in. If she really can't come I'd like her to ring me, of course, but if you could emphasize—"

"I'll tell her, Miss Fane, as soon as she arrives. Then of course it'll be up to her."

"Of course. Oh, thank you! Goodbye, Mr. Carter."

"Goodbye."

Very important. Urgent. What important, urgent thing could Sandra Fane possibly need to tell Josephine Webster? He would, of course, have to find out. And it was strange, as he had listened to her he had realized he still had a slight, irrational sense of unfinished business.

If he got to her flat about three o'clock it would fit with his story of Josephine coming at lunch-time to say goodbye to Cathy, she would be calling on her way home. He just about finished the chest of drawers, working with the balcony doors open and intermittently whistling, hoping now not to hear from the Chief until he'd undressed Josephine for the last time. He wouldn't ring Sandra, he wouldn't risk Josephine's and Neil's voices being heard so close together on the telephone, he would just arrive . . .

If he had been half in love with Sandra Fane her face when she saw Josephine Webster would have grappled him to her.

"Oh, my dear, thank you."

"Neil told me it was important."

"It's my future," she said, with the catch in her voice and the sad smile he was certain would eventually bring her fame. "And Jim's. He's here, I begged him to stay in the hope you would come, or at least ring, and he did. He heard this morning that his partner Dave Earnshaw killed Mrs. Willoughby and the other woman, and I think it's that which has brought things to a head. It's the least of it for me, though, now . . ."

She led the way into her sitting-room, where Jim Grayson sprang up from one of the chintz chairs and stood reddening as the two women came up to him.

"You haven't met, have you?" said Sandra. "But I don't think I need introduce you. Josephine, I want you to help me persuade Jim not to do a dreadful thing. Jim . . ." She took Grayson's arm and led him to the sofa, where they sat down side by side and arm in arm. Her failure to offer Josephine a seat was to Neil a sign of her distraction. He sat down on the edge of a chair opposite and looked at them—both thin, pale and tense. "Jim," said Sandra, "tell Josephine your story first, and then—"

"Please don't tell me anything you'd really rather not," Neil felt obliged to contribute.

"No, I'll tell you," said Grayson heavily. "Because Sandra so much wants me to, and because she trusts you and you're going away."

"I wanted to tell you," said Sandra, "before Jim announced what he says he's going to do. Because the secret is so enormous, if we keep it entirely to ourselves it'll smother us. We've got to let some air in on it, I know we have. And then when Jim told me he was going to—"

"I'll tell her," said Grayson, as Neil's impatience was beginning to demand expression. He looked through Neil. "Mrs. Willoughby didn't take an overdose of Digoxin. I gave it to her."

"You—what?"

"I gave it to her. I knew what she was doing. I knew why Stella Lawrence died."

"But—Sandra!" His mind was whirling, it was a savage effort to maintain Josephine. "You said you hadn't told Jim about the blackmail. Or about . . ." He tailed off, perhaps she still hadn't told Grayson why she had been one of Mrs. Willoughby's victims.

"I told him my secret as soon as we realized we wanted to spend our lives together." The look she turned on Grayson was so intimate, Neil had to drop his eyes. "Each of us knows everything important there is to know about the other." He didn't think he and Cathy would want it quite like that. "The blackmail didn't come into that category and I didn't tell him about it until Stella Lawrence died—I thought he'd insist on my going to the police, and I could cope with things quite easily as they were, I told you she wasn't greedy. But it all seemed much more serious when Mrs. Lawrence walked under that bus. Jim was very upset but he didn't suggest the police, he said he'd try to talk to Mrs. W. When he did—well, she didn't listen to him and—he'll tell you what happened. Of course, after *she* died I told the police Jim hadn't known anything about either my secret or the blackmail—otherwise they would have seen a motive for the murder. I'm sorry I lied to you too, Josephine, but it was vital to give the universal impression that Jim knew nothing."

"You managed it." He had to acknowledge that despite his training, his ingrained habit of questioning every statement he heard, he had never really doubted Jim Grayson's ignorance.

"My grandfather died just then," said Jim, "and I used his death as a screen. I'm not an actor and I don't think I could have hidden from Ma, at least, the fact that I knew what she was doing. As it was, I couldn't look at her again, but she put it down to my grief. I *was* grieved—poor old man, I really feel it now—but at the time I was first and foremost grateful."

"And then you decided to kill her."

"I think at first it was just that I realized I had a very easy, painless way of killing her. But only if she persisted in what she was doing, not if she—I can only think of the biblical word—repented."

"You had a biblical sort of an attitude, didn't you?" He had to keep saying *Josephine* in his head to remind himself he was there as Sandra

Fane's female solicitor friend and not a male arm of the law—in a way he was relieved to find himself having to resist his normal reactions.

" 'Vengeance is mine, saith the Lord,' and I'm not the Lord," said Grayson painfully. "I shouldn't have done it and I wish to God I hadn't. Not just because she loved me. She did, you know, she would never have put me into her book."

"Go on, darling," said Sandra Fane softly.

"I had an appointment that day at lunch-time—I told Dave about it"—briefly Grayson closed his eyes—"but it was cancelled and I knew —I knew it was the time. I usually collected Ma's pills for her, and I'd handed in her prescription for a fresh bottle at the chemist near the office when I got to work, although she still had one or two left. I got home about one and took eight tablets out of the new bottle and crushed them up with some Mogadon—to sweeten any bitter flavour, and make sure she—died in her sleep." He sat silent until Sandra Fane put her hand up to caress his throat. "I mixed some sugar with them, too," he managed then, "and put it all in another small bottle. I put the bottle in my pocket and went upstairs and suggested we have some tea together, which we often did. She liked it very strong, which was part of my opportunity, and the other part was that I was the only person in her life permitted to make it in her kitchen corner." The curious intermittent twitch and thrust of Grayson's head was growing more and more obtrusive. "But first I let her know Sandra had told me about the blackmail. I begged her to stop what she was doing, try and make amends, but I couldn't get through."

"Bless you, Jim," said Sandra Fane in a voice Neil didn't recognize, making him jump. "With my other occupations, it adds up to a nice little business. Nobody gets hurt, and it helps me to manage."

"Don't . . ." choked Grayson, and Sandra Fane hurled herself apologetically upon him. "I mentioned Mrs. Lawrence," said Grayson, when Sandra with a wan smile at Neil had flung back into her seat, "and she just said Mrs. Lawrence was unbalanced, poor lady. I think it was then I realized I was wasting my time. I offered as usual to make the tea, and she graciously agreed. She was nattering on in her usual way all the time I was doing it, but slipping in that she really didn't know what she should do about Miss Fane, who had been so naughty, and when I heard that I stirred my mixture into her mahogany brew. She drank it without any comment and we sat for a time while she said nice things about me and that I was too good for Sandra—Ma wanted everyone for herself, I always knew that—and I noticed she was looking a bit dopey and saying less and less, and then she said she thought she'd go for a nap and I went with her across the landing and saw her on to the bed. She said, 'All right, Jim, we'll have another chat later about Miss Fane,' and then she closed her eyes and I went out and back into the other room and found the key to the middle bit of her wardrobe still in the lock—she must have been far gone already to leave it like that." Grayson groped for Sandra Fane's ready hand. "Then I took her black book out. I'd seen her with it often, marking down transactions, and I thought that if I destroyed it the police might never find out the names of her clients and Sandra wouldn't be connected with any publicity about her death. But there must have been another book or something because they found Sandra's name and her secret . . . I stood on the landing with the book in my hand—I burned it afterwards —just not able to make myself close her doors, shut her in. I don't know why, but I just couldn't . . . So I killed her twice myself, didn't I?" he asked Neil, focusing on Josephine for the first time since he had begun his story. "I left the way open for her other murderer."

"You made sure she didn't feel the scissors," said Sandra. She turned to Neil. "That's all."

"Except that I put the pills she had left in the old bottle into the new one," said Grayson, "and threw the old bottle into her wastepaper basket. I didn't wear gloves because I always had innocent fingerprints on her medicine bottles. The police told me about them and seemed quite happy with my explanation. They were so taken up with the— other murder—I don't think it ever occurred to them that Ma might not have tried to commit suicide."

"It doesn't look as if it did," said Neil, wincing. If he was anyone to go by, it didn't look as if it had done.

"When I'd finished with the pills," said Grayson, "I dashed out of the house. If I hadn't, I suppose I'd have seen Dave. Well, he would have rung my bell to make sure I wasn't there before letting himself into the house—the police told me he'd cut a key from mine—and then he wouldn't have gone upstairs and I'd have been the only one to kill Ma. I suppose he came because I'd told him I was going to be out, but if he'd found me at home it wouldn't have seemed significant—Ma could have killed herself whether or not I was in the house." But if Grayson had come back as Earnshaw was on his way downstairs, it might well have been extremely significant for Grayson. Neil hoped the hypothesis wouldn't present itself to him. "I hadn't intended lying to the police about being in the house when Ma was having that particular cup of tea, I might even have told the whole truth and said I was with her—but when I went upstairs again to see if the mixture had killed her and found . . . then I had to say I hadn't been in, hadn't seen her, and hope no one had seen *me*. Dave, though. I still can't . . . I might have seen him on the stairs," he whispered. "Mrs. Monkton did."

"Don't think of it, you mustn't!" said Neil sharply, his alarm at the look of Grayson's face breaking through the bounds of Josephine. But Grayson and Sandra Fane were too engrossed with themselves to be normally aware of him.

"I'm glad you know, Josephine." Sandra Fane turned her sad smile on him as he smoothed his skirt over his knees in a feeble attempt to restore his femininity. "It won't give us claustrophobia now. And Jim won't be uneasy, because you'll be the other side of the world, and he knows I trust you."

She was, perhaps, seeking a final assurance. "You can, Sandra. You said Jim wanted to do something?"

"He wants to confess to the police that he gave Mrs. Willoughby the lethal dose. Josephine, please help me to persuade him not to. It'll ruin both our lives for absolutely nothing."

"If there's the slightest chance of his being tempted to play God again," said Neil sternly, not having to stop and think, "then I think he's right."

Sandra Fane gave a little moan, and Grayson said, "Never! Never!"

"Then if it's simply for your own conscience, it would be self-indulgence of a very high order." He was neither Josephine Webster nor Detective Inspector Neil Carter of Scotland Yard, he was a scourge of cant. But Grayson must be very near the edge, and needed careful handling. "I'm sorry," he said more gently, "but I had a strong reaction. If you're a hundred per cent certain that was the one and only time you'll condemn another human being to death I think Sandra's right, I don't think you should go to the police." The word brought him back abruptly to himself, made him realize what an officer of the law was in process of saying. But he went on. "Quite apart from the technical fact that you *didn't* kill Mrs. Willoughby—which I know isn't the point that's exercising you—you can't alter what you did by confessing it. The police may not even believe you, and if they do you'll only spoil two lives."

"Not Sandra's," muttered Grayson. The light of obsession still shone in his eyes. "She'll be better off making a fresh start."

"That's cruel," said Neil sharply above Sandra Fane's second agonized moan. It was difficult to sound female and forceful at the same time, but by now his main concern was to get his points across. "And a breach of trust. And it's not as if you're going to escape punishment by not making a statement to the police. You're punishing yourself already, and your sentence will probably be longer than any court would hand out, even though my advice to you"—not as Josephine Webster, not as Detective Inspector Neil Carter, simply as another human being —"is to try at least to live happily ever after."

"I'm listening," whispered Grayson.

"A good self-image is a poor sort of thing," said Neil, "to set against a good partnership." He got to his feet. He mustn't turn it into a sermon, but there was just one more thing to say. "The blackmail story will, I think, have to come out, but the public will judge Mrs. Willoughby less harshly if they think she made amends."

"By taking her life," breathed Sandra Fane. "Yes!"

"I thought of that," said Grayson, reminding Neil of the really quite effective way he had promoted the idea of Mrs. Willoughby's suicide even when he hadn't been able to cite remorse for blackmail, merely the fact of her damaged son (he had been protecting her, rather than himself), "before I decided it was my moral duty to—"

"Think of it again." Josephine rested her hand a moment on his bony arm, and Neil looked into Grayson's eyes and judged them to be coming back to themselves. "Thank you both for your trust. I must go now, you'll understand, and anyway you'll have had enough of a third party."

She didn't contradict him. "I'll see you out."

"Goodbye," said Grayson wearily, sinking back on the sofa. "And thank you."

"Thank you for listening, not telling me to put my own house in order." He followed Sandra out to the hall.

"Goodbye, Josephine. Please write to me, I should hate to lose touch."

They were standing close together and the front door was still shut, but he was without apprehension—she had nothing left over from her love and concern for Grayson.

"Goodbye, Sandra, I'm sure we'll meet again." He'd have to take Cathy to her play, and eventually she'd be ringing up to find out why Josephine hadn't written. "D'you think it will be all right now?"

She nodded, biting her lip. "Thank you," she whispered. "No one else could have done it."

Successfully persuaded a man to defy the law, he thought as he walked away. Oh, well. He was ready now to resume his own life.

Fortunately the Chief had parked in a prominent place. When he got up to the flat he rang the bell instead of using his key.

Cathy's feet came more slowly than usual, and she hardly opened the door.

"Josephine!" she said loudly when she saw him. Then, very softly, drawing him just into the hall, "Thank goodness you saw the car. Miss Prince is back, run through to the bathroom, everything's there, and I've pulled the sitting-room door to." He heard her loud again as he softly shut the bathroom door. "Thanks, Josephine, you could have kept it a bit longer, I wasn't in a hurry. Yes, see you soon." The front door banged and then there was silence as she went back to the Chief, as his love and gratitude surged. When he was ready he thrust all Josephine's props into the clothes basket in case the Chief wanted the loo, then tiptoed past the almost closed sitting-room door, easing the front door open and shut. Outside on the step he discovered he had left his key in Josephine's handbag and was about to ring as Miss Prince appeared.

"Good afternoon, Mr. Carter, Neil, don't tell me you've locked yourself out." At least she hadn't been at her spyhole as he emerged.

"I appear to have done just that, Miss Prince, but not to worry, Cathy's at home."

"Entertaining one of her friends, yes"—she'd seen Cathy let Josephine in and thought that was the end of it—"I'm afraid you'll be among the ladies, Neil. If you don't want to disturb them I can let you have your spare key and then you can—"

"It's all right, Miss Prince." Hastily he rang the bell. "Did you have a good holiday?"

"Oh, lovely, thank you, I hope you and Cathy will come in one evening soon for coffee and look at my photographs."

"How very nice, Miss Prince." Cathy had opened the door and was staring at him in amazement. "Forgot my key, darling," he said, grinning, rejoicing in the amused response he saw she was having difficulty controlling.

"Hello, Miss Prince," she just managed. "Did you have a nice holiday?"

"Lovely, thank you, Cathy. I was just saying to Neil—"

"Forgive us just now," said Cathy apologetically, "but Neil's boss is here."

They left Miss Prince still fluttering her bewilderment on her doorstep, and managed a quick embrace in the hall.

"Forgot my door key," said Neil as he followed Cathy into the sitting-room, where the Chief was sitting in the usual high chair. "Getting flabby, you see, Governor, with nothing to keep me up to the mark."

In view of all that had recently occurred, the comment was so outrageous he hoped it might appeal to the Chief. Watching the as yet expressionless face, he decided to pre-empt even further. "I'm glad my female contact struck lucky. As you know, Governor, I was with Grayson the day Mrs. Monkton was killed, and heard about the man in uniform from him and the child. It made me remember a man who had called here just after Cathy started seeing Mrs. Willoughby, trying to deliver a parcel to the wrong address. It wasn't any kind of evidence but I just wondered . . ." Would he have wondered, if he hadn't seen Earnshaw leaving Miss Littlewood's that first time? "I told her to look out for a superior kind of postman somewhere round Acacia Road W.12, and the rest followed. I—"

"You chose to tell Peter Cummings first, Neil." The Chief's gaze was hard to sustain. "And he told me. So no need to go through it all again if it's still the same."

"Still the same, Governor?" He hoped his air of innocence wasn't too elaborate. "Of course it's still the same. I'm only sorry I can't produce—"

"All right, Neil, all right. You struck lucky too. Very lucky indeed." The gaze intensified almost unbearably before shifting and settling back less like a laser beam. "I'm here to tell you to come in to work on Monday. It's been decided that a fortnight's—idleness"—the word was under stress—"is the punishment to fit your case. No reprimand for your file."

"Thank you, Governor." And for not playing with him, for telling him straight out. The Chief might well have felt justified in taking his time with the best news he could have brought.

"The only stipulation is that you meet Sergeant Jenkins halfway. He's prepared to apologize."

"So am I, Governor."

"That's good, Neil." The Chief got up and lumbered towards the balcony. "Nice view."

"You'll have a drink with us, Governor? I know it's a bit early, but for me it would be a celebration."

"I don't see why not. A glass of that rather good sherry."

"I'll get it," said Cathy.

The Chief sank back into his chair. "Plenty for you on Monday," he said to Neil. "And by the way, there's an idea afloat of having a summer revue as well as the Christmas one. Naturally your name's been associated with it, you being the best drag act the Yard has got. Thought I'd just warn you. No compulsion, of course, any more than there is at Christmas, but it would be appreciated if you agreed to play."

The Chief had raised his big head and was staring at Neil intently. It could be coincidence, or he could be telling him what he suspected.

He would never know which.

He mustn't show a reaction but he must act according to Cathy, standing behind the Chief's chair with the sherry bottle in her hand. He glanced at her, trying to look casual, and she nodded, smiling.

"I don't see why not," he said to the Chief in his turn. "You appear to be telling me I'll have the time for it."

"Back to normal," said Cathy, when he had seen the Chief out. She poured him more sherry. "Oh, Neil, I'm so glad."

"Yes . . . I must just tell you what I found out this afternoon."

Her face altered as she absorbed it, and when he had finished she said, "Excuse me, Neil," and went out of the room.

He forced himself to give her a few moments, then went to look for her. She was in the spare room, staring at the portrait of Mrs. Willoughby, which was lying on the bed.

"I brought it out to destroy it, but it's too good, it's my best work." There was a tear on her cheek, but ruefully she smiled at him. "I wish it wasn't, Neil, but it is."

He put his arm round her waist, and was aware for the first time that it was thickening. "They say the Devil has the best tunes, so one might expect him to corner the art market as well. What will you do with it?"

"I don't want it in the flat. I was going to do some more work on it but I couldn't, now, and anyway I only really had refinements left to add, it'll pass as a finished portrait. I'll varnish it and then put it in the garage, it'll be all right zipped into that old brief-case you gave me. I don't think even Jim Grayson would want it now, I'll probably enter it for the next Society of Arts exhibition. If it isn't accepted, or doesn't sell, I'll think again. I'll take the sketch to school and use it for the mural character, I can't make myself let that go either, I'm afraid." Cathy picked up the portrait and examined it at arms' length. "She had something as well as wickedness, Neil. A pity she didn't use it in a different way. She understood people. And saw things most of us don't see. I know it sounds silly, but I'm convinced she saw Mrs. Lawrence's death in her crystal." She paused, looking at him. "Or her own."

He didn't contradict her, he wasn't certain enough she was wrong. "What will you call it?"

"I'll call it what it is, Neil." She laid the canvas face downwards on the bed. *"Portrait of an Unknown Woman."*

About the Author

Eileen Dewhurst was born in Liverpool and educated at Huyton College, later at Oxford. As a free-lance journalist, she has written numerous articles for such publications as *The Times* and *Punch*, and her plays have been performed throughout England. A NICE LITTLE BUSINESS is her ninth novel for the Crime Club.